THE LOST YEARS OF
MERLIN

T. A. BARRON

THE LOST YEARS OF
MERLIN

Philomel Books

PHILOMEL BOOKS

A division of Penguin Young Readers Group.
Published by The Penguin Group.
Penguin Group (USA) Inc., 375 Hudson Street, New York, NY 10014, U.S.A.
Penguin Group (Canada), 90 Eglinton Avenue East, Suite 700, Toronto, Ontario
M4P 2Y3, Canada (a division of Pearson Penguin Canada Inc.).
Penguin Books Ltd, 80 Strand, London WC2R 0RL, England.
Penguin Ireland, 25 St. Stephen's Green, Dublin 2, Ireland
(a division of Penguin Books Ltd).
Penguin Group (Australia), 250 Camberwell Road, Camberwell, Victoria 3124,
Australia (a division of Pearson Australia Group Pty Ltd).
Penguin Books India Pvt Ltd, 11 Community Centre, Panchsheel Park,
New Delhi - 110 017, India.
Penguin Group (NZ), 67 Apollo Drive, Rosedale, North Shore 0745,
Auckland, New Zealand (a division of Pearson New Zealand Ltd.)
Penguin Books (South Africa) (Pty) Ltd, 24 Sturdee Avenue,
Rosebank, Johannesburg 2196, South Africa.
Penguin Books Ltd, Registered Offices: 80 Strand,
London WC2R 0RL, England.

Published simultaneously in Canada.   Printed in the United States of America.
Design by Gunta Alexander.   The text is set in Galliard.

Library of Congress Cataloging-in-Publication Data
Barron, T. A. The lost years of Merlin / by T. A. Barron.
p. cm. Summary: A young boy who has no identity nor memory of his past
washes ashore on the coast of Wales and finds his true name after a series of
fantastic adventures.
1. Merlin (Legendary character)—Juvenile fiction. [1. Merlin (Legendary
character)—Fiction. 2. Wizards—Fiction. 3. Fantasy.] I. Title.
PZ7.B27567Lo 1996 [Fic]—dc20 96-33920
ISBN 978-0-399-25020-0
1 3 5 7 9 10 8 6 4 2
First Impression

This book is dedicated to
PATRICIA LEE GAUCH
loyal friend, passionate writer, demanding editor

with special appreciation to
BEN
age four, who sees and soars like a hawk

W E
S

L O S

T H E

Ruins of Varigal

be there giants?

dwarves last seen here

Lake of the Face

living stones

Tuatha's Grave

crossing

Crystal Cave of the Grand Elusa

orc

THE MISTED HILLS

The River Un

Cobblers' Rowan

Arbassa, Home of Rhia

DRUMAWOOD

Treelings once lived here

The Last Shomorra

Trouble found here

Forgotten Island

shore of the speaking shells

dunes

Emrys' Landing

I. SCHOENHERR · MCMXCVI

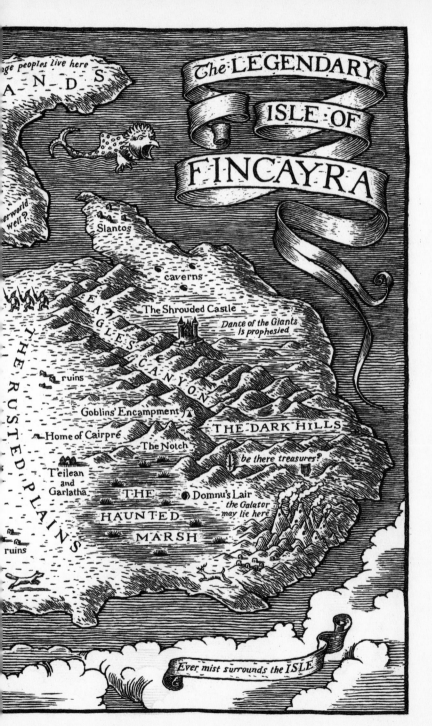

The LEGENDARY
ISLE OF
FINCAYRA

ge peoples live here
A N D S

erworld
well?

Slantos

caverns

EAGLES

The Shrouded Castle

Dance of the Giants
is prophesied

CANYON

ruins

THE·RUSTED·PLAINS

Goblins' Encampment

THE·DARK·HILLS

Home of Cairpré

The Notch

be there treasures?

Teilean
and
Garlatha

THE

HAUNTED

MARSH

Domnu's Lair
the Galator
may lie here

ruins

Ever mist surrounds the ISLE

CONTENTS

PART THREE

AUTHOR'S NOTE

I don't know much about wizards, but I have learned this much: They are full of surprises.

As I finished writing *The Merlin Effect,* a novel that follows a single strand of Arthurian legend from ancient Druid times almost to the dawn of the twenty-first century, I realized that the strand had bound me up so tightly that I could not escape. As I tugged on it, the strand tugged back. As I unraveled it, the strand entangled me more completely.

The strand was Merlin himself. He is a mysterious and captivating fellow, this wizard who can live backward in time, who dares to defy even the Threefold Death, and who can seek the Holy Grail while still speaking with the spirits of rivers and trees. I realized that I wanted to get to know him better.

Modern scholars have argued that the myth of Merlin may have sprung from an actual historical figure, a Druid prophet who lived somewhere in Wales in the sixth century A.D. But that is a matter for historians to debate. For whether or not Merlin was ever real in the realm of history, he is certainly real in the realm of imagination. There he has long lived, and there he continues to thrive. He even accepts visitors on occasion. And since I wanted to write a work of imagination, not history, Merlin's door was wide open.

So before I could even begin to protest, Merlin made his own plans for me. My other books and projects had to wait. It was time to explore another aspect of his legend, one deeply personal to the wizard himself. I suspected that, like most things in life, the more I learned about Merlin, the less I would really know. And, to be sure, I was well aware from the outset that making even a small contribution to such a marvelous body of myth would pose a daunting challenge. But curiosity can be a powerful motivator. And Merlin was insistent.

Then came the wizard's first surprise. As I immersed myself in the traditional tales about Merlin, I found an unexplained gap in the lore. Merlin's youth—the crucial, formative time when he most likely discovered his own shadowy origins, his own identity, and his own powers—was only fleetingly mentioned, if it was mentioned at all. Where he first tasted sorrow, where he first knew joy, where he first gained a particle or two of wisdom, remained unexplored.

Most of the traditional tales follow the same approach as Thomas Malory and ignore Merlin's early life entirely. A few stories speak of his birth, his tormented mother, his unknown father, and his precocious infancy. (In one account, he speaks fluently in his mother's defense when only one year old.) Then we hear nothing more of him—until, when considerably older, he is found explaining the secret of the fighting dragons to the treacherous King Vortigern. In between lies a gap of several years. Perhaps, as some have supposed, he wandered alone in the woods during those years lost from legend. Or perhaps, just perhaps . . . he traveled somewhere else.

This gap in Merlin's early life contrasts starkly with the volumes and volumes of material about his later years. As an adult, he assumes many (sometimes contradictory) forms, being variously described as prophet, magician, Madman of the Forest, trickster, priest, seer, and bard. He appears in some of the earliest myths of Celtic Britain, some of them so ancient that their sources were already obscure when the great Welsh epics of the *Mabinogion* were first set down a thousand years ago. In Spenser's *Faerie Queene* and in Ariosto's *Orlando Furioso,* Merlin the wizard is present. He counsels the young king in Malory's *Morte d'Arthur,* assembles Stonehenge in Robert de Boron's twelfth century poem *Merlin,* delivers many prophecies in Geoffrey of Monmouth's *Historia Regnum Brittaniae.*

More recently, writers as diverse as Shakespeare, Tennyson, Thomas Hardy, T. H. White, Mary Stewart, C. S. Lewis, Nikolai Tolstoy, and John Steinbeck have spent time with this fascinating figure, as have many others in many lands. Yet, with rare exceptions such as Mary Stewart, few have dealt at all with Merlin's youth.

And so the early years of Merlin remain strangely mysterious. We are left wondering about his early struggles, fears, and aspirations. What were his deepest dreams? His passions? How did he discover his own unusual talents? How did he deal with tragedy and loss? How did he come to know, perhaps even to accept, his own dark side? How did he first encounter the spiritual works of the Druids— and, for that matter, the ancient Greeks? How did he reconcile his own yearning for power and his horror at its abuses? In sum, how did he become the wizard and mentor to King Arthur whom we celebrate still today?

Questions such as these are not answered by the traditional lore. Nor do the words attributed to Merlin himself shed much light. Indeed, one gets the impression that he was determined to avoid talking about his own past. A reader of the traditional lore could fairly easily picture Merlin as an old man, seated beside the boy Arthur, musing distractedly about the "lost years" of his youth. Yet one can only speculate whether he might have been remarking on the brevity of life, or perhaps referring to a missing chapter from his own past.

My own view is that, during Merlin's lost years, he not only disappeared from the world of story and song. Rather, I believe that Merlin *himself* disappeared—from the world as we know it.

This tale, spanning a few volumes, will attempt to bridge the gap. The story begins when a young boy, without any name and without any memory of his past, washes ashore on the coast of Wales. It concludes when that same boy, having gained and lost a great deal, is ready to step into a central role in Arthurian legend.

In between, much happens. He discovers his second sight, but pays dearly for the privilege. He begins to speak with animals, trees, and rivers. He finds the original Stonehenge, far older than the circle of stones that tradition credits him with constructing on England's Salisbury Plain. First, however, he must learn the meaning of Stonehenge's Druid name, *Dance of the Giants*. He explores his first crystal cave. He voyages to the lost Island of Fincayra (spelled *Fianchuivé* in the Gaelic), known in Celtic myth as an island beneath the waves, a bridge between the Earth of human beings and the Otherworld of spiritual beings. He encounters some figures whose names are familiar in ancient lore, including the great Dagda, the evil Rhita Gawr, the tragic Elen, the mysterious Domnu, the wise Cairpré, and the vital Rhia. He also encounters others not so familiar, such as Shim, Stangmar, T'eilean and Garlatha, and the Grand Elusa. He learns that true sight requires more than eyes; that true wisdom unites qualities often separated, like faith and doubt, female and male, light and dark; that true love mingles joy with grief. And, most important of all, he gains the name Merlin.

Some words of thanks are necessary: to Currie, my wife and best friend, for guarding so well my solitude; to our pandemonious children Denali, Brooks, Ben, Ross, and Larkin, for their abundant sense of humor and sense of wonder; to Patricia Lee Gauch, for her unwavering faith in the power of a story to be true; to Victoria Acord and Patricia Waneka, for their invaluable assistance; to Cynthia Kreuz-Uhr, for her understanding of the interwoven sources of myth; to those who have encouraged me along the way, especially Madeleine L'Engle, Dorothy Markinko, and M. Jerry Weiss; to all the bards and poets and storytellers and scholars who have contributed over many centuries to the tales of Merlin; and, of course, to the elusive wizard himself.

Come with me, then, as Merlin reveals to us the story of his lost years. In this journey, you are the witness, I am the scribe, and Merlin himself is our guide. But let us beware, for a wizard, as we know, is full of surprises.

T. A. B.

He that made with his hond
Wynd and water, wode and lond;
Geve heom alle good endyng
That wolon listne this talkyng,
And y schal telle, yow byfore,
How Merlyn was geten and bore
And of his wisdoms also
And othre happes mony mo
Sum whyle byfeol in Engelonde.

—From the thirteenth-century ballad
  OF ARTHOUR AND
  OF MERLIN

PROLOGUE

If I close my eyes, and breathe to the rolling rhythm of the sea, I can still remember that long ago day. Harsh, cold, and lifeless it was, as empty of promise as my lungs were empty of air.

Since that day, I have seen many others, more than I have the strength left to count. Yet that day glows as bright as the Galator itself, as bright as the day I found my own name, or the day I first cradled a baby who bore the name Arthur. Perhaps I remember it so clearly because the pain, like a scar on my soul, will not disappear. Or because it marked the ending of so much. Or, perhaps, because it marked a beginning as well as an ending: the beginning of my lost years.

A dark wave rose on the rolling sea, and from it lifted a hand.

As the wave surged higher, reaching toward sky as smoky gray as itself, the hand reached higher as well. A bracelet of foam swirled around the wrist, while desperate fingers groped for something they could not find. It was the hand of someone small. It was the hand of someone weak, too weak to fight any longer.

It was the hand of a boy.

With a deep sucking sound, the wave began to crest, tilting steadily toward the shore. For an instant it paused, hovering between ocean and land, between the brooding Atlantic and the perilous, rock-bound coast of Wales, known in those days as Gwy-nedd. Then the sucking swelled into a crashing roar as the wave toppled over, hurling the boy's limp body onto the black rocks.

His head smacked against a stone, so violently that his skull would surely have split open were it not for the thick mat of hair that covered it. He lay completely still, except when the whoosh of air from the next wave tousled his locks, black beneath the stains of blood.

A shabby seagull, seeing his motionless form, hopped over the jumble of rocks for a closer look. Bending its beak toward the boy's face, it tried to pull a strand of sea kelp that was wrapped around his ear. The bird tugged and twisted, squawking angrily.

At last the kelp broke free. Triumphantly, the bird jumped down to one of the boy's bare arms. Beneath the shreds of a brown tunic still clinging to him, he seemed small, even for a boy of seven years. Yet something about his face—the shape of his brow, perhaps, or the lines around his eyes—seemed far older.

At that instant, he coughed, vomited seawater, and coughed again. With a screech, the gull dropped the kelp and fluttered off to a stony perch.

The boy remained motionless for a moment. All he could taste was sand, slime, and vomit. All he could feel was the painful throb-bing of his head, and the rocks jabbing into his shoulders. Then came another cough, another gush of seawater. A halting, labored breath. Then a second breath, and a third. Slowly, his slender hand clenched into a fist.

Waves surged and subsided, surged and subsided. For a long while, the small candle flame of life in him wavered at the edge of darkness. Beneath the throbbing, his mind seemed strangely empty. Almost as if he had lost a piece of his very self. Or as if a kind of wall had been erected, cutting him off from a portion of himself, leaving nothing but a lingering sense of fear.

His breathing slowed. His fist relaxed. He gasped, as if to cough again, but instead fell still.

Cautiously, the seagull edged closer.

Then, from whatever quarter, a thin thread of energy began to move through his body. Something inside him was not yet ready to die. He stirred again, breathed again.

The gull froze.

He opened his eyes. Shivering with cold, he rolled to his side. Feeling the rough sand in his mouth, he tried to spit, but succeeded only in making himself gag from the rancid taste of kelp and brine.

With effort, he raised an arm and wiped his mouth with the tatters of his tunic. Then he winced, feeling the raw lump on the back of his head. Willing himself to sit up, he braced his elbow against a rock and pushed himself upright.

He sat there, listening to the grinding and splashing sea. Beyond the ceaseless pulsing of the waves, beyond the pounding inside his head, he thought for an instant that he could hear something else—a voice, perhaps. A voice from some other time, some other place, though he could not remember where.

With a sudden jolt, he realized that he could not remember *anything*. Where he had come from. His mother. His father. His name. *His own name.* Hard as he tried, he could not remember. *His own name.*

"Who am I?"

Hearing his cry, the gull squawked and took flight.

Catching sight of his reflection in a pool of water, he paused to look. A strange face, belonging to a boy he did not know, peered back at him. His eyes, like his hair, were as black as coal, with scattered flecks of gold. His ears, which were almost triangular and pointed at the top, seemed oddly large for the rest of his face. Likewise, his brow rose high above his eyes. Yet his nose looked narrow and slight, more a beak than a nose. Altogether, his face did not seem to belong to itself.

He mustered his strength and rose to his feet. Head swirling, he braced himself against a pinnacle of rock until the dizziness calmed.

His eyes roamed over the desolate coastline. Rocks upon rocks lay scattered everywhere, making a harsh black barrier to the sea. The rocks parted in only one place—and then only grudgingly—around the roots of an ancient oak tree. Its gray bark peeling, the old oak faced the ocean with the stance of centuries. There was a deep hollow in its trunk, gouged out by fire ages ago. Age warped its every branch, twisting some into knots. Yet it continued to stand, roots anchored, immutable against storm and sea. Behind the oak stood a dark grove of younger trees, and behind them, high cliffs loomed even darker.

Desperately, the boy searched the landscape for anything he might recognize, anything that might coax his memory to return. He recognized nothing.

He turned, despite the stinging salt spray, to the open sea. Waves rolled and toppled, one after another after another. Nothing but endless gray billows as far as he could see. He listened again for the mysterious voice, but heard only the distant call of a kittiwake perched on the cliffs.

Had he come from somewhere out there, beyond the sea?

Vigorously, he rubbed his bare arms to stop the shivers. Spying a loose clump of sea kelp on a rock, he picked it up. Once, he knew, this formless mass of green had danced with its own graceful rhythm, before being uprooted and cast adrift. Now it hung limp in his hand. He wondered why he himself had been uprooted, and from where.

A low, moaning sound caught his ear. That voice again! It came from the rocks beyond the old oak tree.

He lurched forward in the direction of the voice. For the first time he noticed a dull ache between his shoulder blades. He could only assume that his back, like his head, had slammed against the rocks. Yet the ache felt somehow deeper, as if something beneath his shoulders had been torn away long ago.

After several halting steps he made it to the ancient tree. He leaned against its massive trunk, his heart pounding. Again he heard the mysterious moaning. Again he set off.

Often his bare feet would slip on the wet rocks, pitching him sideways. Stumbling along, his torn brown tunic flapping about his legs, he resembled an ungainly water bird, picking his way across the shoreline. Yet all the time he knew what he really was: a lone boy, with no name and no home.

Then he saw her. Crumpled among the stones lay the body of a woman, her face beside a surging tidal pool. Her long, unbraided hair, the color of a yellow summer moon, spread about her head like rays of light. She had strong cheekbones and a complexion that would be described as creamy were it not tinged with blue. Her long blue robe, torn in places, was splotched with sand and sea kelp. Yet the quality of the wool, as well as the jeweled pendant on a leather cord around her neck, revealed her to have been once a woman of wealth and stature.

He rushed forward. The woman moaned again, a moan of inextinguishable pain. He could almost feel her agony, even as he could feel his own hopes rising. *Do I know her?* he asked himself as he bent over her twisted body. Then, from a place of deeper longing, *Does she know me?*

With a single finger he touched her cheek, as cold as the cold sea. He watched her take several short, labored breaths. He listened to her wretched moaning. And, with a sigh, he admitted to himself that she was, for him, a complete stranger.

Still, as he studied her, he could not suppress the hope that she might have arrived on this shore together with him. If she had not come on the same wave, then at least she might have come from the same place. Perhaps, if she lived, she might be able to fill the empty cup of his memory. Perhaps she knew his very name! Or the names of his mother and father. Or perhaps . . . she might actually *be* his mother.

A frigid wave slapped against his legs. His shivers returned, even as his hopes faded. She might not live, and even if she did, she probably would not know him. And she certainly could not be his mother. That was too much to hope for. Besides, she could not have looked less like him. She looked truly beautiful, even at the edge of death, as beautiful as an angel. And he had seen his own reflection. He knew what he looked like. Less like an angel than a bedraggled, half-grown demon.

A snarl erupted from behind his back.

The boy whirled around. His stomach clenched. There, in the shadows of the dark grove, stood an enormous wild boar.

A low, vicious growl vibrating in its throat, the boar stepped out of the trees. Bristling brown fur covered its entire body except for the eyes and a gray scar snaking down its left foreleg. Its tusks, sharp as daggers, were blackened with the blood of a previous kill. More frightening, though, were its red eyes, which glowed like hot coals.

The boar moved smoothly, almost lightly, despite its hulking form. The boy stepped backward. This beast outweighed him several times over. One kick of its leg would send him sprawling. One stab of its tusk would rip his flesh to shreds. Abruptly the boar stopped and hunched its muscular shoulders, preparing to charge.

Glancing behind, the boy could see only the onrushing waves of the ocean. No escape that way. He grabbed a crooked shard of driftwood to use as a weapon, though he knew it would not even begin to pierce the boar's hide. Even so, he tried to plant his feet on the slippery rocks, bracing for the attack.

Then he remembered. The hollow in the old oak! Although the tree stood about halfway between him and the boar, he might be able to get there first.

He started to dash for the tree, then suddenly caught himself. The woman. He could not just leave her there. Yet his own chance for safety depended on speed. Grimacing, he tossed aside the driftwood and grabbed her limp arms.

Straining his trembling legs, he tried to pull her free from the rocks. Whether from all the water she had swallowed or from the weight of death upon her, she felt as heavy as the rocks themselves. Finally, under the glaring eyes of the boar, she budged.

The boy began dragging her toward the tree. Sharp stones cut into his feet. Heart racing, head throbbing, he pulled with all his power.

The boar snarled again, this time more like a raspy laugh. The whole body of the beast tensed, nostrils flaring and tusks gleaming. Then it charged.

Though the boy was only a few feet from the tree, something kept him from running. He snatched a squarish stone from the ground and hurled it at the boar's head. Only an instant before reaching them, the boar changed direction. The stone whizzed past and clattered on the ground.

Amazed that he could have possibly daunted the beast, the boy quickly bent to retrieve another stone. Then, sensing some movement over his shoulder, he spun around.

Out of the bushes behind the ancient oak bounded an immense stag. Bronze in hue, except for the white boots on each leg that shone like purest quartz, the stag lowered its great rack of antlers. With the seven points on each side aimed like so many spears, the stag leaped at the boar. But the beast swerved aside just in time to dodge the thrust.

As the boar careened and snarled ferociously, the stag leaped once again. Seizing the moment, the boy dragged the limp woman into the hollow of the tree. By folding her legs tight against her chest, he pushed her entirely into the opening. The wood, still charred from some ancient fire, curled around her like a great black shell. He wedged himself into the small space beside her, as the boar and the stag circled each other, pawing the ground and snorting wrathfully.

Eyes aflame, the boar feigned a charge at the stag, then bolted straight at the tree. Hunched in the hollow, the boy drew back as far as he could. Yet his face remained so close to the gnarled bark of the opening that he still could feel the boar's hot breath as its tusks slashed wildly at the trunk. One of the tusks grazed the boy's face, gashing him just below the eye.

At that moment the stag plowed into the flank of the boar. The bulky beast flew into the air and landed on its side near the bushes. Blood oozing from a punctured thigh, the boar scrambled to its feet.

The stag lowered its head, poised to leap again. Hesitating for a split second, the boar snarled one final time before retreating into the trees.

With majestic slowness, the stag turned toward the boy. For a brief moment, their eyes met. Somehow the boy knew that he would remember nothing from that day so clearly as the bottomless brown pools of the stag's unblinking eyes, eyes as deep and mysterious as the ocean itself.

Then, as swiftly as it had appeared, the stag leaped over the twisted roots of the oak and vanished from sight.

PART ONE

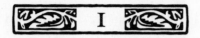

A LIVING EYE

I *stand alone, beneath the stars.*

The entire sky ignites into flame, as if a new sun is being born. People shriek and scatter. But I stand there, unable to move, unable to breathe. Then I see the tree, darker than a shadow against the flaming sky. Its burning branches writhe like deadly serpents. They reach for me. The fiery branches come closer. I try to escape, but my legs are made of stone. My face is burning! I hide my eyes. I scream.

My face! My face is burning!

I awoke. Perspiration stung my eyes. Straw from my pallet scratched against my face.

Blinking, I drew a deep breath and wiped my face with my hands. They felt cool against my cheeks.

Stretching my arms, I felt again that pain between my shoulder blades. Still there! I wished it would go away. Why should it still bother me now, more than five years since the day I had washed ashore? The wounds to my head had long since healed, though I still remembered nothing of my life before being thrown on the rocks. So why should this wound last so much longer? I shrugged. Like so much else, I would never know.

I started to stuff some loose straw back into the pallet when my fingers uncovered an ant, dragging the body of a worm several times its size. I watched, almost laughing, as the ant tried to climb straight up the miniature mountain of straw. It could have easily gone around one side or another. But no. Some mysterious motive drove it to try, spill over backward, try again, and spill again. For several minutes I watched this repeating performance.

At last I took pity on the little fellow. I reached for one of its legs, then realized that it might twist off, especially if the ant struggled. So I picked up the worm instead. Just as I expected, the ant clung to it, kicking frantically.

I carried the ant and its prize up and over the straw, dropping them gently on the other side. To my surprise, when I released my hold on the worm, so did the ant. It turned toward me, waving its tiny antennae wildly. I caught the distinct feeling that I was being scolded.

"My apologies," I whispered through my grin.

The ant scolded me for a few more seconds. Then it bit into the worm and started to drag the heavy load away. To its home.

My grin faded. Where could I find my own home? I would drag behind me this whole pallet, this whole hut if necessary, if only I knew where to go.

Turning to the open window above my head, I saw the full moon, glowing as bright as a pot of molten silver. Moonlight poured through the window, and through the gaps in the thatched roof, painting the interior of the hut with its gleaming brush. For a moment, the moonlight nearly disguised the poverty of the room, covering the earthen floor with a sheath of silver, the rough clay walls with sparkles of light, the still-sleeping form in the corner with the glow of an angel.

Yet I knew that it was all an illusion, no more real than my dream.

The floor was just dirt, the bed just straw, the dwelling just a hovel made of twigs bound with clay. The covered pen for the geese next door had been constructed with more care! I knew, for I sometimes hid myself in there, when the honking and hissing of geese sounded more to my liking than the howling and chattering of people. The pen stayed warmer than this hut in February, and drier in May. Even if I did not deserve any better than the geese, no one could doubt that Branwen did.

I watched her sleeping form. Her breathing, so subtle that it hardly lifted her woolen blanket, seemed calm and peaceful. Alas, I knew better. While peace might visit her in sleep, it escaped her in waking life.

She shifted in her slumber, rolling her face toward mine. In the lunar light she looked even more beautiful than usual, her creamy cheeks and brow thoroughly relaxed, as they were only on such nights when she slept soundly. Or in her moments of silent prayer, which happened more and more often.

I frowned at her. If only she would speak. Tell me what she knew. For if she did know anything about our past, she had refused to discuss it. Whether that was because she truly did not know, or because she simply did not want me to know, I could never tell.

And, in the five years we had shared this hut, she had revealed little more about herself. But for the kind touch of her hand and the ever present sorrow at the back of her eyes, I hardly knew her at all. I only knew that she was not my mother, as she claimed.

How could I be so sure that she was not my mother? Somehow, in my heart, I knew. She was too distant, too secretive. Surely a mother, a real mother, wouldn't hide so much from her own son. And if I needed any more assurance, I had only to look at her face.

So lovely—and so very different from my own. There was no hint of black in those eyes, nor of points on those ears! No, I was no more her son than the geese were my siblings.

Nor could I believe that her real name was Branwen, and that mine was Emrys, as she had tried to convince me. Whatever names we had possessed before the sea had spat us out on the rocks, I felt sure somehow that they were not those. As many times as she had called me Emrys, I could not shake the feeling that my true name was . . . something else. Yet I had no idea where to look for the truth, except perhaps in the wavering shadows of my dreams.

The only times that Branwen, if that was really her name, would show even a hint of her true self were when she told me stories. Especially the stories of the ancient Greeks. Those tales were clearly her favorites. And mine, too. Whether she knew it or not, some part of her seemed to come alive when she spoke of the giants and gods, the monsters and quests, in the Greek myths.

True, she also enjoyed telling tales of the Druid healers, or the miracle worker from Galilee. But her stories about the Greek gods and goddesses brought a special light into her sapphire eyes. At times, I almost felt that telling these stories was her way of talking about a place that she believed really existed—a place where strange creatures roamed the land and great spirits mingled with humans. The whole notion seemed foolish to me, but apparently not to her.

A sudden flash of light at her throat curtailed my thoughts. I knew that it was only the light of the moon reflected in her jeweled pendant, still hanging from the leather cord about her neck, although the green color seemed richer tonight than ever before. I realized that I had never seen her take the pendant off, not even for an instant.

Something tapped on the dirt behind me. I turned to see a bundle of dried leaves, slender and silvery in the moonlight, bound with a knot of grass. It must have fallen from the ridge beam above, which supported not only the thatch but also dozens of clusters of herbs, leaves, flowers, roots, nuts, bark shavings, and seeds. These were only a portion of Branwen's collection, for many more bundles hung from the window frame, the back of the door, and the tilting table beside her pallet.

Because of the bundles, the whole hut smelled of thyme, beech root, mustard seed, and more. I loved the aromas. Except for dill, which made me sneeze. Cedar bark, my favorite, lifted me as tall as a giant, petals of lavender tingled my toes, and sea kelp reminded me of something I could not quite remember.

All these ingredients and tools she used to make her healing powders, pastes, and poultices. Her table held a large assortment of bowls, knives, mortars, pestles, strainers, and other utensils. Often I watched her crushing leaves, mixing powders, straining plants, or applying a mixture of remedies to someone's wound or wart. Yet I knew as little about her healing work as I did about her. While she allowed me to watch, she would not converse or tell stories. She merely worked away, usually singing some chant or other.

Where had she learned so much about the art of healing? Where had she discovered the tales of so many distant lands and times? Where had she first encountered the teachings of the man from Galilee that increasingly occupied her thoughts? She would not say.

I was not alone in being vexed by her silence. Oftentimes the villagers would whisper behind her back, wondering about her healing powers, her unnatural beauty, her strange chants. I had even heard the words *sorcery* and *black magic* used once or twice, although it did not seem to discourage people from coming to her when they needed a boil healed, a cough cured, or a nightmare dispelled.

Branwen herself did not seem worried by the whisperings. As long as most people paid her for her help, so that we could continue to make our way, she did not seem to care what they might think or say. Recently she had tended to an elderly monk who had slipped on the wet stones of the mill bridge and gashed his arm. While binding his wound, Branwen uttered a Christian blessing, which seemed to please him. When she followed it with a Druid chant, however, he scolded her and warned her against blasphemy. She replied calmly that Jesus himself was so devoted to healing others that he might well have drawn upon the wisdom of the Druids, as well as others now called pagan. At that point the monk angrily shook off her bandage and left, though not before telling half the village that she was doing the work of demons.

I turned back to the pendant. It seemed to shine with its own light, not just the moon's. For the first time I noticed that the crystal in its center was not merely flat green, as it appeared from a distance. Leaning closer, I discovered violets and blues flowing like rivulets beneath its surface, while glints of red pulsed with a thousand tiny hearts. It looked almost like a living eye.

Galator. The word sprung suddenly into my mind. *It is called Galator.*

I shook my head, puzzled. Where did that word come from? I could not recall ever having heard it. I must have picked it up from the village square, where numerous dialects—Celt, Saxon, Roman, Gaelic, and others even more strange—collided and merged every day. Or perhaps from one of Branwen's own stories, which were sprinkled with words from the Greeks, the Jews, the Druids, and others more ancient still.

"Emrys!"

Her shrill whisper startled me so much that I jumped. I faced the bluer-than-blue eyes of the woman who shared with me her hut and her meals, but nothing more.

"You are awake."

"I am. And you were staring at me strangely."

"Not at you," I replied. "At your pendant." On an impulse, I added, "At your *Galator.*"

She gasped. With a sweep of her hand she stuffed the pendant under her robe. Then, trying to keep her voice calm, she said, "That is not a word I remember telling you."

My eyes widened. "You mean it is the real word? The right word?"

She observed me thoughtfully, almost started to speak, then caught herself. "You should be sleeping, my son."

As always, I bristled when she called me that. "I can't sleep."

"Would a story help? I could finish the one about Apollo."

"No. Not now."

"I could make you a potion, then."

"No thanks." I shook my head. "When you did that for the thatcher's son, he slept for three and a half days."

A smile touched her lips. "He drank a week's dose at once, poor fool."

"It's almost dawn, anyway."

She gathered her rough wool blanket. "Well, if you don't want to sleep, I do."

"Before you do, can't you tell me more about that word? Gal— Oh, what was it?"

Seeming not to hear me, she wrapped herself in her customary cloak of silence, even as she wrapped herself in the wool blanket and closed her eyes once more. In seconds, she seemed to be asleep again. Yet the peace I had seen in her face before had flown.

"Can't you tell me?"

She did not stir.

"Why don't you ever help me?" I wailed. "I need your help!"

Still she did not stir.

Ruefully, I watched her for a while. Then I rolled off the pallet, stood, and splashed my face with water from the large wooden bowl by the door. Glancing again at Branwen, I felt a renewed surge of anger. Why wouldn't she answer me? Why wouldn't she help me? Yet even as I looked upon her, I felt a small prick of guilt that I had never been able to bring myself to call her Mother, although I knew how much it would please her. And yet . . . what kind of mother would refuse to help her son?

I tugged against the rope handle of the door. With a scrape against the dirt, it opened, and I left the hut.

II

AN OWL IS COMING

The western sky had darkened, as the moon had nearly set. Streaks of silver, shading into gray, lined the thick clouds above the village of Caer Vedwyd. In the dim light, its humped roofs of thatch looked like a group of shadowed boulders. Somewhere nearby I heard lambs crying. And my friends, the geese, began to wake up. A cuckoo in the bracken called twice. Under the dripping oak and ash trees, the fresh scent of bluebells mingled with the smell of wet thatch.

It was May, and in May even a dreary village before dawn could seem lovely. I pulled a burr from the sleeve of my tunic, listening to the quiet stirrings. This month excited me like no other. Flowers opened their faces to the sky, lambs birthed, leaves sprouted. And as the flowers blossomed, so did my dreams. Sometimes, in May, I swallowed my doubts and believed that one day I would find the truth. Who I really was, where I really came from. If not from Branwen, then from someone else.

In May, anything seemed possible. If only I could learn to harness time itself. To make every month like May! Or, perhaps, to live *backward* in time, so that whenever the end of the month arrived, I could turn May right around and live it all over again.

I chewed my lip. Whatever the month, this village would never be my favorite place. Nor my home. I knew this early hour would be the finest of the day, before the sun's rays revealed its tattered huts and fearful faces. Like most villages in this rolling, thickly wooded country, Caer Vedwyd existed only because of an old Roman road. Ours ran along the north bank of the River Tywy, which flowed south all the way to the sea. Although the road had once carried streams of Roman soldiers, it now carried mainly vagabonds and wandering traders. It was a towpath for horses bringing barges of grain down the river, a route for those seeking the Church of Saint Peter in the city of Caer Myrddin to the south, and also, as I remembered well, a passage to the sea.

A metal tool clanged in the smith's shop under the great oak. I could hear a horse tramping somewhere up the towpath, its bridle jingling. In another hour, people would be gathering in the square under the tree, where the village's three main paths converged. Soon the sounds of bartering, arguing, cajoling, and of course thieving, would fill the air.

Five years in this place, and it still did not feel like home. Why? Perhaps because everything, from the local gods to the local names, was changing. Fast. The newly arrived Saxons had already started to call Y Wyddfa, whose icy ridges towered over everything, Snow Hill or Snowdon. Likewise, people were now calling this region, long known as Gwynedd, the country of Wales. But to call it a country at all was to imply a kind of unity that did not really exist. Given the number of travelers and dialects that passed through just our little village every day, Wales seemed to me less a country than a way station.

Following the path down to the mill house, I saw the last traces of moonlight touching the slopes of Y Wyddfa. The sounds of the waking village melted into the splashy clatter of the river flowing under the stone bridge by the mill. A frog bellowed, somewhere by the mill house, the only building in the village made of real brick.

Without warning, a quiet voice within me whispered, *An owl is coming.*

I whirled about just in time to see the square head and massive brown wings sail past me as fast as the wind and as silent as death. Two seconds later it dropped into the grass behind the mill house, its talons squeezing the life out of its prey.

Stoat for supper. I grinned to myself, pleased that I had somehow known that the owl was approaching, and that its invisible quarry was a stoat. How did I know? I had no idea. I simply knew, that's all. And I supposed that any reasonably observant person would have known as well.

More and more, though, I wondered. I did sometimes seem a step ahead of other people in sensing what was about to happen. This talent, if you could call it a talent, had only just appeared in the last few weeks, so I didn't even begin to understand it. And I hadn't shared it with Branwen, or with anyone else. It could be nothing more than a string of lucky guesses. But if, in fact, it was something more, it might at least provide some entertainment. Or even prove useful in a pinch.

Only the day before, I had seen some village boys chasing one another with imaginary swords. For a brief moment, I longed to be one of them. Then the group's leader, Dinatius, spied me and pounced on me before I could get away. I had never liked Dinatius, who had spent the years since his mother's death as the smith's servant. He struck me as mean, stupid, and quick-tempered. But I had tried never to offend him, less out of kindness than the fact that he was much older and much larger than I—or any other boy in the village. More than once, I had seen him struck by the smith's powerful hand for shirking his duties, and just as often I had seen Dinatius do the same to someone smaller. Once he badly burned the arm of another boy who had dared to question his Roman ancestry.

All this ran through my mind the day before as I struggled to get away from him. Then I chanced to see a low-flying gull overhead. I pointed to the bird and cried, "Look! Treasure from the sky!" Dinatius turned his face skyward at just the moment that the bird released an especially pungent sort of treasure—which splatted him right in the eye. While Dinatius cursed and tried to wipe his face, the other boys laughed, and I escaped.

Smiling, I thought of yesterday's close call. For the first time, I wondered whether I might possess a talent—a power—even more precious than predicting events. Suppose, just suppose . . . I could actually *control* events. Make something happen. Not with my hands, my feet, or my voice. With nothing but my thoughts.

How exciting! It was probably just another May dream. But what if it was more? I would give it a try.

As I approached the stone bridge over the river, I knelt beside a low, tightly cupped flower. Concentrating all my thoughts on the flower, I grew oblivious to everything else. The chilled air, the crying lambs, the smith's noises, all faded away.

I studied the flower's lavender hue, touched on the east by the golden light of the emerging sun. Minuscule hairs, wearing droplets of dew, embroidered the edges of each petal, while a tiny brown aphid scurried across the collar of fringed leaves at the top of the stalk. Its aroma seemed fresh, but not sweet. Somehow I knew that its hidden center must be the color of aged yellow cheese.

Ready at last, I began willing the flower to open. *Show yourself,* I commanded. *Open your petals.*

I waited for a long moment. Nothing happened.

Again I focused on the flower. *Open. Open your petals.*
Still nothing happened.

I started to stand. Then, very slowly, the collar of leaves began to flutter as if touched by the barest of breezes. A moment later one of the lavender petals stirred, unfurling an edge ever so slightly, before gradually beginning to open. Another petal followed, and another, and another, until the whole flower greeted the oncoming dawn with petals outstretched. And from its center sprouted six soft sprigs, more like feathers than petals. Their color? Like aged yellow cheese.

A brutal kick struck me in the back. Coarse laughter filled the air, crushing the moment as swiftly as a heavy foot crushed the flower.

III

RIDING
THE STORM

With a groan, I pushed myself to my feet. "Dinatius, you pig."

The older boy, square-shouldered with bushy brown hair, smirked at me. "You're the one with pointed ears like a pig. Or like a demon! Anyway, better a pig than a bastard."

My cheeks grew hot, but I held my temper. I looked into his eyes—gray as a goose's back. This required me to tilt my head back, since he was so much taller. Indeed, Dinatius' shoulders could already lift loads that made many grown men wobble. In addition to stoking the smith's fire—hot, heavy work on its own—he cut and carried the firewood, worked the bellows, and hauled iron ore by the hundredweight. For this the smith gave him a meal or two a day, a sack of straw to sleep on, and many a blow about the head.

"I am no bastard."

Dinatius slowly rubbed the stubble on his chin. "Where then is your father hiding? Maybe he's a pig! Or maybe he's one of those rats who lives with you and your mother."

"We don't have any rats in our home."

"Home! You call that a home? It's just a filthy hole where your mother can hide and do her sorcery."

My fists clenched. The taunts about me cut deep enough, but it was his crass mention of *her* that made my blood boil. Still, I knew that Dinatius wanted me to fight him. I also knew what the outcome would be. Better to hold my temper, if I could. It would be very hard to keep my arms still. But my tongue? Even harder.

"He who is made of air should not accuse the wind."

"What do you mean by that, bastard whelp?"

I had no idea where the words came from that I spoke next. "I mean that you should not call somebody else bastard, since your father was just a Saxon mercenary who rode through this village one night and left nothing but you and an empty flask in his wake."

Dinatius' mouth opened and then closed without a word. I realized that I had spoken words he had always feared, but never admitted, were true. Words that struck more violently than clubs.

His face reddened. "Not so! My father was a Roman, and a soldier! Everyone knows that." He glared at me. "I'll show you who's the bastard."

I stepped backward.

Dinatius advanced on me. "You are nothing, bastard. Nothing! You have no father. No home. No name! Where did you steal the name Emrys, bastard? You are nothing! And you'll never be more!"

I winced at his words, even as I saw the rage swell in his eyes. I glanced about for some way to escape. I couldn't possibly outrun him. Not without a head start. But there were no birds flying overhead today. A thought hit me. *No birds flying overhead.*

Just as I had done yesterday, I pointed to the sky and cried out, "Look! Treasure from the sky!"

Dinatius, who had just leaned forward to lunge at me, did not look skyward this time. Instead, he hunched as if to protect his head from a blow. That was all that I could hope for. I turned and ran as fast as a frightened rabbit across the rain-soaked yard of the mill house.

Roaring with rage, he flew after me. "Come back, coward!"

I cut across the grass, leaped over a broken grinding stone and some scraps of wood, and dashed over the bridge, my leather boots slapping on the stones. Even before I reached the opposite side, I could hear Dinatius' footsteps above my own panting. Veering sharply, I turned up the old Roman road on the riverbank. To my right, the Tywy's waters churned. To my left, dense forest stretched unbroken, except by the pathways of deer and wolves, all the way to the slopes of Y Wyddfa.

I sped up the stony path for sixty or seventy paces, all the while hearing him draw closer. As I topped a small rise, I left the path, hurling myself into the thicket of bracken bordering the forest. Despite the thorns tearing into my calves and thighs, I plunged frantically ahead. Then, breaking free of the bracken, I jumped a fallen branch, leaped a rivulet, and scrambled up the mossy outcropping of rock on the other side. Finding a slender deer trail, winding like an endless snake along the forest floor, I raced along until I found myself in a grove of towering trees.

I stopped just long enough to hear Dinatius crashing through the branches behind me. Without pausing to think, I crouched on the cushion of needles underfoot and sprung up to the lowest branch of a great pine tree. Like a squirrel, I worked my way upward, one branch after another, until I had climbed to the height of three men above the ground.

At that very instant, Dinatius entered the grove. Directly above him, I clung to the branch, heart racing, lungs aching, legs bleeding. I tried to remain motionless, to breathe quietly, though my lungs screamed for more air.

Dinatius stared to his left and to his right, straining to see in the dimly lit grove. At one point, he looked up, but caught a flake of bark in his eye and thundered, "Curse this forest!" Hearing some slight rustling beyond the grove, he threw himself in that direction.

For most of the morning, I waited on that branch, observing the slow sweep of light over the needled boughs, and the still slower movement of wind walking among the trees. At length, convinced that I had eluded Dinatius, I dared to move. But I did not climb down.

I climbed up.

Ascending the stairway of branches, I realized that my heart was still racing, though not with fear, nor with exertion. It pounded with anticipation. Something about this tree, this minute, thrilled me in a way I could not explain. Each time I tugged my body to a higher branch, I found my own spirits lifted as well. It was almost as if I could see farther, hear clearer, and smell deeper the higher I climbed. I imagined myself soaring beside the small hawk that I could see circling above the trees.

The vista below me enlarged. I followed the course of the river as it wound its way down from the hills to the north. The river reminded me of a huge serpent, something out of Branwen's stories. And the hills sat in rumpled rows, like the folds of an ancient, exposed brain. What thoughts, I wondered, had that brain produced over the great stretch of time? Was this forest one of them? Was this day one of them?

Out of the mists curling among the steepest hills rose the great mass of Y Wyddfa, its summit gleaming, cloaked in white. Cloud shadows, dark and round, moved across its ridges like the footprints of giants. If only I could see the giants themselves! If only I could witness their dance!

In the western sky the clouds themselves gathered, though I could still see the occasional glint and sparkle of light on the sunlit sea. The sight of the endless ocean filled me with a vague, indefinable longing. Somehow I knew. My true home, my true name, lay out there . . . somewhere. Currents as bottomless as the sea itself churned within me.

Reaching for the next limb, I struggled to pull myself higher. I clasped my hands around the base of the branch, then threw one leg over. Several twigs broke off and spiraled gracefully to the ground. With a grunt, I pulled as hard as I could and finally mounted it.

Ready to rest, I wedged myself into the notch of the branch and leaned back against the trunk. Feeling my hands, so sticky from pine sap, I brought them to my face. I filled my lungs with the sweet, resiny smell.

Suddenly something brushed my right ear. I spun my head around. A bristling brown tail disappeared around the trunk. As I stretched to peer behind the trunk, I heard a loud whistle. The next instant, I felt tiny feet scamper lightly across my chest and down my leg.

I sat up again, just in time to see a squirrel leap from my own foot to a lower branch. Grinning, I watched the bustling animal chatter and squeak. The squirrel dashed up the trunk and then down and then up again, waving its tail like a furry flag, all the while chewing on a pinecone almost as large as its head. Then, as if it had just noticed me, it stopped short. It considered me for a few seconds, squealed once, and jumped to the outstretched bough of a neighboring tree. From there it scurried down the trunk and out of sight. I wondered whether I had looked as amusing to the squirrel as the squirrel had looked to me.

The thrill rose in me again, driving me to climb. As the wind lifted, so did the elixir of scents from the trees. Resins from chafing branches on every side poured over me, immersing me in a river of aromas.

Again I saw the hawk, still circling overhead. I could not be sure, but I felt somehow that it was watching me. Observing me, for reasons of its own.

The first rumble of thunder came as I hauled myself up to the highest branch that could support my weight. With it came a rumble more powerful still, the collective calling of thousands of trees bending with the same wind. I gazed across the sea of trees, their branches rippling like waves on water. I found that beneath the rumble I could hear their varying voices: the deep sighing of oak and the shrill snapping of hawthorn, the whooshing of pine and the cracking of ash. Needles clicked and leaves tapped. Trunks groaned and hollows whistled. All these voices and more joined to form one grand, undulating chorus, singing in a language not so distant from my own.

As the wind swelled, my tree started to sway. Almost like a human body it swung back and around, gently at first, then more and more wildly. While the swaying intensified, so did my fears that the trunk might snap and hurl me to the ground. But in time my confidence returned. Amazed at how the tree could be at once so flexible and so sturdy, I held on tight as it bent and waved, twisted and swirled, slicing curves and arcs through the air. With each graceful swing, I felt less a creature of the land and more a part of the wind itself.

The rain began falling, its sound merging with the splashing river and the singing trees. Branches streamed like waterfalls of green. Tiny rivers cascaded down every trunk, twisting through moss meadows and bark canyons. All the while, I rode out the gale. I could not have felt wetter. I could not have felt freer.

When, at last, the storm subsided, the entire world seemed newly born. Sunbeams danced on rain-washed leaves. Curling columns of mist rose from every glade. The forest's colors shone more vivid, its smells struck more fresh. And I understood, for the first time in my life, that the Earth was always being remade, that life was always being renewed. That it may have been the afternoon of this particular day, but it was still the very morning of Creation.

IV

THE RAG PILE

Late afternoon light heightened the hues and deepened the shadows before I felt a subtle pang in my abdomen. Quickly the pang grew. I was hungry. Hungry as a wolf.

Taking a last look at the vista, I could see a golden web of light creeping across the hills. Then I began to climb down from my perch. When at last I reached the bottommost branch, still wet from rain, I wrapped my hands around the bark and let myself drop over the side. For a moment I hung there, swaying like the tree in the gale. For some reason, I realized, the usual ache between my shoulder blades had not bothered me since I had first ascended the branches. I let go, falling into the bed of needles.

Gently, I placed my hand upon the ridged trunk of the old tree. I could almost feel the resins moving through the tall, columnar body, even as the blood moved through my own. With a simple pat of my hand, I gave thanks.

My gaze fell to a bouquet of tan mushrooms wearing shaggy manes, nestled among the needles at the base of the pine. From my forages with Branwen, I knew them to be good eating. I pounced. In short order, I had consumed every one—as well as the roots of a purple-leafed plant growing nearby.

I found the deer trail and followed it back to the rivulet. Cupping my hands, I drank some of the cold water. It chilled my teeth and awakened my tongue. A new lightness in my step, I returned to the towpath leading to the village.

I crossed the bridge. Beyond the mill, the thatched roofs of Caer Vedwyd clustered like so many bundles of dry grass. In one of them, the woman who called herself my mother was probably mixing her potions or tending to someone's wound, ever secretive and silent. To my own surprise, I found myself hoping that, one day, this place might yet feel like home.

Entering the village, I heard the playful shouts of other boys. My first impulse was to seek out one of my usual hideaways. Yet . . . I felt a new surge of confidence. This was a day to join in their games!

I hesitated. What if Dinatius was about? I would need to keep a wary eye on the smith's shop. Still, perhaps even Dinatius might soften in time.

Slowly, I approached. Beneath the great oak tree, where the three main pathways converged, I saw farmers and merchants gathered, peddling their goods. Horses and donkeys stood tethered to posts, their tails swishing at flies. Nearby, a bard with a somber face was entertaining a few listeners with a ballad—until one of the swishing tails slapped him right in the mouth. By the time he quit gagging and composed himself again, he had lost his audience.

Four boys stood at the far side of the square, practicing their aim by throwing rocks and sticks at a target—a pile of torn rags stuffed against the base of the oak. When I saw that Dinatius was not among them, I breathed easier. Soon I drew near enough to call out to one of the boys.

"How is your throw today, Lud?"

A squat, sandy-haired boy turned to me. His round face and small eyes gave him the look of being perpetually puzzled. Although he had not been unfriendly to me in the past, today he seemed cautious. I could not tell whether he was worried about Dinatius—or about me.

I stepped nearer. "Don't worry. No birds are going to empty themselves on your head."

Lud watched me for an instant, then started to laugh. "A good shot, that was!"

I grinned back. "A very good shot."

He tossed me a small stone. "Why not try your aim?"

"Are you sure?" one of the other boys asked. "Dinatius won't like it."

Lud gave a shrug. "Go ahead, Emrys. Let's see you throw."

The boys traded glances as I hefted the stone in my palm. With a snap of my arm, I threw at the rag pile. The stone flew high and wide, hitting the goose pen and causing a great commotion of honking and flapping.

I muttered sheepishly, "Not too good."

"Maybe you should get closer," ridiculed one of the boys. "Like right under the tree."

The others laughed.

Lud waved them quiet and tossed me another stone. "Try again. Some practice is what you need."

Something about his tone restored my confidence. As they all watched, I took aim again. This time, as I positioned myself, I took a moment to gauge the distance to the target and the weight of the stone in my hand. Keeping an eye on the pile of rags, I wound back my arm and released.

The stone made a direct hit. Lud clucked in satisfaction. I could not keep from smiling proudly.

Then something odd caught my attention. Instead of sailing

through the rags and hitting the trunk of the tree behind, my stone had bounced away, as if the rags themselves were made of something solid. As I looked more closely, my heart missed a beat. For as I watched, the rag pile shifted. From it came a piteous groan.

"It's a person!" I cried in disbelief.

Lud shook his head. "That's no person." He waved carelessly at the rag pile. "That's a Jew."

"A filthy Jew," echoed one of the other boys. He hurled his own stone at the rags. Another hit. Another groan.

"But—but you can't." I started to say more, then caught myself. That would risk losing any chance I might have to be accepted by the group.

"Why not?" Lud reared back to throw a weighty stick. "The Jew should never have come through here. They are Hell born, like demons, with horns and tails. They carry diseases. Bring bad luck."

The rag pile whimpered.

I swallowed hard. "I don't believe it. Why don't we let the beggar go and aim at something else instead?"

Lud eyed me strangely. "You'd best not defend the Jew. People might wonder whether . . ." He paused, picking his words. "Whether you come from the same stock."

Before I could reply, Lud let fly the heavy stick.

With a sweep of my arm, I cried out. "No! Don't hit him!"

The stick abruptly stopped its flight in midair and fell to the ground.

It was as if the stick had slammed into an invisible wall of air. The boys stood astonished. My jaw dropped. I was no less amazed than they were.

"A spell," whispered one boy.

"Sorcery," said another.

Lud's round face whitened. Slowly, he backed away from me. "Get away, you— you—"

"Demon's child," finished another voice.

I turned to find myself face-to-face with Dinatius, his tunic ripped and splattered with mud from his long trek through the forest. Despite his grimace, he looked satisfied at having cornered his prey at last.

I straightened my back, which only made me more aware of his considerable size advantage. "Let's not be enemies."

He spat on my cheek. "You think I would be the friend of a demon's whelp like you?"

My dark eyes narrowed as I wiped my face clean. It was all I could do to contain my anger enough to try again. My voice shaking, I declared, "I am no demon. I am a boy just like you."

"I know what you are." Dinatius' voice rolled down on me like a rock slide. "Your father was a demon. And your mother does the wicked work of demons. Either way, you are a child of the devil!"

With a shout, I lunged at him.

Deftly, Dinatius stepped to one side, swung me into the air, and threw me hard to the ground. He kicked me in the side for good measure, sending me rolling in the dirt.

I could barely sit up for the pain in my ribs. Above me towered Dinatius, his bushy head thrown back in laughter. The other boys laughed, too, even as they urged him on.

"What's your trouble, demon's child?" taunted Dinatius.

Though my pain was great, my rage was greater. Clutching my side, I struggled to roll onto my knees, then rise to my feet. I growled like a wounded beast, then charged again, arms flailing.

An instant later, I found myself facedown in the grass, barely able to breathe. I could taste blood in my mouth. The thought of playing dead crossed my mind, in the hope that my tormentor would lose interest. But I knew better.

Dinatius' laughter ceased as I forced myself to stand, blood trickling down my chin. I planted my unsteady feet and looked into his eyes. What I found there caught me off guard.

Beneath his belligerence, he was clearly surprised. "God's sweet death, but you're stubborn."

"Stubborn enough to stand up to you," I replied hoarsely. My hands clenched into fists.

At that moment, another figure swept out of nowhere to stand between us. The boys, except for Dinatius, fell back. And I gasped in surprise.

It was Branwen.

Though a shadow of fear crossed his face, Dinatius spat at her feet. "Move aside, she-demon."

Eyes alight, she glared at him. "Leave us."

"Go to the devil," he retorted. "That's where you both belong."

"Is that so? Then it is you who had better flee." She raised her arms menacingly. "Or I will bring the fires of Hell down on you."

Dinatius shook his head. "You will be the one to burn. Not me."

"But I am not afraid of fire! I cannot be burned!"

Lud, watching Branwen nervously, pulled on Dinatius' shoulder. "What if she speaks the truth? Let's go."

"Not until I finish with her whelp."

Branwen's blue eyes flashed. "Leave now. Or you shall burn."

He stepped backward.

She leaned toward him, then spoke a single word of command. "Now."

The other boys turned and ran. Dinatius, seeing their flight, looked uncertain. With both hands, he made the sign to protect himself from the evil eye.

"Now!" repeated Branwen.

Dinatius glowered at her for a moment, then retreated.

I took Branwen's arm. Together, we walked in slow procession back to our hut.

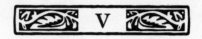

SACRED TIME

Stretched out on my pallet, I winced as Branwen massaged my bruised ribs. Odd patches of light, streaming through the holes in the thatched roof, fell on her left shoulder and hand. Her brow wrinkled in concern. Those blue eyes studied me so intensely that I could almost feel them boring into my skin.

"Thank you for helping me."

"You're welcome."

"You were wonderful. Really wonderful! And you appeared just in time, out of empty air. Like one of your Greek gods—Athena or somebody."

Branwen's wrinkles deepened. "More like Zeus, I'm afraid."

I laughed, which I regretted because it made my side hurt. "You mean you showered them with thunder and lightning."

"Instead of wisdom." She gave a sullen sigh. "I only did what any mother would do. Even if you never . . ."

"What?"

She shook her head. "It doesn't matter."

She rose to prepare a poultice that smelled of smoke and cedar. I heard her chopping and grinding for several minutes before returning to my side. Then, placing the poultice against my ribs, she laid her hands on top, pressing gently. Gradually I felt a steady warmth flowing into my bones, as if the marrow itself had turned into fire coals.

In time she closed her eyes and began to sing a low, slow chant that I had heard her use before in her healing work. In the past, I had never been sure whether she sang it to heal the person in her care or, in some way I could not understand, to heal herself. This time, studying her face, I had no doubt: The chant was for her, not for me.

> *Hy gododin catann hue*
> *Hud a lledrith mal wyddan*
> *Gaunce ae bellawn wen cabri*
> *Varigal don Fincayra*
> *Dravia, dravia Fincayra.*

The words, I felt, came from another world, an ocean away. I waited until she opened her eyes, then asked what I had wondered so often before, not expecting to receive any answer.

"What does it mean?"

Again she examined me with eyes that seemed to pierce my very soul. Then, choosing her words with care, she replied, "It is about a place, a magical place. A land of allurement. And also illusion. A land called Fincayra."

"What do those words at the end say? *Dravia, dravia Fincayra.*"

Her voice dropped to a whisper. "Live long, live long Fincayra." She lowered her eyes. "Fincayra. A place of many wonders, celebrated by bards of many tongues. They say it lies halfway between our world and the world of the spirit—neither wholly of Earth nor wholly of Heaven, but a bridge connecting both. Oh, the stories I could tell you! Its colors are more bright than the brightest sunrise; its air more fragrant than the richest garden. Many mysterious creatures are found there—including, legend has it, the very first giants."

Shifting my hips on the straw, I rolled so that my face was closer to hers. "You make it sound like a real place."

Her hands tightened against my ribs. "No more than any other place I've told you stories about. Stories may not be real in the same way as this poultice, my son, but they are real nonetheless! Real enough to help me live. And work. And find the meaning hidden in every dream, every leaf, every drop of dew."

"You don't mean that stories—like the ones about the Greek gods—are true?"

"Oh, yes." She thought for a moment. "Stories require faith, not facts. Don't you see? They dwell in sacred time, which flows in a circle. Not historical time, which runs in a line. Yet they are true, my son. Truer in many ways than the daily life of this pitiful little village."

Puzzled, I frowned. "But surely the Greeks' mountain Olympus is not the same as our mountain Y Wyddfa."

Her fingers relaxed slightly. "They're not so different as you think. Mount Olympus exists on land, and in story. In historical time, and in sacred time. Either way, Zeus and Athena and the others can be found there. It is an *in between place*—not quite our world and not quite the Otherworld, but something in between. In the same way that mist is not really air and not really water, but something of both. Another place like that is the Isle of Delos, the Greek island where Apollo was born and makes his home."

"In story, sure. But not in reality."

She eyed me strangely. "Are you sure?"

"Well . . . no, I guess not. I've never been to Greece. But I've seen Y Wyddfa a hundred times, right out that window. There are no Apollos walking around here! Not on that mountain, and not in this village."

Again she eyed me strangely. "Are you sure?"

"Of course I'm sure." I grasped a handful of straw from my pallet and threw it in the air. "This is the stuff of this village! Dirty straw, broken walls, angry people. Ignorant, too. Why, half of them think you really are a sorceress!"

Lifting the poultice, she examined the bruise running down my ribs. "Yet they still come here to be healed." She reached for a wooden bowl containing a greenish brown paste that smelled pungent, like overripe berries. Tenderly, using two fingers of her left hand, she began to apply the paste to my bruise.

"Tell me this," she said without taking her eyes off my wound. "Have you ever been out walking, away from the clatter of the village, when you felt the presence of a spirit, of something you couldn't quite see? Down by the river, perhaps, or somewhere in the forest?"

My thoughts drifted back to the great pine tree swaying in the storm. I could almost hear the swishing of branches, the wafting of resins, the feeling of bark on my hands. "Well, sometimes, in the forest . . ."

"Yes?"

"I've felt as if the trees, the oldest trees especially, were alive. Not just like a plant, but like a person. With a face. With a spirit."

Branwen nodded. "Like the dryads and hamadryads." She gazed at me wistfully. "I wish I could read to you some of the stories about them, in the Greeks' own words. They tell them so much better than I can! And those books . . . Emrys, I have seen a room full of books so thick and musty and inviting that I would sit down with one on my lap and do nothing but read all day long. I would keep on reading late into the night until I fell asleep. And then, as I slept, I might be visited by the dryads, or by Apollo himself."

She stopped short. "Have I never told you any stories about Dagda?"

I shook my head. "What does that have to do with Apollo?"

"Patience." Taking another scoop of the paste, she continued working. "The Celts, who have lived in Gwynedd long enough to know about sacred time, have many Apollos of their own. I heard about them as a child, long before I learned to read."

I jolted. "You are Celtic? I thought you came from . . . wherever I came from, over the sea."

Her hands tensed. "I did. But before I went there, I lived here, in Gwynedd. Not in this village but in Caer Myrddin, which was not so crowded as it is today. Now let me continue."

I nodded obediently, feeling buoyed by what she had said. It wasn't much, but it was the first time she had ever told me anything about her childhood.

She resumed both her work and her story. "Dagda is one of those Apollos. He is one of the most powerful Celtic spirits, the god of complete knowledge."

"What does Dagda look like? In the stories, I mean."

Branwen took the last of the paste from the bowl. "Ah, that's a good question. A very good question. For some reason known only to him, Dagda's true face is never seen. He assumes various forms at various times."

"Like what?"

"Once, in a famous battle with his supreme enemy, an evil spirit named Rhita Gawr, both of them took the forms of powerful beasts. Rhita Gawr became a huge boar, with terrible tusks and eyes the color of blood." She paused, trying to remember. "Oh, yes. And a scar that ran all the way down one of its forelegs."

I stiffened. The scar under my eye, where the boar's tusk had ripped me five years ago, started to sting. On many a dark night since that day, the same boar had appeared again, and attacked again, in my dreams.

"And in that battle, Dagda became—"

"A great stag," I completed. "Bronze in color, except for the white boots. Seven points on each side of its rack. And eyes as deep as the spaces between the stars."

Surprised, she nodded. "So you have heard the story?"

"No," I confessed.

"Then how could you know?"

I exhaled long and slow. "I have seen those eyes."

She froze. "You have?"

"I have seen the stag. And the boar as well."

"When?"

"On the day we washed ashore."

She studied me closely. "Did they fight?"

"Yes! The boar wanted to kill us. Especially you, I would guess, if it really was some kind of evil spirit."

"Whatever makes you say that?"

"Well, because you were . . . you! And I was just a scrawny little boy then." I cast an eye over myself and grinned. "As opposed to the scrawny big boy I am now. Anyway, that boar would surely have killed us. But then the stag appeared, and drove it off." I touched the spot under my eye. "That's how I got this."

"You never told me."

I glanced at her sharply. "There is much you have never told me."

"You're right," she said ruefully. "We may have shared a few stories about others, but very few about ourselves. It's my fault, really."

I said nothing.

"But I will share this much with you now. If that boar—Rhita Gawr—could have killed just one of us, it would not have been me. It would have been *you.*"

"What? That's absurd! It's you who has such knowledge, such powers to heal."

"And you have powers more vast by far!" Her gaze locked into mine. "Have you begun to feel them yet? Your grandfather told me once that his came in his twelfth year." She caught her breath. "I did not mean to mention him."

"But you did! Now can you tell me more?"

Grimly, she shook her head. "Let's not talk about it."

"Please, oh please! Tell me something, at least. What was he like?"

"I can't."

My cheeks grew hot. "You must! Why did you mention him at all unless there was something about him I should know?"

She ran a hand through her yellow locks. "He was a wizard, a formidable one. But I will tell you only what he said about you. Before you were born. He told me that powers such as he possessed often skipped a generation. And that I would have a son who . . ."

"Who what?"

"Who would have powers even greater than his own. Whose

magic would spring from the very deepest sources. So deep that, if you learned to master them, you could change the course of the world forever."

My jaw fell open. "That's not true. And you know it. Just look at me!"

"I am," she said quietly. "And while you are not now what your grandfather described, perhaps you will be someday."

"No," I protested. "I don't want that. I only want my memory back! I want to know who I really am."

"What if who you are involves such powers?"

"How could it?" I scoffed. "I'm no wizard."

She cocked her head. "One day you might be surprised."

Suddenly I remembered what had happened to Lud's stick. "Well . . . I *was* surprised. Out there, before you came. Something strange happened. I'm not even sure I did it. But I'm not sure I didn't, either."

Without saying a word, she retrieved a torn piece of cloth and started wrapping it around my ribs. She seemed to be observing me with new respect, perhaps even a touch of fear. Her hands moved more gingerly, as if I were almost too hot to touch. Whatever she was feeling, whatever I was sensing, it made me very uncomfortable. In the same moment that I had started to feel closer to her, it made her seem more distant than ever.

At length, she spoke. "Whatever you did, you did from your powers. They are yours to use, a gift from above. From the greatest of the gods, the one I pray to more than any other, the one who gave each of us whatever gifts we have. I have no idea what your powers might be, my son. I only know that God didn't give them to you without expecting you to use them. All God asks is that you use them *well*. But first you must, as your grandfather put it, come to master them. And that means learning how to use them with wisdom and love."

"But I didn't ask for powers!"

"Nor did I. Just as I did not ask to be called a sorceress. But with every gift comes the risk that others may not understand it."

"Aren't you afraid, though? Last year in Llen they burned someone they said was a sorceress."

She raised her eyes to the shafts of light coming through the holes above our heads. "Almighty God knows I am no sorceress. I only try to use whatever gifts I may have as best I can."

"You try to blend the old wisdom with the new. And that frightens people."

Her sapphire eyes softened. "You see more than I realize. Yes, it frightens people. So does almost everything these days."

She gently tied off the bandage. "The whole world is changing, Emrys. I have never known a time like this, even in . . . the other place. Invasions from across the sea. Mercenaries whose loyalties shift overnight. Christians at war with the old beliefs. Old beliefs at war with the Christians. People are afraid. Deathly afraid. Anything unknown becomes the work of demons."

Stiffly, I sat up. "Don't you sometimes wish . . ." My voice disappeared, and I swallowed. "That you didn't have your gifts? That you weren't so different? That nobody thought you were a demon?"

"Of course." She bit her lip thoughtfully. "But that's where my faith comes in. You see, the new wisdom is powerful. Very powerful. Just see what it did for Saint Brigid and Saint Colombe! Yet I know enough about the old wisdom to know it has great power, too. Is it too much to hope that they can live together, old and new? That they can strengthen each other? For even as the words of Jesus touch my soul, I cannot forget the words of others. The Jews. The Greeks. The Druids. The others, even older."

I watched her somberly. "You know so much. Not like me."

"There you are wrong. I know so little. So very little." A sudden look of pain crossed her face. "Like . . . why you never call me *Mother.*"

An arrow jabbed my heart. "That is because . . ."

"Yes?"

"Because I really don't believe you are."

She sucked in her breath. "And do you believe that your true name is Emrys?"

"No."

"Or that my true name is Branwen?"

"No."

She tilted her head upward. For a long moment, she stared into the thatch over our heads, blackened with the soot of countless cooking fires. At length, she looked at me again.

"About my own name, you are right. After we landed here, I took it from an old legend."

"The one you told me? About Branwen, daughter of Llyr?"

She nodded. "You remember it? Then you remember how Branwen came from another land to marry someone in Ireland. Her life began with boundless hope and beauty."

"And ended," I continued, "with so much tragedy. Her last words were, *Alas that I was ever born.*"

She took my hand in her own. "But that is about my name, not yours. My life, not yours. Please believe what I am telling you! Emrys is your name. And I am your mother."

A sob rose inside my throat. "If you are really my mother, can't you tell me where my home is? My true home, the place I really belong?"

"No, I can't! Those memories are too painful for me. And too dangerous for you."

"Then how do you expect me to believe you?"

"Hear me, please. I don't tell you only because I care for you! You lost your memory for a reason. It is a blessing."

I scowled. "It is a curse!"

She watched me, her eyes grown misty. It seemed to me that she was about to speak, to tell me at last what I most wanted to know. Then her hand squeezed mine—not in sympathy, but in fright.

FLAMES

A shape filled the doorway, blocking the light.

I jumped up from the pallet, knocking over Branwen's wooden bowl. "Dinatius!"

A hefty arm pointed at us. "Come out, both of you."

"We will not." Branwen rose to her feet and stood beside me.

Dinatius' gray eyes flashed angrily. He shouted over his shoulder, "Take her first."

He entered the hut, followed by two of the boys from the village square. Lud was not with them.

I grabbed Dinatius by the arm. He shook me off as if I were a fly, throwing me backward into the table bearing Branwen's utensils and ingredients. Spoons, knives, strainers, and bowls sprayed across the dirt floor of the hut as the table collapsed under my weight. Liquids and pastes splattered the clay walls, while seeds and leaves flew into the air.

Seeing him wrestling with Branwen, I sprung to my feet and leaped at him. He wheeled around and smacked me with such force that I flew backward into the wall. I lay there, momentarily dazed.

When my head cleared, I realized that I was alone in the hut. At first, I wasn't certain what had happened. Then, hearing shouts outside, I stumbled over to the doorway.

Branwen lay twenty or thirty paces away, in the middle of the path. Her hands and legs were bound with a length of spliced rope. A wad of cloth, torn from her dress, had been stuffed into her mouth so she could not cry out. Apparently the merchants and villagers in the square, busy with their work, had not yet noticed her—or not wanted to intervene.

"Look at her," laughed a slim, grimy-faced boy, pointing at the crumpled figure on the path. "She's not so scary now."

His companion, still holding some rope, joined the laughter. "Serves the she-demon right!"

I started to run to her aid. Suddenly I caught sight of Dinatius, bending over a pile of loose brush that had been stacked under the wide boughs of the oak. As he slid a shovel full of flaming coals from the smith's shop under the brush, fear sliced through me. *A fire. He's starting a fire.*

Flames began crackling in the brush. A column of smoke swiftly lifted into the branches of the tree. At this point Dinatius stood upright, hands on his hips, surveying his work. Silhouetted before the fire, he looked to me like a demon himself.

"She says she is not afraid of fire!" declared Dinatius, to the nods of the other boys. "She says she cannot be burned!"

"Let's find out," called the boy with the rope.

"Fire!" shouted one of the merchants, suddenly aware of the flames.

"Put it out!" cried a woman emerging from her hut.

But before anyone could move, the two boys had already grabbed Branwen by the legs. They began dragging her toward the blazing tree, where Dinatius stood waiting.

I ran out of the hut, my eyes fixed on Dinatius. Rage swelled within me, such rage as I had never known before. Uncontrollable and unstoppable, it coursed through my body like an enormous wave, knocking aside every other sense and feeling.

Seeing my approach, Dinatius grinned. "Just in time, whelp. We'll cook you both together."

A single wish overwhelmed me: *He should burn. Burn in Hell.*

At that instant, the tree shuddered and cracked, as if it had been ripped by a bolt of lightning. Dinatius whirled around just as one of the biggest branches, perhaps weakened by his fire, broke loose. Before he could escape, the branch fell directly on top of him, pinning his chest and crushing his arms. Like the breath of a dozen dragons, the blaze leaped higher. Villagers and merchants scattered. Branches exploded into flames, the sound of their snapping and splitting nearly drowning out the cries of the trapped boy.

I rushed to Branwen. She had been dropped only a few paces from the burning tree. Fire was licking at the edges of her robe. Quickly I pulled her away from the searing flames and untied her bonds. She pulled the wad from her mouth, staring at me with both gratitude and fear.

"Did you do that?"

"I—I think so. Some kind of magic."

Her sapphire eyes fixed on me. "Your magic. Your power."

Before I could reply, a spine-shivering scream erupted from inside the inferno. It went on and on, a cry of absolute agony. Hearing that voice—that helpless, human voice—my blood froze within my veins. I knew at once what I had done. I also knew what I must do.

"No!" protested Branwen, clutching at my tunic.

But it was too late. I had already plunged into the roaring flames.

VII

HIDDEN

Voices. Angelic voices.

I sat bolt upright. Could they really be angels? Was I really dead? Darkness surrounded me. Blacker than any night I had ever known.

Then: the pain. The pain on my face and my right hand told me I must indeed be alive. It was searing pain. Clawing pain. As if my very skin were being ripped away.

Beneath the pain, I grew aware of a strange weight on my brow. Cautiously, I reached my hands to my face. The fingers of my right hand, I realized, were bandaged. So were my brow, my cheeks, my eyes—swathed in cold, wet clothes that smelled of pungent herbs. Even the barest touch cut me with daggers of pain.

A heavy door creaked open. Across an expanse of stone floor, footsteps approached, echoing from a high ceiling above my head. Footsteps whose cadence I thought I recognized.

"Branwen?"

"Yes, my son," answered the voice in the darkness. "You have awakened. I am glad." Yet she sounded more dismal than glad, I thought, as she lightly caressed the back of my neck. "I must change your bandages. I am afraid it will hurt."

"No. Don't touch me."

"But I must, if you are to heal."

"No."

"Emrys, I must."

"All right, but be careful! It hurts so much already."

"I know, I know."

I tried my best to remain still as she carefully unwrapped the bandages, touching me as delicately as a butterfly. While she worked, she dripped something over my face which smelled as fresh as the forest after a rain and seemed to numb the pain a little. Feeling somewhat better, I spouted questions like a fountain. "How long have I slept? Where is this place? Who are those voices?"

"You and I—forgive me if this stings—are at the Church of Saint Peter. We are the guests of the nuns who live here. It is they you hear singing."

"Saint Peter! That's in Caer Myrddin."

"So it is."

Feeling a cold draft from a window or door somewhere, I drew my rough wool blanket about my shoulders. "But that is several days' travel, even with a horse."

"So it is."

"But—"

"Be still, Emrys, while I untie this."

"But—"

"Still, now . . . that's right. Just a moment. Ah, there."

As the bandage fell away, so did my questions about how we had come to be here. A new question crowded out all the rest. For although my eyes were no longer covered, I still could not see.

"Why is it so dark?"

Branwen did not answer.

"Didn't you bring a candle?"

Again she did not answer.

"Is it nighttime?"

Still she did not answer. Yet she did not need to, for the answer came from a cuckoo, alive with song, somewhere nearby.

The fingers of my unbandaged hand quivered as I touched the tender area around my eyes. I winced, feeling the blotches of scabs, the still-burning skin underneath. No hair on my eyebrows. No eyelashes, either. Blinking back the pain, I traced the edges of my eyelids, crusted and scarred.

I knew my eyes were wide open. I knew I could see nothing. And, with a shiver, I knew one thing more.

I was blind.

In anguish, I bellowed. Suddenly, hearing again the sound of the cuckoo, I flung off my blanket. Despite the weakness of my legs, I forced myself to rise from the pallet, pushing away Branwen's hand as she tried to stop me. I staggered across the stones, following the sound.

I tripped on something and crashed to the floor, landing on my shoulder. Stretching out my arms, I could feel nothing but the surface of the stones beneath me. They felt hard and cold, like a tomb.

My head spun. I could feel Branwen helping me to my feet, even as I could hear her muffled sobs. Again I pushed her away. Staggering forward, my hands hit a wall of solid rock. The sound of the cuckoo drew me to the left. The groping fingers of my unbandaged hand caught the edge of a window.

Grasping the sill, I pulled myself closer. Cool air stung my face. The cuckoo sang, so close to me that I might have reached out and touched its wing. For the first time, it seemed, in weeks, I felt the splash of sunshine on my face. Yet as hard as I tried to find the sun, I could not see it.

Hidden. The whole world is hidden.

My legs buckled beneath me. I fell to the floor, my head upon the stones. And I wept.

VIII

THE GIFT

During the weeks stretching into months that followed, my torment filled the halls of the Church of Saint Peter. The nuns residing there, moved both by the strength of Branwen's piety and the severity of my burns, had opened the gates of their sanctuary. They must have found it difficult to feel anything but sympathy for this woman who did little else but pray all day and tend to her wounded boy. As to the boy himself, they mostly avoided me, which suited me just fine.

For me, every day was dark—in mood as well as sight. I felt like an infant, barely able to crawl around the cold stone chamber that I shared with Branwen. My fingers came to know well its four rigid corners, its uneven lines of mortar between the stones, its lone window where I sometimes stood for hours, straining to see. Instead of lighting me, though, the window only tortured me with the jovial call of the cuckoo and the distant bustle of Caer Myrddin's marketplace. Occasionally the smell of someone's cooking pot or a flowering tree might waft to me, mingling with the scents of thyme and beech root that rose from Branwen's low table by her pallet. But I could not go out to find such things. I was a prisoner, confined in the dungeon of my blindness.

Two or three times, I summoned the courage to walk, feeling

with my hands past the heavy wooden door and into the maze of corridors and chambers beyond. By listening carefully to the echoes of my footsteps, I discovered that I could judge the length and height of passageways and the size of rooms.

One day I found a stairway whose stone steps had been worn into shallow bowls over the years. Feeling the wall carefully as I descended, I pushed open a door at the bottom and found myself in a fragrant courtyard. Wet grass touched my feet; warm wind breathed on my face. I remembered, all at once, how good it felt to be outdoors, on the grass, in the sun. Then I heard the nuns singing in the cloisters nearby. I started walking faster, eager to find them. Without warning, I strode right into a stone column, so hard that I fell over backward into a shallow pool of water. As I struggled to get up, I stepped on a loose rock and pitched sideways. The left side of my face bashed against the base of the column. Bruised and bloody, my bandages torn, I lay there sobbing until Branwen found me.

After that I didn't stir from the pallet in my chamber, convinced I would spend the rest of my days as a helpless burden to Branwen. Even when I tried to think of other things, my mind always returned to the day that had been my undoing. The sight of her, bound and gagged by the tree. The rage that boiled over so violently. The laughter, melting into shrieks, of Dinatius. The searing flames all around. The crushed arms and broken body beneath the branches. The sound of my own screams when I realized that my face was burning.

I could not remember our trek to the walls of Caer Myrddin, though from Branwen's spare description I could imagine it well enough. I could almost see Lud's round face watching us ride over the hill in the cart of the passing trader who had taken pity on the woman with sapphire eyes and her badly burned son. I could almost feel the swaying of the horse-drawn cart, almost hear the squealing of the wheels and the pounding of the hooves on the towing path. I could almost taste my own charred skin, almost hear my own delirious wailing as we rode through those long days and nights.

Now, very little broke the regularity of my days. The singing of the nuns. The shuffling of their footsteps to cloisters, to meals, to meditations. Branwen's quiet prayers and chants as she did her best to heal my skin. The continuing calls of the cuckoo, perched in a rustling tree that I could not name.

And darkness. Always darkness.

Sometimes, as I sat on my pallet, I ran my fingers gingerly over the scabs on my cheeks and under my eyes. The ridges on my skin felt terribly deep, like the bark of a pine tree. I knew that, despite Branwen's skills, my face would be scarred forever. Even if, by some miracle, my sight were ever restored, those scars would announce my folly to the world. I knew, of course, that such thoughts were foolishly vain. Yet they came to me anyway.

Once I found myself longing to grow a beard. I imagined a great, flowing beard—the kind an ancient sage, hundreds of years old, might wear. What a beard that was! All curly and white, it covered my face like a mass of clouds. I even suspected that a bird or two might try to nest there.

But such wistful moments never lasted long. Increasingly, I felt gripped by despair. Never again would I climb a tree. Never again would I run freely through a field. Never again would I see Branwen's face, except in memory.

I began to leave my meals untouched. Despite Branwen's insistence that I eat more, I had no desire. One morning, she knelt beside me on the stones of our chamber, wordlessly dressing my wounds. As she tried to replace my bandage, I leaned away from her, shaking my head.

"I wish you had left me to die."

"It was not your time to die."

"How do you know?" I snapped. "I feel like I've died already! This is not a life! This is endless torture. I prefer to live in Hell than to live here."

She seized me by the shoulders. "Don't talk that way! It is blasphemy."

"It is the truth! See what your powers, the ones you called a gift from God, have done for me? Curse these powers! I'd be better off dead."

"Stop it!"

I shook free, my heart pounding. "I have no life! I have no name! I have nothing!"

Branwen, swallowing her sobs, began to pray. "Dear Lord, Savior of my soul, Author of all that is written in the Great Book of Heaven and Earth, please help this boy! Please! Forgive him. He knows not what he says. If only you would restore his sight, even a little, even for a while, I pledge to you he will earn your forgiveness. He will never use his powers again, if that is what it takes! Only help him. Please help him."

"Never use my powers again?" I scoffed. "I would gladly give them up in exchange for sight! I never wanted them anyway."

Bitterly, I tugged the bandage on my brow. "And what kind of life do you have now? Not much better than mine! It's true. You may talk bravely. You may fool those nuns out there. But not me. I know you are miserable."

"I am at peace."

"That's a lie."

"I am at peace," she repeated.

"At peace!" I shouted. "At peace! Then why are your hands so chafed from all your wringing? Why are your cheeks so stained with your—"

I never finished the sentence.

"Good God," she whispered.

"I . . . don't understand." Hesitantly, I extended a hand toward her face, lightly brushing her cheek.

In that instant, we both realized that I could, somehow, *sense* her tear stains. Though I could not see them with my eyes, I nonetheless knew they were there.

"It is another gift." Branwen's voice was full of awe. She clasped my hand tightly. "You have the *second sight*."

I didn't know what to think. Was this the same ability that I once used to open a flower's petals? No. It felt different. Less willful somehow. What about seeing the colors inside the flower before it opened? Perhaps. Yet this felt different from that, too. More like . . . an answer to Branwen's prayer. A gift from God.

"Can it be?" I asked meekly. "Can it really be?"

"Thanks to God, it can."

"Test me," I demanded. "Hold up some fingers."

She obliged.

I bit my lower lip, trying to perceive her fingers.

"Two?"

"No. Try again."

"Three?"

"Try again."

Focusing my thoughts, I instinctively closed my eyes, though of course that made no difference. After a long pause, I said, "Two hands, not one. Am I right?"

"Right! Now . . . how many fingers?"

Minutes passed. Perspiration formed on my scarred brow, stinging the sensitive skin. But I didn't waver. At length, I asked a hesitant question.

"Could it be seven?"

Branwen sighed with relief. "Seven it is."

We embraced. I knew, in that moment, that my life had changed completely. And I suspected that, for the rest of my days, I would continue to ascribe special importance to the number seven.

Most important of all, though, I knew that a promise had been made. It didn't matter whether it had been made by me, by Branwen, or by us both. I would never again move objects with my mind. Not even a flower petal. Nor would I read the future, or try to master whatever other powers might once have been mine. But I could see again. I could live again.

Right away, I started eating. And hardly stopped—especially if I could get bread-in-milk, my favorite. Or blackberry jam on bread crusts. Or mustard mixed with raw goose eggs, which gave me the added fun of making any nearby nuns ill. One afternoon, Branwen went out to the market and found a single, succulent date—which was, for us, as splendid as a royal feast.

And my spirit revived along with my appetite. I began to explore the hallways, the cloisters, the courtyards of Saint Peter. The whole church was my domain. My castle! Once, when no nuns were about, I stole into the courtyard and took a bath in the shallow pool. The most difficult part was to resist singing at the top of my lungs.

Meanwhile, Branwen and I worked together every day for long hours, trying to sharpen my second sight. For my first practice sessions, we used spoons, pottery bowls, and other ordinary utensils that she found somewhere in the church. In time, I moved on to a small altar with subtle contours and grains in its wood. Eventually, I graduated to a two-handled chalice with intricate carvings on its surface. Although it took the better part of a week, I finally came to read the words inscribed on its rim: *Ask, and ye shall receive.*

As I practiced, I realized that I could see objects best if they were stationary and not far away. If they moved too quickly or remained too distant, I often lost them. A flying bird simply melted into the sky.

Furthermore, as the light around me grew dimmer, so did my second sight. At dusk I could see only the blurred outlines of things. I could not see anything at night, unless a torch or the moon pushed back the darkness. Why my second sight should need light at all, I could only wonder. It was, after all, not like normal sight. So why should darkness smother it? Then again, second sight seemed to be partly inward, and partly outward. Perhaps it relied on what was left of my eyes, in some way I could not comprehend. Or perhaps it required something else, something inside me, which failed to pass the test.

Thus, while second sight was certainly better than no sight at all, it was not nearly as good as the eyesight I had lost. Even in daylight, I could discern only the barest wisps of colors, leaving most of the world painted in variants of gray. So while I could tell that Branwen now wore a cloth veil around her head and neck, and that it was lighter in color than her loose robe, I could not tell whether the veil was gray or brown. I began to forget much of what I had learned about the colors of things since arriving in Gwynedd.

Yet I could accept such limitations. Oh, yes—and gladly. With my emerging ability, I walked to the cloisters or to meals with Branwen. I sat beside a nun and conversed for some time, seeming to look at her with my eyes, without her suspecting that those eyes remained useless. And one morning I actually ran around the courtyard, weaving in and out of the columns, leaping right over the pool.

That time I didn't hold back my singing.

THE YOUNG BIRD

$\mathbf{A}$s my second sight improved, Branwen helped me to read the Latin inscriptions in the religious manuscripts at the church. Strong smells of leather and parchment washed over me every time I cracked open one of those volumes. And the images, stronger still, carried me away—to the flaming chariot of Elijah, the last supper of Jesus, the stone tablets of Moses.

Sometimes, as I pored over those texts, my troubles melted away. I became one with the words, seeing deeds and colors and faces with richness and clarity that I could never see with my eyes. And I came to understand, in a way I never had before, that books are truly the stuff of miracles. I even dared to dream that someday, somehow, I might surround myself with books from many times and many tongues, just as Branwen had once done.

With each passing day, my vision grew a little stronger. One morning I discovered that I could read Branwen's expression by the curl of her lips and the glint in her eyes. Another morning, as I stood by my window watching the wind toss the branches, I realized that the rustling tree where the cuckoo lived was a hawthorn, broad and dark. And one night I glimpsed, for the first time since before the fire, a star shining overhead.

On the next night, I positioned myself in the center of the

courtyard, far from any torches. Low on the northern horizon, a second star glittered. The next night, three more. Then five more. Eight more. Twelve more.

Branwen joined me in the courtyard the following evening. Together we lay on our backs on the stones. With a sweep of her hand, she pointed out the constellation Pegasus. Then, slowly and rhythmically, she told me the tale of the great winged horse. As she spoke, I felt I was soaring through the sky on Pegasus' broad back. We leaped from one star to another, sailed past the moon, galloped across the horizon.

Every night after that, unless clouds completely covered the sky, Branwen and I lay there under the dome of darkness. As much as I loved reading the church's manuscripts, reading the manuscript of the heavens thrilled me even more. With Branwen as my guide, I spent my evenings in the company of Cygnus, Aquarius, and Ursa—whose claws raked my back several times. I tied the sails of Vela, swam far with Pisces, marched beside Hercules.

Sometimes, while exploring the stars, I imagined the entire sky shrinking down into a single, glorious cape. In a flash, I would put it on. Deep blue, studded with stars, the cape fell over my back, sparkling as I moved. The stars riding my shoulders. The planets ringing my waist. How I would love to own a cape like that one day!

Yet even as I celebrated, I could not forget how much lay hidden from me. The clouded sky obscured some of the stars; my clouded vision obscured more. Still, the thrill of all I could see far outweighed the frustration with what I could not. Despite the clouds, the stars had somehow never seemed so bright.

And yet . . . there remained a dark place inside of me that even the light from stars could not reach. The ghosts of my past continued to haunt me. Especially what I had done to Dinatius. I still heard his screams, still saw the terror in his eyes, still felt the twisted and useless remains of his arms. When I asked Branwen whether he had survived, she couldn't say. She only knew that he was still hovering at the edge of death when we had left the village. Still, this much was clear. While he had done plenty to provoke my rage, his brutality could not obscure my own.

On top of that, something else continued to plague me, something deeper than guilt. Fear. About myself, and my dreadful powers. The merest thought of them threw up a wall of flames in my mind, flames that seared my very soul. If I lacked the strength to keep my promise, would I use those powers or would they use me? If, in the grip of uncontrollable rage, I could destroy both a person and a tree with such ease, what else might I one day destroy? Could I annihilate myself completely, as I did my own eyes?

What kind of creature am I, really? Perhaps Dinatius had been right after all. Perhaps the blood of a demon really did flow through my veins, so that terrible magic could rise out of me at any moment, like a monstrous serpent rising out of the darkest depths of the sea.

And so it was, even in the new brightness of my days, that I remained troubled by the darkness of my own fears. As the weeks passed, my vitality, as well as my vision, continued to grow. Yet my unease continued to grow as well. I knew, down inside, that I could never put my fears to rest—until I somehow learned my true identity.

There came an afternoon when I heard a new sound outside the window of my chamber. Eagerly, I moved closer. By stretching my second sight, I found the source of the sound, nestled among the boughs of the hawthorn tree. I watched and listened for a while. Then I turned back to Branwen, who sat in her customary place on the floor next to my pallet, grinding some herbs.

"The cuckoo has nested in the hawthorn tree." I spoke with a mixture of certainty and sadness that made Branwen put down her mortar and pestle. "I have watched her—seen her—sitting in the nest every day. She laid her only egg there. She guarded it from enemies. And now, at last, the egg has hatched. The young bird has emerged from the darkness."

Branwen studied my face carefully before responding. "And," she asked in a trembling voice, "has the young bird flown?"

Slowly, I shook my head. "Not yet. But very soon he must."

"Can he not . . ." She had to swallow before trying again. "Can he not stay with his mother for a while longer, sharing their nest for a little more time?"

I frowned. "All things must fly when they are able."

"But where? Where will he go?"

"In this case, he must find his own self." After a pause, I added, "To do that, he must find his own past."

Branwen clutched at her heart. "No. You don't mean that. Your life will be worth nothing if you go back . . . there."

"My life will be worth nothing if I stay here." I took a step toward her. Though my eyes were useless, I probed her with my newfound gaze. "If you cannot, or will not, tell me where I came from, then I must find out myself. Please understand! I must find my true name. I must find my true mother and father. I must find my true home."

"Stay," she begged in desperation. "You are only a boy of twelve! And half blind, as well! You have no idea of the risks. Listen to me, Emrys. If you stay with me for just a few more years, you will reach manhood. Then you can choose whatever you want to be. A bard. A monk. Whatever you like."

Seeing my blank look, she tried a different approach. "Whatever you do, don't decide right now. I could tell you a story, something to help you think through this madness. What about one of your favorites? The one about the wandering Druid who saved Saint Brigid from slavery?" Without waiting for me to answer, she began. "There came a day in the life of young Brigid when she—"

"Stop." I shook my head. "I must learn my own story."

Weakly, Branwen clambered to her feet. "I left behind more than you will ever know. Do you know why? So we could be safe, you and I. Is that not enough for you?"

I said nothing.

"Must you really do this?"

"You could come with me."

She leaned against the wall for support. "No! I could not."

"Then tell me how to get back there."

"No."

"Or at least where to begin."

"No."

I felt a sudden urge to probe the inside of her mind, as if it were the inside of a flower. Then the flames ignited, overwhelming my thoughts. I remembered my promise—and also my fears.

"Tell me just one thing," I pleaded. "You told me once that you knew my grandfather. Did you also know my father?"

She winced. "Yes. I knew him."

"Was he, well, not human? Was he . . . a demon?"

Her whole body stiffened. After a long silence she spoke, in a voice that seemed a lifetime away. "I will say only this. If ever you should meet him, remember: He is not what he may seem."

"I will remember. But can't you tell me anything more?"

She shook her head.

"My own father! I just want to know him."

"It is better you do not."

"Why?"

Instead of answering, she just shook her head sadly. She went to the low table bearing her collection of healing herbs. Deftly, she picked a few, then ground them into a coarse powder which she poured into a leather satchel on a cord. Handing me the satchel, she said resignedly, "This might help you live a little longer."

I started to respond, but she spoke again.

"And take this, from the woman who would have you call her Mother." Slowly, she reached into her robe and pulled out her precious pendant.

Despite my limited vision, I could see the flash of glowing green.

"But it's yours!"

"You will need it more than I."

She removed the pendant and squeezed its jeweled center one last time before placing the leather cord around my neck. "It is called . . . the *Galator*."

I caught my breath at the word.

"Guard it well," she continued. "Its power is great. If it cannot keep you safe, that is only because nothing outside of Heaven can."

"You kept me safe. You built a good nest."

"For a while, perhaps. But now . . ." Tears brimmed in her eyes. "Now you must fly."

"Yes. Now I must fly."

Gently, she touched my cheek.

I turned and left the room, my footsteps echoing down the corridor of stone.

X

THE OLD OAK

As I stepped through the carved wooden gates of the Church of Saint Peter, I entered the bustle and confusion of Caer Myrddin. It took some time for my dim vision to adjust to all the commotion. Carts and horses clattered along the stony streets, as did donkeys, pigs, sheep, and a few hairy dogs. Merchants bellowed about their wares, beggars clutched at the robes of passersby, spectators gathered around a man juggling balls, and people of all descriptions strode past, carrying baskets, bundles, fresh greens, and stacks of cloth.

I glanced over my shoulder at the hawthorn tree, whose branches I could barely make out above the church wall. For all the pain I had experienced in that place, I would miss the quiet calm of my room, the slow singing of the nuns, the bird in the boughs of that tree. And, more than I ever expected, I would miss Branwen.

Watching the blur of people, animals, and goods, I noticed some sort of shrine on the opposite side of the street. Curious, I decided to get closer, although that would require swimming across the fast-flowing river of traffic. Biting my lip, I started across.

Instantly, I was pushed and kicked, turned and buffeted. Since I could not see well enough to stay out of the way, I crashed into a man carrying a load of firewood. Sticks flew in all directions. So did curses. Then I walked straight into the flank of a horse. Seconds later, I nearly lost my toes under a cart wheel. Somehow, though, I made it to the other side. I approached the shrine.

It was not much of a monument, just a carved image of a hawk above a bowl of muddy water. If any people took care of it, they had not done so in years. The hawk's wings had broken off. The stones around the base were crumbling. Probably only a handful of the people who strode by here every day even noticed it.

Yet something about this old, forgotten shrine intrigued me. I drew closer, touched the hawk's worn beak. I knew enough from Branwen's descriptions to guess that the shrine was probably made to honor Myrddin, one of the ancient Celts' most revered gods, who sometimes took the form of a hawk. One of their Apollos, as she would say. Although I still could not quite accept her notion that such spirits still walked the land, I wondered again about the stag and the boar who had fought over us so long ago. If they were, in fact, Dagda and Rhita Gawr, was it just possible that the spirit of Myrddin still lived as well?

A donkey, loaded down with heavy sacks, knocked into me. I fell into the shrine, plunging my hand into the murky water. As I stood and shook my hand dry, I tried to imagine what Caer Myrddin might have looked like centuries ago. Branwen had told me that, instead of a bustling city, it was just a peaceful hill with a spring where wandering shepherds might pause to rest. Then, over time, it grew into a trade center, taking goods from the farms of Gwynedd, and regions as distant as Gwent, Brycheiniog, and Powys Fadog. When the Romans came, they built a fortress on the River Tywy's high banks. And now the old military roads, such as the one to Caer Vedwyd, linked the city to the lush valleys and deer-filled forests of the north, and also down the river to the sea. Whether or not anyone today took the time to remember such things, this crumbling shrine—and the name of the city itself—still connected Caer Myrddin to its distant past.

That, I realized, was the purpose of my own journey. To connect myself with my past. To find my name. My home. My parents. And though I had no idea where this journey might take me, nor where it might end, I suddenly knew where it should begin.

The sea. I must return to the sea. To the very spot where I had tumbled onto the rocky shore more than five years ago.

Perhaps, when I arrived at that forbidding shore, I would find nothing but jagged rocks and screeching gulls and pulsing waves. Or perhaps I would find the clue that I sought. Or at least a clue to the clue. It was not much of a hope, but it was the only hope I had.

For what seemed like hours, I wandered through the city, trying to keep to the smaller side streets to avoid being trampled in the traffic. As if I were not already aware of the limits of my vision, I tripped and stumbled enough times to make my toes horribly tender within my leather boots. Even so, I made my way. While I am sure many people concluded—correctly—that I was a clumsy oaf, I am just as sure none of them guessed that my eyes were totally useless. The occasional words of sympathy I received were for my scars, not for my blindness.

At last, I found my way to the road that ran beside the River Tywy. I knew that if I followed it far enough to the north, I would return to my old village. From there I would make my way to the sea.

At last I came to the walls of the city, ten paces thick and twice as tall. I crossed the wide bridge, taking care not to trip on the uneven stones. Then I continued into the wooded valley beyond.

As I plodded along beside the river, I concentrated on each step. If my attention wavered, even briefly, I was likely to end up on the ground. Too often, I did. Once I tripped in the middle of a village square, where a donkey almost stepped on my back.

Still, I managed well enough. For three days I walked, eating raspberries and bramble berries along with the round of cheese given to me by one of the nuns. During that time I spoke to no one, and no one spoke to me. One day at dusk I helped a shepherd pull his lamb out of a pit, receiving a crust of bread in thanks, but that was my only contact with others.

In time the road turned into the old towpath through Caer Vedwyd. Barges floated down the river, sliding past the families of ducks and swans. As I drew near the village, I kept to the cover of the woods, staying parallel to the path without actually walking on it. That way no one saw me. Occasionally, I feasted on roots and berries and edible leaves. I drank once again from the rivulet below the great pine tree where I rode out the gale, but I wished that I had never climbed down. In a strange way I felt more at home here, in the wild woods, than anywhere else in Gwynedd.

Late that afternoon, I paused near the bridge at Caer Vedwyd. I caught a glimpse of a tall but twisted figure standing at the other end of the bridge. I strained to make it out more clearly, as the wind swelled around me. It could have been a decrepit tree, except that I had never noticed a tree in that spot before. I could not shake the feeling that it was, instead, the bent body of a person—a person with nothing but stumps for arms.

I did not linger. Despite the obstacles, I tromped through the woods for some distance, avoiding the next several villages as well. As the shadows grew longer, my vision worsened and my progress slowed. Finally, having left any signs of people behind, I broke into a wide meadow. Scraped from my falls and exhausted from my trek, I found a hollow in the soft grass and curled up to sleep.

Sunlight on my face woke me. Crossing the meadow, I rejoined the road near the point where it left the river. But for one elderly man, whose scraggly white beard bounced on his chest as he walked, I met no one else on this stretch. I observed the old man, wishing again that I too could grow a beard, to hide those miserable scars. One day, perhaps. If I lived so long.

Despite the lack of settlements, I did not feel disoriented. My memories of the way to the sea remained surprisingly clear. For though I had traveled this route only once in my life, I had walked it many times in my dreams. My slow shuffle started to gain speed. I could almost hear the distant sound of slapping waves.

Every so often, I reached into my tunic and touched the Galator. As little as I knew about it, I felt oddly comforted to know it was there. The same was true for Branwen's leather satchel, slung over my shoulder.

The old road gradually deteriorated until it became no more than a grassy trail. At last it passed through a cleft in a wall of crumbling cliffs. I smelled the barest whiff of salt on the air. I knew this place, knew it in my bones.

Black rock rose vertically to twenty times my own height. Kittiwakes called and swooped among the crags. The trail bent sharply to the right, ending where I knew it would.

At the ocean.

Before me stretched the gray-blue waters, without any end and without any bottom. The smell of kelp tickled my nostrils. Waves rushed forward and withdrew, grinding sand against rock. Gulls, circling above the shore, shrieked noisily.

I crossed the black barrier of rocks, stepping over tidal pools and shards of driftwood. Nothing has changed, I told myself. As waves washed over my feet, I gazed westward. The fog of my vision merged with the fog on the water. I strained to see more clearly, but it was impossible.

Nothing has changed. The black rocks, the briny breeze, the endless rhythm of the waves. Just like before. Did they hide a clue somewhere? If so, how could I ever hope to find it? The sea was so enormous, and I was so . . . tiny. My head dropped lower on my chest. Aimlessly, I started to walk, my leather boots splashing in the chill water.

Then I saw one shape that had changed. The ancient oak, though still mammoth, had been shorn of most of its bark, which sat in tattered strips among the roots. Several branches, broken and splintered, lay strewn across the rocky beach. Even the hollow in the trunk, where I had endured the attack of the boar, had been punctured, its walls split and buckled. The old tree had finally died.

As I approached its remains, I tripped, stabbing my shin on a pointed rock. But I cut short my own howl of pain, not wanting to alert any wild boars that might be near. Whether or not the boar I had met here was really Rhita Gawr, it had certainly wanted blood on its tusks. If a boar appeared now, I would have no place to hide. And, almost certainly, no Dagda to rescue me.

My shoulders ached, as did my legs. I sat down on the lifeless roots. As I ran my hand along the edge of the hollow, I could still feel the marks of the boar's slashing tusks. That experience felt so close. So recent. And yet this ancient tree, whose strength had then seemed eternal, was now nothing more than a skeleton.

I kicked at a shred of bark by my foot, knowing that I myself had fared little better. I had returned to this spot, if not yet dead, then perilously close. I was nearly blind. I was utterly lost.

I sat there, my head in my hands. Absently, I stared at the shoreline. The tide, I could tell, was beginning to retreat. Gradually, the border widened between the harsh rocks and the sea, leaving a strip of sand whose contours contained their own tiny mountains and oceans.

A hermit crab skittered across this landscape of sand. I watched as the crab wrestled with a half-buried shell at the edge of a tidal pool. After much clawing and scraping, the crab finally retrieved its prize, a conch streaked with a color that reminded me vaguely of orange. I imagined the crab celebrating that it had, at last, found a new home. But before it could savor its success, a sudden sea breeze blew the shell out of its grasp. The shell slid into the shallow pool, floating like a tiny raft, bouncing on the ripples.

Seeing the stranded crab watch its hard-earned treasure float away, I allowed myself a sardonic grin. That is how it works. You think you have found your dream, then you lose it forever. You think you have found your home, then you see it float away.

Float away. Despite my better judgment, I felt suddenly possessed by an idea. A wild, hopeless, mad idea.

I would build a raft! Perhaps this very tree, which had helped me once before, could help me again. Perhaps this very tide, which had borne me once to shore, could bear me out to the sea. I would trust. Simply trust. In the tree. In the tide.

I had nothing to lose except my life.

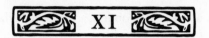

SAILING

Using the broken limbs of the ancient oak, lashed together with ropelike shreds of bark, I built my raft. Relying only on my second sight, I often misjudged the fit of limbs and the strength of knots. Yet plank by plank my raft came together. In its center, I placed a large slab from the hollow of the tree, which provided a slightly cupped seat where I could ride. Finally, I bound the edges with several long strands of kelp that I found among the rocks.

By the time I finished, the sun was starting to set. I dragged the meager craft to the edge of the waves. On a whim, before pushing off, I ran back to the tidal pool where the conch shell still drifted. Scooping it up, I dropped it on the sand so that the crab might find its home again.

Gulls screeched, in laughter it seemed, as I waded into the cold waves. Before climbing on my feeble vessel, I hesitated. Opposing worlds tugged at me. I stood exactly on the edge—of land and sea, of past and future. For a moment I lost my resolve. Water lapped about my thighs, the same water that had nearly drowned me before. Perhaps I was acting too hastily. Perhaps I should return to shore to think of a better plan.

Just then I noticed a hint of gold shining on the remains of the old tree. The sunset had struck the trunk, etching it in fire. It reminded me of another tree on fire, a tree whose flames still burned me deeply. And I knew I must try to find the answers to my questions.

I pulled myself aboard the raft. Settling into the cupped center, I folded my legs in front of me. I looked one more time at the black cliffs, then turned away from shore. Dipping my hands in the chilly water, I paddled for some distance, until my arms grew too tired. The fading sun, still strong enough to warm my wet skin, made the water sparkle with many more colors than I could detect. Yet even though I could not truly see, I could sense the web of pink and golden light dancing just beneath the waves.

As the tide carried me farther from shore, a breeze leaned against my back. Where the sea might take me, I did not know. All I could do was trust.

I thought about ancient seafarers like Bran the Blessed, Odysseus, and Jonah, whose tales I had heard from Branwen. And I wondered whether anyone but Branwen would ever care about my own ocean voyage. I wished that someday I might be able to describe it to her. But in my heart I knew that I would never see her again.

A black-headed gull swooped past, skimming the surface of the waves in search of supper. With a loud squawk, it careened toward the raft and settled on one of the strands of kelp dangling from the side. Clamping its beak on a green frond, it pulled and twisted madly.

"Away!" I waved my hands in its face. The last thing I needed at this moment was to have my little craft pulled apart by a hungry bird.

The gull dropped the kelp, lifted off with a screech, then circled the raft. A few seconds later it landed again—this time on my knee. The bird's eye, which seemed as yellow as the sun, examined me.

Apparently concluding that I looked too large (or too tough) for a ready meal, the gull cocked its black head and took flight, heading back to shore.

As I watched the gull depart, I yawned. The continuous rocking of the waves was making me drowsy, more so because I was spent from my days of trekking from Caer Myrddin. Yet how could I sleep? I could fall off the raft, or worse, miss something important.

I tried to rest without sleeping. Curling my back, I leaned my head against my knees. To keep myself awake, I concentrated on the slowly setting sun. By now the great burning globe was resting just above the water, sending a shimmering band of light across the waves, right to my raft. It might have been an avenue of gold, a pathway across the water.

I wondered where that path might lead. Just as I wondered where my own might lead.

Checking over my shoulder, I could tell that I had already drifted some distance from shore. Although the breeze had subsided, I realized that the raft might have caught a current. I bounced over the waves, which splashed me constantly. Despite the jostling, my lashings looked still taut, the wood still sturdy. Licking my lips, I tasted the salty spray. As I laid my head again on my knees, I could not help but yawn again.

The sun, swollen and scarlet, ignited the clouds with colors, colors that I could see only subtly. The shape of the sun I could sense more clearly, as it grew flatter on the horizon. An instant later, as if it were a bubble that had finally burst, it disappeared below the waves.

But I did not notice the onset of darkness, for I had fallen asleep.

A sudden splash of cold water woke me. Night had arrived. A host of stars clustered around the thinnest crescent moon I had ever known. I listened to the ceaseless heaving and sucking of the waves, to the bashing of water against wood. I slept no more during that night. Shivering, I drew my legs tightly to my chest. I could only wait for whatever the sea wished to show me.

As the sun rose behind me, I discovered that the coast of Gwynedd had disappeared. Not even the imposing cliffs were visible anymore. Only a faint wisp of a cloud stretched like a pennant from what I guessed might be the summit of Y Wyddfa, though I could not be sure.

I spied a timber that had slipped out of its lashing, and quickly bound it up again. As the day dragged on, my back and legs grew painfully stiff, but I couldn't stand to stretch them without flipping over. Waves slapped relentlessly against the raft and against me. The hot sun burned the back of my neck. Meanwhile, my mouth and throat felt an even stronger burning, which increased as the day wore on. Never before had I felt so thirsty.

Just at sunset, I perceived a group of large, streamlined bodies leaping above the ocean surface. Although seven or eight individuals comprised the group, they swam in perfect unity. They moved like a single wave, surging and subsiding. Then, as they passed near my raft, they changed direction and swam a complete circle around me. Once, twice, three times, they ringed me, leaping in and out of the bubbles of their own wakes.

Were they dolphins? Or sea people, perhaps? The ones Branwen called *people of the mer,* who were said to be part human and part fish? I could not see well enough to tell. Yet the glimpse of them filled me with wonder. As they swam away, their bodies gleaming in the golden light, I promised myself that if I should ever live long enough, I would do whatever I could to explore the mysterious depths under the sea.

Another night passed, as cold as before. The crescent moon vanished completely, swallowed by the stars. Suddenly I remembered the constellations, and Branwen's stories about their origins. After much searching, I managed to find a few, including my favorite, the winged Pegasus. I imagined that the constant rocking of my raft was the galloping, galloping of the steed across the sky.

I fell asleep, dreaming that I was carried aloft on the back of some great winged creature, although whether or not it was Pegasus I could not be sure. Suddenly we were swooping into battle. A darkened castle, manned by ghostly sentinels, rose up before us. And yes! The castle was spinning, turning on its foundation. It drew us down, down, toward its spinning edifice. I tried with all my might to change course, yet I could not. In seconds we would slam straight into the castle walls.

At that point, I woke up. I shivered, from more than cold. The dream filled my thoughts deep into the following day, though its meaning continued to elude me.

Late that afternoon, the western horizon grew dark. Waves rose to new heights, throwing my vessel this way and that, as winds hurled sheets of spray. The raft groaned and creaked. Several strands of kelp burst apart, and a crack appeared in the large slab of wood from the hollow of the old oak. Still, for the most part, the storm passed me by. With twilight, calmer waters returned. I was soaked, to be sure, and terribly thirsty, but both my craft and I remained intact.

That night, I did my best to repair the broken lashing. Then, as I sat cross-legged, a biting wind smacked my face. Another shadow, darker than before, swept across the stars. Swiftly it covered the southern sky, then the dome above me, until finally the entire sky went black.

As darkness swallowed me, my second sight flickered out, useless in such utter blackness. I couldn't see! I was no less blind than I had been on the day I first arrived at the church.

Mighty waves began lifting and swirling, tossing my raft around like a mere twig. Water drenched my face, my back, my arms and legs. And this time the storm did not dissipate. Rather, it swelled, gathering strength with each passing minute. Bending low in my seat, I curled up as tight as I could, like a hedgehog fearing for its life. I wrapped my hands around the outermost edges of the raft, clinging to the scraps of wood that were keeping me afloat.

My powers! For an instant I considered calling on them. Perhaps I could bind the raft together, or even calm the waves! But no. I had promised. Besides, those powers frightened me deeply, even more than this terrible gale. The truth was I knew nothing about magic except its terrible consequences—the smell of scorched flesh, the screams of another person, the agony of my own burning eyes. However my powers might have helped me, I knew that I would never use them again.

All through the black night the storm howled and raged. Curtains of water fell on me. Enormous waves pounded me. At one point I recalled the story of Bran the Blessed surviving a fierce storm at sea, and it gave me a brief burst of hope that I, too, might survive. Yet this hope was soon drowned in the ocean's onslaught.

Both of my hands went numb with the cold, yet I dared not release their grip to try to warm them. More of my lashing popped. One timber split down the middle. My back ached, though not as much as my heart. For something inside me knew that this storm would spell the end of my voyage.

The rising sun brightened the sky only a little, but it was enough that I could begin to sense shapes again. My second sight had only barely returned when a powerful wave crashed down so hard that it knocked the breath right out of me. The raft buckled and finally broke apart.

In that terrifying instant I was cast down into the seething sea, battered by the currents. By luck I touched a floating timber and grasped it. Another wave toppled over me, and another, and another.

My strength ebbing, I started to lose my grip. The wild storm continued thrashing and pounding. As the new day dawned, I felt sure that it would be my last. I barely noticed the odd-shaped cloud hovering low over the water, though it looked almost like an island made of mist.

With a plaintive cry, I let go. Water poured into my lungs.

PART TWO

FALLEN WARRIOR

Not swaying anymore.

Not drowning anymore.

Once again, I awoke to find myself on an unknown shore. The same sound of surf filled my ears. The same brackish taste soured my mouth. The same feeling of dread twisted my stomach.

Were the torments of my years in Gwynedd just a dream? A terrible, twisted dream?

I knew the answer, even before my sand-crusted fingers touched my scarred cheeks, my useless eyes. And the Galator dangling from my neck. Gwynedd had been real. As real as the strange, potent smell that spiced the air of this place, wherever this place might be.

I rolled onto my side, crunching a shell under my hip. Sitting up, I drank in the air. Sweet as a summer meadow it tasted, but with an edge to it. Sharper. Truer.

While I could hear the waves sloshing and slapping, not far away, I could not view them with my second sight. That was not because of my poor vision, however. The waves lay hidden behind a rolling wall of mist, mist so thick that it obscured everything beyond.

Within the wall of mist, curious shapes seemed to coalesce, hold together for a few seconds, then vanish. I saw something like a great archway, with a door swinging closed. As it melted away, it was replaced by a spiked tail, big enough for a dragon. Then, as I watched, the tail transformed into an enormous head with a bulbous nose. Like a giant made of mist, it turned slowly toward me, moving its mouth as if to speak, before dissolving into the shifting clouds.

Turning my stiff back, I looked around. This beach, unlike the north coast of Gwynedd, formed a gentle meeting of land and sea. No piles of jagged rocks littered the coast, only shells of pink and white and purple, strewn over the fine-grained sand. Next to my foot, a leafy vine crawled across the beach like a shiny green snake.

Pink. Purple. Green. My heart leaped. I could sense colors! Not so well as my memories before the fire, perhaps, but much better than before the sea tore my raft to shreds.

But wait. That could not be true. As I examined my own skin, and then the folds of my tunic, I knew that they were no more brightly colored than before.

With a glance back at the beach, I understood. It was not that I could see any better. It was that this landscape simply radiated color. The shells, the shining leaves, even the sand of this place felt brighter and deeper somehow. If they seemed this vivid with only my second sight, how vivid they would be if I had eyes that could truly see!

I picked up one of the spiral-shaped shells. Purple lines wound around its body of gleaming white. It felt comfortable in my hand, like one friend meeting another.

I put the shell to my ear, expecting to hear the watery sound within its chambers. Instead, I heard a strange, breathy sound, like the voice of someone far away. Whispering to me in a language I could not understand. Trying to tell me something.

I caught my breath. Lowering the shell, I peered into its chamber. It seemed ordinary enough. I must have just imagined it. Again I brought it to my ear. The voice again! This time clearer than before.

In spite of myself, I thought I heard it say *bewaaare . . . bewaaare*.

Quickly, I put down the shell. My palms felt sweaty, my stomach knotted. I stood up. My legs, arms, and back ached with stiffness. I glanced down at the shell, then shook my head. Seawater in my ears. Maybe that was it.

Water. I must find fresh water. If only I could find some to drink, I would feel more alive.

I climbed to the ridge of a dune arching above the beach. What I saw took my breath away.

A dense forest, where colorful birds flitted among the spires of towering trees, stretched far to the west. Near the horizon rose waves of misty hills, where the green of the forest deepened into blue. Between here and there, a lush valley unfurled as soft as a carpet. Sunlit streams cascaded out of the woods and over the meadows, merging into a great river that rushed toward the sea. In the distance, more trees grew, though in orderly rows that seemed less wild than the forest, more like an orchard that someone had planted long ago.

I was about to descend into the valley and quench my thirst when something else caught my attention. Although I could see only a little of the eastern bank of the river, it seemed far less green than the other side. Rather, it looked brownish red, the color of dried leaves. Or rust. At first it gave me an unsettled feeling, but then I realized that it was probably just some strange sort of vegetation. Or perhaps a trick of the light, caused by the mass of dark clouds hovering over the eastern horizon.

Feeling my parched throat, I turned back to the verdant valley and forest before me. Time for that drink! Then I would investigate this mist-shrouded island, if indeed it was an island. Although I could not quite put my finger on it, something about this place made me want to stay and explore—despite the strange experience with the shell. It might have been the vibrant colors. Or it might have been the simple fact that I had trusted in the waves and they had brought me here. Whatever the reason, I would remain for a while—but only for a while. If I did not discover any clues to my past, I would promptly leave. I would build myself another boat, sturdier than the last, and continue my quest.

I started down the dune. The sand soon gave way to grasses, their slender stalks bowing in the fragrant breeze. Though still stiff from my voyage, I gathered speed as I descended. Soon I was running across the open field. Feeling the wind in my face, I realized that this was the first time I had run since leaving Caer Myrddin.

Approaching a stream of bright water, I knelt by the mossy stones along its border. Immediately I immersed my whole head in it. The cold, clear water slapped my skin, shocking me no less than the colors and smells of this land had first shocked me. I swallowed enough to feel bloated, belched, then swallowed some more.

Satisfied at last, I leaned on my elbow, now drinking not the water but the crisp, spicy air. Grasses tickled my chin. With so much tall grass surrounding me, anyone passing near might have thought me just a brown log by the streambed. I listened to the subtle rustling of stems rubbing together, the rising and falling of wind in the forest, the steady dancing of the stream. A long-legged beetle, red in hue, crawled lazily across the folds of my tunic.

A sudden whoosh of air, just above my head, jolted me out of my reverie. Whatever it was had flashed past with the speed of an arrow, so fast that I had no idea what it could have been. Cautiously, I lifted myself higher. My second sight detected some movement in the grass downstream. I rose to my feet.

A piercing whistle erupted from the grass, followed by hissing and snarling. The angry sounds swelled as I approached. A few steps later, I halted, amazed.

The largest rat I had ever seen, as thick as my own thigh, with powerful legs and teeth as sharp as dagger points, wrestled before me. Its adversary was a small hawk with a banded brown tail and gray back. A merlin. Despite the fact that the rat was at least three times the bird's size, they appeared evenly matched.

Furiously, they battled. The merlin's strong talons clung tight to the back of the rat's neck. The rat writhed, trying to bite and claw its enemy's head, bashing the bird against the ground. But the bird's courage outweighed its compact body, for it only screeched and dug its talons deeper, drawing blood from the rat's tough hide. Feathers flew, as blood splattered the grass. Clawing, biting, and snarling, they tumbled over each other in a wild frenzy.

This fight might have continued for some time with no victor, except that another rat emerged from a thicket by the stream. Whether out of loyalty to its kind, or more likely, desire for some easy prey, it joined in the fray. Clamping its jaws on one of the merlin's wings, it tore at the bird viciously.

The merlin shrieked in pain, but somehow held on. The second rat, its face ripped by the bird's beak, released its grip and circled around to the other side. Meanwhile, the merlin's torn wing hung at its side, flapping uselessly, while one of its talons came loose. Sensing victory at hand, the second rat brushed away some feathers caught in its teeth. Its legs tensed as it readied to pounce on the weakened bird.

At that instant I ran forward and kicked the second rat in the chest, so hard that it rolled into the thicket. Seeing this, the first rat stopped its thrashing, glaring at me with blood red eyes. With a violent shake, it threw the merlin to the grass. The bird lay on its back, too weak to move.

The rat hissed shrilly. I took a step closer. Then I raised my hand as if to strike. The rat, apparently tired of battling for the moment, turned and slipped away through the blades of grass.

I stooped to examine the merlin. Although its eyes, two dots of black encircled in yellow, remained barely half open, they watched me intensely. As I reached for the bird, it whistled and lashed out with one of its talons, slashing the skin of my wrist.

"What are you doing, fool bird?" I yelped, sucking the bloody wrist. "I'm trying to help you, not hurt you."

Again I reached toward the fallen warrior. Again the bird whistled and struck with its talon.

"Enough of this!" Shaking my head in dismay, I rose to leave.

As I left the spot, I glanced one more time at the merlin. Its eyes had finally closed. It lay there on the grass, shivering.

I took a deep breath, and returned. Cautiously, I picked up the bird, avoiding the talons in case it suddenly came alive again. I held the warm, feathered body in my hand, wondering that any creature so fierce could also feel so soft. Stroking the injured wing, I could tell that, while skin and muscles had been shredded, no bones had been broken. I reached into the satchel that Branwen had given me, removed a pinch of the dried herbs, and added to this a few drops of water from the stream. Using the edge of my tunic, I cleaned the gashes made by the teeth of the rat. There were several deep ones, especially along the wing's upper edge. Carefully I applied the herbs as a poultice.

The merlin stiffened and opened an eye. This time, however, it did not slash at me. Apparently too weak even to whistle, it could only watch me warily.

When I had finished, I held the small bird and pondered what to do next. Leave it here by the stream? No, the rats would surely return and finish their work. Take it with me? No, I had no need for a passenger, certainly not one so dangerous.

Spotting an oak with wide branches at the edge of the woods, an idea came to me. I put down the bird long enough to pull up some grasses and twist them together into a rough-hewn nest. Gathering both the nest and the bird under my arm, I climbed to a low branch that wore a rich coat of moss. I wedged the nest into place where the branch joined the trunk, then placed the helpless bird within.

I looked into the defiant, yellow-rimmed eyes for a moment. Then I climbed down and strode into the forest.

A BUNDLE OF
LEAVES

As I walked among the spires and the intertwined branches of this ancient forest, an odd sensation crept up on me.

It had nothing to do with my second sight, although the light proved dim indeed in these dark groves where only occasional rays reached all the way to the forest floor. It had nothing to do with the resins filling the air, stronger than I had ever smelled, although they brought back the memory of the day I outlasted the storm in the arms of the great pine beneath Y Wyddfa. It had nothing to do with the sounds all around me—winds rushing through leaves, branches clacking and creaking, needles crunching underfoot.

The odd sensation stemmed from none of these things. Or perhaps it came from all these things combined. A sound. A smell. A dimly lit grove. Above all, a feeling. That something in this forest knew I was there. That something was watching me. That a strange whispering, much like what I had heard in the shell, was now happening all around me. I spotted a knobby stick, nearly as tall as myself, leaning against the trunk of an old cedar. A good staff might help me work my way through the dimly lit groves of this forest. I reached for it. Just as my hand was about to squeeze its middle, where a cluster of twigs protruded, I gasped and pulled back.

The stick moved! The twigs, joined by others above and below, began churning like little legs. The knobby shaft bent as it clambered down the cedar's flaky bark, over the roots, and into a patch of ferns. In a few seconds, the stick creature had vanished. So too had my desire to find a staff.

Then I felt a familiar urge. Climb one of these trees! Not all the way to the top, perhaps, but high enough to gain a view of the upper canopies of branches. Choosing a lanky linden tree, whose heart-shaped leaves trembled like the surface of a running river, I started up. My feet and hands found plenty of holds, and I moved swiftly higher.

From the distance of five times my own height above the ground, the view changed dramatically. Much more light pierced the mesh of limbs, improving my vision. Through the quivering linden leaves I noticed a round, green clump of moss near my head—although given my experience with the stick I decided not to touch it. Then I glimpsed a pair of orange and blue butterflies floating among the branches. A spider, its web pearled with dew, swung freely from a nearby limb. Squirrels with large eyes chattered noisily. A golden-plumed bird moved from branch to branch. Yet one quality from the forest floor did not change: The strange whispering continued.

Turning toward the edge of the forest, I could make out the grassy field where I had encountered the merlin. Just beyond, flowing toward the wall of mist that I knew marked the sea, I spied the sparkling water of the great river. To my surprise, a strange wave lifted from its rapids, a wave that seemed almost like a huge hand. I knew that it could not be so. Yet as the hand of water emerged from the river, dripping water through its broad fingers before plunging back down with a splash, I felt a surge of wonder and fear.

Then, from far above me, a huge bundle of leaves broke loose. Rather than falling straight downward, though, it flew outward and across to another tree. Miraculously, the second tree's branches caught the bundle, cradling it in sturdy boughs, before flinging it outward again. Another branch caught it, bent with the weight, then flung it back. The bundle spun through the air, sailing over branches and between trunks, spinning like a dancer. It seemed almost as if the trees of this grove were playing catch with one another, throwing this bundle as children might throw a ball of string.

In time, the bundle of leaves dropped lower and lower among the limbs. Finally, it rolled onto the forest floor, coming to rest at last in a bed of brown needles.

I gasped. From the bundle, a long, leafy branch suddenly protruded. No, not a branch. An arm, wearing a sleeve of woven vines. Then another arm. One leg, then another. A head, its hair bedecked with shining leaves. Two eyes, as gray as beech bark with a touch of blue.

The leaf-draped figure rose and laughed out loud. The laughter, full and clear, rang through the trees with all the beauty of a bell.

I leaned forward on my limb, trying to discern more detail. For I could tell already that this bundle of leaves was, in truth, a girl.

XIV

RHIA

Without warning, the limb gave way. I tumbled to the ground, my fall broken by several boughs along the way. My chest smacked hard into one limb, as did my lower back, my shoulder, and both thighs. With a thud, I landed in a cushion of needles.

Groaning, I rolled to the side. In addition to the stiffness from my voyage, and the usual pain between my shoulder blades, my entire body ached. Slowly, I sat up—and found myself face-to-face with the girl.

Her laughter ceased.

For a long moment, neither of us moved. Although the light was spare, I could tell that she was about my own age. She watched me, standing as still as one of the trees. But for the touch of blue in her eyes, her garb of woven vines consisted of so much green and brown that she could almost have passed for a tree. Yet the eyes could not be missed. They flashed angrily.

She uttered a command in a strange, rustling language, waving her hand as if to brush away a fly. Immediately, the heavy branches of a hemlock wrapped themselves around my middle, as well as my arms and legs. The branches held me tightly, and the more I struggled the harder they squeezed. Swiftly they lifted me into the air. I hung there, suspended, unable to move.

"Let me down!"

"Now you will not fall again." The girl spoke in my own tongue, the Celtic language I had spoken in Gwynedd, but with a curious, lilting accent. Her expression shifted from wrath to mirth. "You remind me of a big brown berry, though not a tasty one."

She picked a plump purple berry growing in the moss by her feet and put it in her mouth. Puckering, she spat it out again. "Ecchh. No sweetness left."

"Let me down!" I roared. I twisted to break free, but the branch around my chest tightened so much that I could hardly breathe. "Please," I croaked. "I meant . . . no harm."

The girl eyed me severely. "You broke the law of Druma Wood. No outsiders are allowed here."

"But . . . I didn't . . . know," I wheezed.

"Now you do." She plucked another berry. Evidently it tasted better than the first, because she bent and picked another one.

"Please . . . let me . . . down."

Ignoring me completely, the girl went about her berry picking, swallowing them almost as fast as she plucked them. At length she started to leave the glade, not bothering even to glance in my direction.

"Wait!"

She stopped. Looking annoyed, she faced me. "You remind me of a squirrel who has stolen someone else's nuts and gets caught. Now you want to give them back, but it's too late. I'll come back for you in a day or two. If I remember."

She turned to go, stepping quickly away.

"Wait!" I gasped.

She disappeared behind a curtain of branches.

I tried again to wriggle free. The hemlock squeezed tighter, pressing the Galator, still under my tunic, deep into my ribs. "Wait! In the name of . . . the Galator."

The girl's face reappeared. Tentatively, she returned to the grove. She stood beneath the mighty hemlock, looking up at me for some time. Then she flicked her wrist and spoke more rustling words that I could not understand.

Instantly, the branches unfurled. I dropped facedown onto the ground. Pulling a handful of needles out of my mouth, I struggled to stand.

She held her hand up to me. Not wishing to be imprisoned by branches again, I obeyed and did not move.

"What do you know about the Galator?"

I hesitated, realizing that the Galator must be famous indeed to be known even in this remote land. Cautiously, I revealed as much as I dared. "I know what it looks like."

"So do I, at least by legend. What else do you know?"

"Only a little."

"Pity," she said, more to herself than to me. Drawing closer, she peered at me curiously. "Why do your eyes look so far away? They remind me of two stars that are hidden by clouds."

I stiffened. Defensively, I snapped, "My eyes are my eyes."

Again she studied me. Then, without a word, she pressed the last of her purple berries into my hand.

Unsure, I sniffed them. Their aroma brought back just how hungry I was, so against my better judgment I popped one into my mouth. A sudden burst of sweetness struck my tongue. I ate the rest in another swallow.

The girl studied me thoughtfully. "I see that you have suffered."

I frowned. She had noticed the scars. As would anyone who looked at my face. And yet . . . it seemed as though she had seen something beneath the surface, as well. I felt an inexplicable urge to unburden myself to this strange girl of the woods. Yet I resisted. I didn't know her, after all. Only a moment ago she would have abandoned me to the trees. No, I would not be so foolish as to trust her.

She rotated her head slightly, listening to some distant whispering of the branches. I noticed the intricate dressing of leaves in her curly brown hair. Although I could not be sure in the dim light of the grove, it appeared that her ears were somewhat triangular in shape, pointed at the top much like my own.

Did that mean that she, like myself, had endured teasing from others for having ears like a demon? Or . . . might everyone in this strange land have pointed ears? Was it possible that this girl and I actually belonged to the same race?

I shook myself back to reality. It was just as likely that angels themselves would have pointed ears. Or that demons would have lovely white wings!

I continued to watch her as she listened. "Do you hear something?"

Her gray-blue eyes swiveled back to me. "Only the words of my friends. They tell me that an outsider is in the forest, but that I already know." She paused. "They also tell me *beware*. Should I?"

I tensed, recalling the voice of the shell. "A person should always beware. But you need not be frightened of me."

She seemed amused. "Do I look frightened?"

"No." I felt myself grinning, as well. "I'm not very scary, I suppose."

"Not very."

"Your friends you spoke of. Are they . . . the trees?"

"They are."

"And you speak with them?"

Once again the bell-like laughter echoed in the grove. "Of course! Just as I speak with the birds and beasts and rivers."

"And also the shells?"

"Naturally. Everything has its language, you know. You only need to learn how to hear it." She raised an eyebrow. "Why do you understand so little?"

"I come from . . . far away."

"So that is why you know nothing of Druma Wood, or its ways." Her brow furrowed. "Yet you know of the Galator."

"Only a little, as I said before." I added wryly, "Although I would have said anything to get those horrible branches off me."

The hemlock boughs overhead wavered slightly. The sight made me cringe.

"You know more than a little about the Galator," declared the girl confidently. "One day you will tell me." She began to walk, somehow certain that I would follow. "But first, tell me your name."

I stepped carefully over a fallen branch. "Where are we going?"

"To get something to eat, of course." She bore to the left, following a trail that only she could detect through a patch of hip-deep fern. "Now will you tell me your name?"

"Emrys."

She glanced at me in a way that told me she did not quite believe me. But she said nothing.

"And what is yours?"

She stopped beneath a beech tree, which, though old and twisted, had bark as smooth as a young sapling. Raising a hand toward the graceful boughs, she said, "My friend will answer."

The leaves of the old beech stirred in gentle rustling. At first the sound meant nothing at all to me. I looked at the girl quizzically. Then, slowly, I began to hear a particular cadence. *Rrrrhhhhiiiaaaa. Rrrrhhhhiiiaaaa. Rrrrhhhhiiiaaaa.*

"Your name is Rhia?"

Again she started walking, passing through a stand of long-needled pines, sturdy and straight. "Rhiannon is my full name, though I don't know why. The trees call me Rhia."

Curious, I questioned her. "You don't know why? Didn't your parents tell you?"

She hopped across a slow-moving stream, where a plump mallard drifted among the reeds. "I lost my family when I was young, very young. The whole thing reminds me of a fledgling who falls out of the nest before she can fly." Without turning toward me, she added, "It also reminds me of you."

I stopped short, grabbed her by the arm. Seeing some branches bend menacingly lower, I released my grip. "What makes you say such a thing?"

She looked straight at me. "You seem lost, that's all."

We strode farther into the forest without speaking, past a red-tailed fox who did not stir from a meal of fresh grouse. The terrain began to slope upward, rising into a steep hill. Yet even as the walking grew more arduous, Rhia's pace did not slacken. In fact, it seemed to me that her pace only increased. Puffing hard, I struggled to keep up with her.

"You're like . . . Atalanta."

Rhia slowed a bit, her expression quizzical. "Who is that?"

"Atalanta," I panted. "A heroine . . . in a Greek legend . . . who could run . . . so fast . . . nobody could . . . catch her . . . until somebody . . . finally tricked her . . . with some . . . golden apples."

"I like that. Where did you ever learn such a story?"

"From . . . someone." I mopped my brow. "But I . . . wish I had . . . some of . . . those apples . . . right now."

Rhia smiled, but did not slow down.

As we ascended, enormous boulders, cracked and covered with pink and purple lichens, sprouted like giant mushrooms from the forest floor. The spaces between the trees grew wider, allowing more sunlight through the canopy of branches. More ferns, as well as sprinklings of flowers, crowded around massive roots and tumbled trunks.

At one point, Rhia paused to wait for me beneath a white-barked tree by a ledge. As I labored to catch up with her, she cupped her hands to her mouth and made a curious hooting sound. An instant later, three small owl faces, flat and feathery with enormous orange eyes, poked out of a hole about halfway up the trunk. The owls watched us intently. Then they hooted twice in unison and disappeared back inside the hole.

Rhia turned to me and smiled. Then she continued to climb the hill. At long last she reached the crest and halted, hands on her hips, taking in the view. Even before I caught up, I sniffed a new, juicy fragrance in the air. When at last I stood beside her, panting, the sight before me took away what little breath I still had.

In the rounded clearing before us, trees of all sizes and shapes and colors twined together, covering the entire top of the hill. Their branches, heavy with fruit, draped almost to the grass. And what fruit! Bright orange spheres, slender green crescents, tightly packed bunches of yellow and blue gleamed amidst the flashing wings of butterflies and bees. Round ones. Square ones. Hefty ones. Wispy ones. Most of the varieties of fruit I had never seen, nor even dreamed of, before. But that did not stop my mouth from watering.

"My garden," announced Rhia.

Seconds later, we were devouring whatever fruits we chose. Juices ran down my chin, my neck, my hands, my arms. Seeds stuck to my hair, while half-chewed rinds clung to my tunic. From a distance, I might have passed for a fruit tree myself.

The orange spheres exploded with tangy flavor, so I peeled and ate my fill of them before I started trying other kinds. One variety, shaped like an urn, contained so many seeds that I spat it out in disgust. Rhia laughed, as did I. Then I tried another, circular with an open hole in the middle. To my relief, it tasted like sweet milk and bore no seeds at all. Next I swallowed half of a gray, egg-shaped fruit. Although it had almost no taste, it somehow made me feel sad, aching with longing for all the things my life lacked.

When she saw that I had tried that particular kind, Rhia pointed me toward a spiral-shaped fruit, pale purple in color. I took a bite. A flavor like purple sunshine burst in my mouth. Somehow, it swept all the aching feelings away.

For her part, Rhia swallowed a huge quantity of tiny red berries growing in bundles of five or six on a stem. I tried one, but it was packed with such overpowering sweetness that it made me nauseous. I had no desire to eat more.

I watched in astonishment as Rhia downed them ten at a time. "How can you eat so many of those?"

She ignored me and continued eating.

At last, I started to feel full. More than full. I sat down, leaning against one of the thickest trunks in the garden. Afternoon light sifted through the leaves and fruit, as a gentle breeze flowed over the hill. I watched as Rhia eventually reached her limit of the sweet red berries. She joined me by the trunk, her shoulder nudging my own.

She opened her arms to the wondrous array of trees around us. "All this," she said gratefully, "from a single seed."

My eyes widened. "A single seed? You can't mean that."

"Oh yes! The seed of the shomorra tree yields not just one tree, but many, not just one fruit, but hundreds. And though the shomorra yields so much, it is so difficult to find that its scarceness is legendary. *As rare as a shomorra*, the old saying goes. In all the Druma, there is but this one."

I drank deeply of the scented air of this clearing. "This is not my home, yet I feel I could stay here long and gladly."

"Where then is your home?"

I sighed. "I don't know."

"So you are searching for that?"

"That and more."

Rhia twirled a vine from her sleeve. "Isn't your home wherever you are?"

"You aren't serious," I scoffed. "Home is the place you come from. The place where your parents live, where your past is hidden."

"Hidden? What in the world do you mean by that?"

"I have no memory of my past."

Although she seemed intrigued, Rhia asked no more questions. Instead, she reached for another cluster of red berries and popped them in her mouth. Through this mouthful, she said, "Perhaps what you are seeking is nearer than you know."

"I doubt it." I stretched my arms and shoulders. "I will explore some more of this place, but if I can't learn anything about my past, I will build a new boat and sail as far as I must. To the very horizon, if that's what it takes."

"Then you won't be long here, I suppose."

"Probably not. Where is here, anyway? Does this place have a name?"

"It has."

"What is it?"

Her expression darkened. "This place, this island, is called Fincayra."

XV

TROUBLE

I jumped as if I had been struck by a whip. "Fincayra?"

Rhia eyed me with interest. "You have heard of it?"

"Yes. Someone told me a little. But I never imagined it could be real."

She sighed somberly. "Fincayra is real enough."

So it is, I thought to myself. As real as Y Wyddfa. As real as Olympus. If only I could tell Branwen! I tried to call back what she had said about Fincayra. *A place of many wonders,* she had called it. *Neither wholly of Earth nor wholly of Heaven, but a bridge connecting both.* She had mentioned bright colors, too. That part I knew was true! And something else. Something about giants.

As we sat together in silence, immersed in private thoughts, the blanket of evening began to envelop the garden of the shomorra. With each passing minute, colors became shadows and shapes became silhouettes.

Finally, Rhia stirred. She rubbed her back against the trunk. "Night already! We have no time to travel to my house."

Feeling drowsy after our feast, I slid lower on the bed of soft grass beneath the tree. "I have slept in worse places."

"Look." Rhia pointed to the sky, where the first stars glimmered through the branches laden with fruit. "Wouldn't you love to be able to fly? To sail among those stars, to be one with the wind? I wish I had wings. Real wings!"

"So do I," I replied, searching for some sign of Pegasus.

She turned to me. "What else do you wish for?"

"Well . . . books."

"Really?"

"Yes! I would love, really love, to bury myself in a whole room full of books. With stories from all peoples, all times. I heard about such a room once."

She watched me for a moment. "From your mother?"

I drew a long breath. "No. From a woman who wanted me to believe that she was."

Rhia seemed puzzled, but said nothing.

"The room," I continued, "would have every kind of book imaginable. Surrounding me, everywhere I turned. Being in a room like that would be a lot like flying, you know. I could fly through those pages, anywhere I like."

Rhia laughed. "I'd rather have real wings! Especially on a night like this. See?" She looked up through the branches. "You can already see Gwri of the Golden Hair."

"That's a new constellation for me. Where is it?"

"Right there."

Though I strained with my second sight, I could see nothing in that part of the sky but a single star that I knew would eventually become part of Pegasus' wing. "I don't see it."

"Can't you see a maiden?"

"No."

She took my arm and aimed it upward. "Now?"

"No. All I see is a star that will be part of Pegasus. And there. I can see another star for Pegasus."

Rhia shot me a puzzled look. "Stars? Constellations of stars?"

Puzzled myself, I demanded, "What else?"

"My constellations are not made from the stars, but from the spaces *between* the stars. The dark places. The open places, where your mind can travel forever and ever."

From that instant onward, I could not view the heavens in the same way. Just as I could not view the girl beside me in the same way. "Tell me more. About what you see up there."

Rhia tossed back her brown curls. In a lilting voice, she began to explain some of the strange wonders of the Fincayran sky. How the broad band of stars across the middle of the night sky was truly a seam sewn in the two halves of time, one half always beginning, the other half always ending. How the longest patches of darkness were really the rivers of the gods, connecting this world and others. How the spinning circle of the stars was actually a great wheel, whose endless revolutions turned life into death, death into life.

Late into the night we drew pictures in the sky and traded tales. When at last we slept, it was soundly. And when warm rays awoke us, we realized that we did not want to leave this place. Not yet.

So for another day and another night we lingered at the bountiful hilltop, feasting on fruit and conversation. Though I remained guarded about discussing my deepest feelings, I discovered more than once that Rhia had an unnerving way of reading my thoughts as if they had been her own.

We sat beneath the fruity canopy, eating a hearty breakfast of tangy orange spheres (for me) and sweet red berries (for her). As we finished the meal by sharing one of the spiral-shaped fruits, Rhia turned to me with a question.

"That woman, the one who said she was your mother. What was she like?"

I looked at her with surprise. "She was tall, with very blue—"

"No, no, no. I don't care what she looked like. What was she *like*?"

For a moment I considered Branwen. "Well, she was kind to me. More kind than I deserved. Most of the time, anyway. Full of faith—in her God, and in me. And quiet. Too quiet. Except when she told me stories. She knew a lot of stories, more than I can begin to remember."

Rhia examined a berry for a moment before dropping it into her mouth. "I'm sure she learned some of them in that room full of books."

"That's right."

"And even though she wasn't your real mother, did you feel different because she was there, beside you? A little less lonely? A little . . . safer?"

I swallowed. "I guess so. Why are you so curious about her?"

Her face, which usually seemed at the very edge of laughter, turned serious. "I was just wondering what a mother, a real mother, would be like."

I lowered my eyes. "I wish I knew."

Rhia nodded. She ran her hand along a drooping bough of fruit, though she seemed to be looking past it, to some place or time far away.

"So you don't remember your mother?"

"I was so very young when I lost her. I only remember feelings. Being safe. And warm. And . . . held. I'm not even sure I really remember those things. It might just be my longing for them."

"What about your father? Any brothers or sisters?"

"I lost them. All of them." She spread her arms to the branches above us. "But I found the Druma. This is my family now. And while I don't have a true mother, I do have someone who protects me. And holds me. She is almost my mother."

"Who is that?"

Rhia smiled. "A tree. A tree named Arbassa."

I imagined her seated in the boughs of a great, sturdy tree. And I, too, smiled.

Then I thought about Branwen, my own almost-mother, as a strange warmth filled my chest. She was so distant from me and yet, at times, so close. I thought about her stories, her healing work, her sorrowful eyes. I wished that she had been willing to share more, about her own struggles as well as my mysterious past. I hoped that I might see her once again someday, although I knew it could not be so. Haltingly, I said a silent prayer to the God to whom she prayed so often, a prayer that wished her the peace she so longed to find.

Suddenly a sharp whistle pierced the air above my head. I looked up to find a familiar form perched on one of the branches.

"I don't believe it."

"A merlin," observed Rhia. "A young male. And look. His wing is hurt. See how it's missing some feathers." She twitched her neck, in the way a hawk often does, and released a sharp whistle of her own.

The bird, cocking his head, whistled back. This time the whistle warbled a bit, incorporating some more throaty tones.

Rhia's thick eyebrows lifted. She turned to me. "He said to me—not very politely, I might add—that you saved his life a while ago."

"He told you that?"

"Is it not true?"

"Yes, yes, it's true. I patched him up after he got into a fight. But how did you learn to talk with birds?"

Rhia shrugged as if the answer were obvious. "It's no more difficult than talking with trees." She added a bit sadly, "Those that are still awake, that is. Anyway, who was the merlin fighting?"

"I couldn't believe his pluck. Or foolishness. He picked a fight with two giant rats, each of them at least three times his size."

"Giant rats?" Rhia's whole body stiffened. "Where? In the Druma?"

I shook my head. "No, but right on the edge. Near a little stream that flows out of the trees."

Gravely, Rhia glanced at the merlin, who was pecking ravenously at a spiral-shaped fruit. "Killer rats, on our side of the river," she muttered, shaking her head. "They are forbidden to enter Druma Wood. That's the first time I've heard of them so close. Your friend the merlin may not have any manners, but he was right to attack them."

"That bird just likes fighting, if you ask me. It could just as easily have been you or me that he attacked. He is no friend of mine."

As if to contradict me, the merlin fluttered down from the fruit and landed on my left shoulder.

Rhia laughed. "Looks like he disagrees with you." She observed the hawk thoughtfully. "It's possible, you know, that he came to you for a reason."

I grimaced. "The only reason is the same bad luck that follows me everywhere."

"I don't know. He doesn't seem like such bad luck to me." Whistling in a light, friendly cadence, she extended her hand toward the merlin.

With a screech, the bird lashed out with one of his talons. Rhia quickly withdrew, though not before the talon sliced across the back of her hand.

"Oh!" Scowling, she licked the blood from her wound, then whistled a sharp reprimand.

The merlin reprimanded her in return.

"Stop that," I barked. I tried to brush the merlin off my shoulder, but the talons held tight, piercing my tunic and digging into my skin.

"You keep him away from me," declared Rhia. "That bird is trouble."

"I told you so."

"Don't act so smug!" She got up to leave. "Just rid us of him."

I rose also, with the unwanted passenger still on my shoulder. "Can't you help me somehow?"

"He's your friend." She stalked off, heading down the hill.

Again I tried to remove the merlin. But he refused to budge. Fixing an eye on me, he whistled angrily, as if he were threatening to tear off my ear if I did not cooperate.

Growling with frustration, I ran after Rhia as she disappeared into the forest. The bird clung tight to my shoulder, wings flapping. When I finally caught up with her, she was sitting on a low, rectangular rock, licking her gash.

"I don't suppose you could fix my hand the way you fixed your friend's wing."

"He's not my friend!" I shook my left shoulder, but the merlin hung on, eyeing me coldly. "Can't you see? It's more like he's my master and I'm his slave." I glared at the bird. "I can't make him leave."

Rhia's expression turned sympathetic. "I'm sorry. It's just that my hand hurts so."

"Let me see it." I took her hand, studying the deep cut. Blood continued to flow. Swiftly, I reached into my satchel and sprinkled some of the powdered herbs into the open wound. Pulling a broad leaf off a nearby bush, I laid it over the gash, taking care to draw the skin together as I had seen Branwen do dozens of times. Then, using a vine from Rhia's own sleeve, I wrapped her hand securely.

She lifted her hand gratefully. "Where did you learn to do this?"

"From Branwen. The woman who told me stories. She knew a lot about healing." I closed the satchel. "But she could only heal wounds to the skin."

Rhia nodded. "Wounds to the heart are much more difficult."

"Where are you going next?"

"To my house. I hope you will come." She waved at the hawk, who raised a vicious talon in response. "Even with your, ah, companion there."

"Generous of you," I replied grimly. Despite the bothersome bird, my curiosity to learn more about this place, and about Rhia herself, remained strong. "I would like to come. But I won't stay for long."

"That's fine. As long as you take that bird with you when you go."

"Do I have any choice?"

With that, we strode into the forest. For the rest of that morning and well into the afternoon we followed a trail only visible to Rhia. We rounded hills, leaped streams, and slogged through marshes where the air hummed with all kinds of insects.

Halfway across one such marsh, Rhia pointed to a dead tree that seemed to be painted bright red. She clapped her hands once. A split second later, a scarlet cloud billowed out of its branches. Butter-flies—hundreds of them, thousands of them—rose into the air, leaving the tree as bare as a skeleton.

I watched the scarlet cloud rise. So bright were the wings of the butterflies, flashing in the sun, that I wondered whether slices of the sun itself had been set like jewels within them. And I began to hope that my second sight was continuing to improve. If I could see such a stunning burst of color as this without my eyes, then one day, perhaps, I might be able to see all the world's colors as vividly as I had seen them before the fire.

On we went, stepping through glades of hip-high fern, crossing over tumbled trees whose trunks and limbs were melting steadily into soil, passing beneath roaring waterfalls. When we paused to gather some berries or take a drink of water, it was only briefly. Yet those moments were always long enough to glimpse the tail of a scurrying beast, catch the spicy scent of a flower, or hear the several voices of a stream.

I did my best to keep up, although Rhia's pace and my poor vision in shadowy places kept my chest heaving and my shins bruised. All the while, the bird continued to pinch my shoulder. I started to doubt that those talons would ever let me go.

As the late afternoon light wove luminous threads through the loom of branches, Rhia came to a sudden halt. I approached, huffing, to find her looking up at the trunk of a linden tree. There, wrapped around the middle of the trunk, hung a spiky wreath of glittering gold.

"What is it?" I asked in wonderment.

Rhia smiled at me. "Mistletoe. The golden bough. See how it holds the light of the sun? It is said that one who wears a mantle of mistletoe may find the secret path to the Otherworld of the spirits."

"It's beautiful."

She nodded. "Second only to the long-tailed alleah bird, it's the most beautiful sight in the forest."

I studied the shining wreath. "It seems so different from other plants."

"And so it is! It's neither a plant nor a tree, but a little of both. It's something in between."

Something in between, I repeated to myself, remembering the words. Once Branwen had used them to describe those special places, like the Greeks' Mount Olympus, where mortals and immortals could live side by side. And those special substances, like mist, where elements as distinct as air and water could merge to form something both alike and unlike themselves. Something in between.

Rhia beckoned. "We should go. We will need to move quickly to reach my house before dark."

Through the towering trees we marched. As the light grew dim, my ability to see grew worse. As did my bruises and scrapes. Despite Rhia's repeated urgings, I lost speed in the darkening forest. I stumbled more and more often, tripping on roots and rocks. Every time I fell, the merlin dug in his talons and screeched at me angrily, so loud that my ear stung as much as my shoulder. The trek became a torture.

At one point, I misjudged a branch and walked straight into it. The branch jabbed one of my sightless eyes. I howled in pain, but Rhia was too far ahead to hear. Then, trying to regain my balance, I did not see an animal's den and stepped in it, twisting my ankle.

I crumpled on a fallen trunk, my eye stinging and my ankle throbbing. I lowered my head toward my knees, prepared to wait out the night if necessary.

To my surprise, the merlin finally lifted off. An instant later, he pounced on a mouse, bit the creature's neck in two, then carried it aloft. He landed next to me on the trunk and began attacking his meal. While sorry for the mouse, I rubbed my sore shoulder thankfully. But my relief was muted. I felt sure that the bird, who continued to eye me even as he ate, would soon return to his favorite perch. Why, of all the places in this entire forest, did he have to choose my poor shoulder?

"Emrys!"

"Over here," I answered dismally. Even the sound of Rhia's voice failed to lift my spirits, for I did not look forward to telling her that I could not see well enough to go any farther that night.

I heard a crackling of twigs, and she appeared out of the darkness. Suddenly I realized that she had not come alone. Beside her stood a slight figure, thin as a sapling, whose long face remained hidden in shadow. And although I could not be sure, the figure seemed to exude a potent fragrance, as sweet as apple blossoms in the spring.

I rose to meet them. My ankle felt somewhat stronger, but I still wobbled unsteadily. With the onset of night, I could see less well by the minute.

Rhia indicated her thin companion. "This is Cwen, my oldest friend. She took care of me when I was young."

"Sssso young you could not sssspeak, nor even feed yoursssself," whispered Cwen in a voice like the wind rustling a field of dry grasses. Sounding wistful, she added, "You were assss young then assss I am old now." She pointed a narrow, knobby arm at me. "And who issss thissss?"

At that instant a deafening whistle and a flapping of wings filled the air, followed by a shriek from Cwen. Rhia swatted at something, then pulled her friend away. I myself cried out as sharp talons closed once more on my left shoulder.

"Akkkhh!" hissed Cwen, glaring at the merlin. "That thing attacksssss me!"

Furious, Rhia whistled at the bird. Yet he merely cocked his head at her, not even bothering to respond.

Rhia glared at me. "That bird is trouble! Nothing but trouble!"

With a glance at my shoulder, I nodded glumly. "I wish I knew how to lose him."

"Sssskewer him," urged Cwen, keeping her distance. "Pluck out hissss featherssss!"

The merlin ruffled his pointed wings and she fell silent.

Rhia scratched her chin thoughtfully. "This bird reminds me of a shadow, the way he sticks to you."

"He reminds me more of a curse," I grumbled.

"Hear me out," Rhia went on. "Is there any possibility, no matter how small, that you might be able to tame him?"

"Are you insane?"

"I am serious!"

"But why should I want to tame him?"

"Because if you can come to know him, even a little, you might find out what he really wants. And then you might find some way to free yourself from him."

Cwen scoffed. "Nonssssense."

As the darkness closed in, I didn't feel at all hopeful. "It will never work."

"Do you have a better idea?"

I shook my head. "I suppose, if I am going to try to tame him—and I would have better luck taming a dragon, I think—then I should first give him a name."

"Right," agreed Rhia. "But the name will be tricky. It must be something fitting."

I groaned. "That part is easy. You just said it yourself. The name for him is Trouble. Nothing but Trouble."

"Good. Now you can start his training."

Dejectedly, I turned to the dark form on my shoulder.

"Come then," said Rhia as she took Cwen's thin arm. "We are only a few hundred paces from my house."

I brightened a bit. "Really?"

"Yes. You are welcome there, so long as that bird is not too much—"

"Trouble," finished Cwen.

XVI

ARBASSA'S
DOOR

As Rhia led us out of the deep forest into a nearby clearing, I noticed the sudden brightness of the night sky. Then, as the web of branches fell away, I wondered whether a star might be exploding above us, filling the sky with light. At once I realized that the light came not from a star, nor even from the sky.

It came from Rhia's house. From the center of the clearing rose a great oak, mightier than any tree I had ever seen. Its burly branches reached outward and upward from the trunk, so thick that it seemed to be made of several trunks fused together. Set in the midst of those branches, glowing like a giant torch, was an aerial cottage whose beams and walls and windows curled with the twisting limbs. Layers of leaves overlaid the tree house, so that the light radiating from its windows shone through multiple curtains of green.

"Arbassa." Rhia lifted her arms high as she spoke the name.

In response, the branches above her head shimmered just enough to drop a light rain of dew on her upturned face.

I watched, my chest feeling warm again, as Rhia approached the base of the tree. Peeling off her snug shoes, which appeared to be made of a leathery type of bark, she stepped into a cup-shaped portion of the massive roots. As she spoke a quiet, swishing phrase, the root gradually closed around her feet, so that she and the tree stood planted together as one single being. Rhia stretched her arms wide and embraced the great trunk, even though she could only reach a tiny portion of the way around. At the same time, one of the tree's enormous branches unfurled like the frond of a fern, wrapping itself over her back to return the embrace.

A few moments later, the branch lifted and the root parted. With a creaking sound, the trunk creased, cracked, and opened into a small doorway. Rhia ducked her head and entered. Cwen, walking stiffly, slipped in beside her.

"Come." Rhia motioned to me to join her.

As I stepped toward the cavern, however, the tree shuddered. The bark-edged doorway began to close. Rhia shouted a sharp command, but the tree ignored her and continued to seal itself. I called out to her, while Trouble fluttered his wings nervously. Despite Rhia's protests, the doorway shut tight.

Helpless, I stood before the tree. I knew as little about what this meant as I knew what to do about it. But one thing was clear. I had been rejected—no doubt thanks to the troublesome bird on my shoulder.

Just then the trunk creased again. The door reopened. Rhia, her face red from shouting, beckoned to me to come. Glancing uncertainly at the fidgeting bird, I entered the dark cavern.

Rhia said nothing. She merely turned and started to climb the spiraling stairway within the trunk. I followed, hoping that Trouble would not cause any.

The gnarled platforms of the stairs grew right out of the inner walls of the trunk, so that the whole stairway smelled as rich and moist as a glade after a rain. As we climbed higher, the stairs grew lighter, revealing intricately carved script that flowed over the inner walls. Thousands of lines of this tightly written script covered the stairwell, as beautiful as it was indecipherable. I wished I could read what it said.

At last we reached an open platform. Rhia pushed against a drapery of leaves, and entered her house. I came right behind, although Trouble clawed angrily at the leaves when they brushed against his feathers.

I found myself standing on a floor of tightly meshed boughs, sturdy yet uneven. A fire burned in the hearth in the middle of the room, so bright that I wondered what fuel could be burning within it. The branches of the great tree curled around us, though they were not as closely woven as the floor, so that window slats opened in all directions.

Every piece of furniture in this one-room house rose out of the branches, as naturally as the branches themselves sprang from the trunk. A low table by the hearth, a pair of simple chairs, a cabinet containing utensils made of carved wood and beeswax, all were produced by living branches twisted into shape. Next to the cabinet, Cwen was stirring something.

I stepped closer to Rhia. "What happened down there?"

Cautiously, she looked from me to the sharp-taloned bird on my shoulder. "My friend Arbassa did not want to let you in."

"That much I could tell."

"It would only have done that for one reason. To keep out of my home someone who could do me great harm."

I felt a new surge of resentment against Trouble. If his presence had almost prevented me from entering Rhia's house, might it also prevent me from finding my past, my identity? "I wish I'd never met this cursed bird!"

Rhia frowned. "Yes. I know." She waved toward Cwen, still bending over the cabinet. "Come. Let's have some supper."

The slim figure poured something that looked like honey over her concoction, a platter of rolled leaves crammed with reddish-brown nuts. The whole thing gave off a hearty, roasted smell. As she carried the platter over to the low table by the hearth, she glanced sharply at Trouble. "I have no ssssupper for that vicioussss beasssst."

For the first time, I realized that Cwen was truly more tree than human. Her skin, gnarled and ridged, looked very much like bark, while her tangled brown hair resembled a mass of vines. Her root-like feet remained unshod, and she wore no adornment but the silver rings on the smallest of her twelve knobby fingers. Beneath her robe of white cloth, her body moved like a tree bending with the wind. Yet her age must have been considerable, for her back bent like a trunk leaning under a winter's weight of snow, and her neck, arms, and legs seemed twisted and frail. Even so, the fragrance of apple blossoms wafted around her. And her recessed brown eyes, shaped like slender teardrops, shone as bright as the fire.

Staying clear of me, and especially my passenger, she set down the platter. Her aim was off, however, and she knocked over an oaken flask of water on the table.

"Cursssse thessssse old handsssss!" Cwen grabbed the flask and brought it over to the cabinet. As she refilled it, I heard her muttering, "The cursssse of time, the cursssse of time." She continued to grumble as she returned it to the table.

Rhia sat in one of the chairs, indicating with a nod for me to take the other. I watched as she took one of the rolled leaves in her hand. This she plunged into the jar of honey on the platter.

She flashed me a slightly guilty smile. "A person can never get enough honey."

I grinned. Tilting my head toward Cwen, I whispered, "She is not a person, like you or me, is she?"

Rhia looked at me curiously. "A person, she certainly is. But like us, she is not. She is the last survivor of the treelings—a race of part trees, part people. They used to be common in Fincayra, back in the days when giants were the masters of this land. But they are gone now, except for Cwen."

She stuffed the food, dripping with honey, into her mouth, then reached for the flask of water. After several swallows, she offered it to me. Since by then I had tried some myself and found the rolled leaves so sticky that they were very difficult to chew, I accepted the water gladly.

As I replaced the flask on the table, I noticed that the fire, intensely bright though it was, produced no smoke and no heat. In a flash I understood that this fire was really not a fire at all. Thousands of tiny beetles, pulsing with light of their own making, crawled across a pile of rounded river stones in the center of the hearth. The stones appeared to be their home, for the beetles crawled over and under them continuously, like bees in a hive. While each one of the beetles comprised only a subtle spot of light, collectively they produced a powerful glow which illuminated the entire tree house.

As I finally swallowed the sticky food, Trouble shifted on my shoulder, digging his talons deep into my skin. I cried out, then turned angrily toward him. "Why do you punish me like this? Get off my shoulder, I say! Get off!"

Trouble merely stared at me, unblinking.

I turned to Rhia. "How am I supposed to tame him? Not even the Galator could tame him!"

Cwen, standing near one of the window slats, stiffened.

Caught off guard, I instinctively touched the tunic over my chest, feeling the pendant hanging beneath. Then, realizing what I had done, I did my best to disguise the motion, reaching higher to rub my free shoulder. In a casual voice, I said to Rhia, "Wouldn't it be wonderful to find something magical, like the Galator? But if I ever did, I wouldn't waste it on the bird. I'd use it to mend my sore body."

Rhia nodded sympathetically. "Where are you sore?"

"My legs mostly. But I also have this ache between my shoulder blades. It's been with me for as long as I can remember."

Her eyebrows lifted, but she remained silent. I somehow had the feeling that she, too, knew more than she was saying.

She reached beneath the table and pulled out two small, silvery blankets, made from the most delicate linen I had ever seen. She spread one over her thighs, then handed the other to me. "A good night's sleep will help."

I held the shimmering blanket up to the light. "What is this cloth?"

"It is silk, made by moths."

"Moths? You're joking."

She smiled. "Their silk is just as warm as it is light. Try it yourself."

Keeping a safe distance from the hawk, Cwen approached. "Would a ssssong be ssssoothing to you?"

"Please," Rhia answered. "It reminds me of all the times you sang to me when I was small."

Cwen nodded, her teardrop eyes expressionless. "I will ssssing you a ssssong that ussssed to help you ssssleep."

As she passed a thin hand over the glowing beetles, their light dimmed. Then, like an old tree weaving in the wind, Cwen began to project a rolling, vibrating sound. It swelled and faded, repeating a comforting pattern over and over again. Almost a voice, yet not quite a voice, the sound wound wordlessly around us. Coaxing us to relax, to let go. I pulled the blanket over my chest and leaned back in the chair, my eyes feeling heavy. Rhia, I could tell, was already asleep, and even Trouble's head had drooped low on his chest. I watched Cwen's flowing motions for a while, but it was not long before I too drifted into slumber.

I dreamed that I lay alone, fast asleep, in a deep forest. Tall trees surrounded me, weaving in the wind. Honey, from somewhere, dripped into my mouth. Then, all at once, enemies appeared. I couldn't see them. But I could feel them. They were hiding in the trees. Or perhaps they were the trees themselves! Worse yet, as hard as I tried, I couldn't wake up, not even to protect myself. Slowly, one of the thin, twisted trees nearby bent down over my sleeping form, slipping a fingerlike branch into my tunic. *The Galator. It wants the Galator.* With a supreme effort, I managed to rouse myself.

I was still sitting in the chair by the dimly glowing hearth. The silk blanket had fallen to the floor beside me. I reached for the Galator, and to my relief, felt it was still there under my tunic. Listening, I heard the sporadic chattering of birds outside, telling me that sunrise was an hour or so away. Rhia slept curled as tight as a ball in her chair, while Cwen lay snoring on the floor by the cabinet. Trouble sat on my shoulder, his yellow-rimmed eyes wide open.

I wondered whether Arbassa itself ever slept. Even now, as it held us in its arms, was it still watching the hawk with concern? I wished I could ask the great tree whether Fincayra held the answers to my questions. Had the time come to leave Druma Wood and explore other parts of this island? Or should I be building a boat to search for another place entirely?

I sighed. For I knew once again, in that hour before dawn, how little I really did know.

 XVII

THE ALLEAH
BIRD

Rhia shrieked suddenly. She sat rigid in her chair, not moving, not breathing. Even the golden light of sunrise, pouring through the window slats and over her suit of leafy vines, could not hide the look of terror on her face.

I bounced out of my chair. "What's wrong?"

Her wide eyes peered into mine. "Everything."

"What do you mean?"

She shook the forest of curls on her head. "A dream. So real, like it was truly happening." She took a deep breath. "It frightened me."

I watched her, remembering my own dream.

Cwen's slender form approached. "What dream wassss thissss?"

Rhia faced her. "Every night I dream about the Druma. Without fail."

"Sssso? I do assss well."

"It's always safe. Always comforting. Always . . . home. Even when I go to sleep worried about the troubles in other parts of Fincayra—which happens more and more—I know I can always find peace in my dreams of the Druma."

Cwen wrung her knobby hands. "You don't sssseem sssso peaceful now."

"I'm not!" Rhia's eyes filled with terror again. "Last night I dreamed that the whole Druma—all the trees, the ferns, the animals, the stones—started bleeding! Bleeding to death! I tried and tried, but I couldn't do anything to stop it. The forest was dying! The sky darkened. Everything turned the color of dried blood. The color of—"

"Rust," I finished. "Same as the other side of the river."

She nodded grimly, then lifted herself from her chair and strode to the eastern wall, where rays of lavender and pink now mixed with gold. Propping her hands on both sides of a slat, she gazed at the dawn. "For months, I've tried to convince myself that the sickness across the River Unceasing would never reach the Druma. That only the Blighted Lands would fall, not the whole of Fincayra."

"Sssso wrong," put in Cwen. "In all my yearssss, which are now sssso very many, I have never felt the Druma in ssssuch danger. Never! If we are to ssssurvive, we need new ssssstrength—from whatever ssssource." The last phrase rang rather ominously, though I was not sure why.

Rhia's brow creased. "That too was part of my dream." She paused, thinking. "A stranger came into the forest. A stranger who knew no one at all. He had some sort of power . . ." She swung around to face me. "And he—and only he—could save the Druma."

I blanched. "Me?"

"I'm not sure. I woke up before I could see his face."

"Well, I'm not your savior. That's certain."

She watched me closely, though she didn't say anything.

Trouble's talons squeezed tighter on my shoulder.

I turned from Rhia to Cwen and back to Rhia. "You're mistaken! Badly mistaken. Once I had . . . But I can't . . . I can't do anything like that! And even if I could, I have my own quest to follow." I shook my left arm. "Despite this bird on me."

"Your own quesssst?" demanded Cwen. "Sssso you care nothing for otherssss?"

"I didn't say that."

"But you did." Rhia looked at me sharply. "You care about your own quest more than you care about the Druma."

"If you put it that way, yes." My cheeks burned. "Don't you understand? I have to find my own past! My own name! The last thing I need is to get caught up in whatever is happening here. You can't ask me to give up my quest just because you had one bad dream!"

She glared at me. "And how far would your quest have gone if the Druma had not been kind to you?"

"Far enough. I got here on my own, didn't I?"

"You remind me of a baby who says he fed himself on his own."

"I am no baby!"

Rhia sucked in her breath. "Listen. I'm the only creature of my kind who lives in this forest. No other woman or man or child can be found here, except for the rare outsider who slips through, as you did. But do I think, even for an instant, that I live here alone? That I could have survived without the others—like Arbassa, or Cwen, or the alleah bird, whose beauty I treasure even if I should never be lucky enough to see it again? If the Druma is in trouble, then all of them are in trouble. And I'm in trouble, too."

Imploringly, she opened her hands to me. "Please. Will you help?"

I looked away.

"He will not help ussss," spat Cwen.

Rhia strode to the stairway entrance. "Come. I want you to see what else will die if the Druma dies."

As she started down the stairs within Arbassa's trunk, I followed her, but only reluctantly. For the feeling was growing inside me that my own quest must take me elsewhere—to other parts of Fincayra, and perhaps beyond. In any case, to places far from the Druma. And even if I stayed here for a while, how could I try to help Rhia without being tempted to call on my forbidden powers? I shook my head, certain that our new friendship was already lost.

I glanced over my shoulder at Cwen. She showed no emotion at my departure—with one exception. Her teardrop eyes glared at Trouble, making clear that she was glad to see the irascible bird go. As if in response, he lifted one leg and raked his talons savagely in her direction.

Winding down the stairway, I smelled the familiar moist fragrance, all the while doubting I would ever stand here, in this great tree, again. I paused to examine the curious script that covered Arbassa's walls.

Rhia, already at the bottom, called up to me. "Let's go."

"I am just taking a last look at this writing."

Even in the spare light of the stairwell, her puzzlement was clear. "Writing? What writing?"

"On the wall here. Don't you see it?"

She climbed back up to me. After staring at the spot where I pointed, she seemed baffled, as if she saw nothing there. "Can you read it?"

"No."

"But you can see it?"

"Yes."

For a moment she scrutinized me. "There is something different about the way you see, isn't there?"

I nodded.

"You see without your eyes."

Again I nodded.

"And you can see something I can't see *with* eyes." Rhia bit her lip. "You are even more of a stranger to me now than when I first met you."

"Maybe it's better for you I stay a stranger."

Trouble fluttered his wings nervously.

"He doesn't like it in here," she observed, heading down the stairs.

I followed. "He probably knows what Arbassa thinks of him." After a pause, I added, "Not to mention what I think of him."

The doorway creaked, then opened. We stepped through it into the morning light scattered by the leafy boughs overhead, even as the passage snapped shut behind us.

Rhia glanced upward into the broad boughs of Arbassa, then quickly moved into the forest. As I followed, my walking jarred Trouble, and his talons squeezed me tighter than ever.

Before long, she came to a large beech tree, its gray bark folded with age. "Come here," she called. "I have something to show you."

I approached. She took her hand and laid it flat against the trunk.

"No tree is as ready to speak as a beech. Especially an elder. Listen."

Gazing up into the branches, she started making a slow, swishing sound with her voice. Immediately, the branches began to wave in response, whispering gently. As she varied her pace, pitch, and volume, the tree seemed to reply in kind. Soon the girl and the tree were engaged in full and lively conversation.

After a time, Rhia turned to me and spoke again in our own language. "Now you try it."

"Me?"

"You. First put your hand on the trunk."

Still doubtful, I obeyed.

"Now before you speak, listen."

"I already heard the branches."

"Don't listen with your ears. Listen with your *hand*."

My palm pressed into the folds of the trunk; my fingers joined with the cold, smooth bark. Presently I could feel a vague pulsing at the edges of my fingertips. The pulsing moved gradually into my whole hand and then up my arm. I could almost feel the subtle rhythm of air and earth flowing through the body of the tree, a rhythm that combined the power of an ocean wave surging with the tenderness of a small child breathing.

Without thinking, I started making a swishing sound like Rhia. To my surprise, the branches responded, waving gracefully above me. A whisper stirred the air. I nearly smiled, knowing that while I did not understand its words, the tree was indeed speaking to me.

Both to Rhia and the old beech, I said, "One day I would like to learn this language."

"It would do you no good if the Druma dies. Only here are the trees of Fincayra still awake enough to talk."

I hunched my shoulders. "What can I possibly do for you? I already told you I'm not the person in your dream."

"Forget my dream! There is something remarkable about you. Something . . . special."

Her words warmed me. Even if I didn't really believe them, it meant something that she did. For the first time in what seemed like ages, I thought of myself, seated on the grass, concentrating on a flower, making it open its petals one by one. Then I remembered where that path had taken me, and I shuddered. "Once there was something special. But that part of me is gone."

Her gray-blue eyes burrowed deeper. "Whatever it is you have, it is with you right now."

"I have only myself and my quest—which will probably take me far from here."

Adamantly, she shook her head. "That is not all you have."

All at once I understood what she must be talking about. The Galator! She didn't want me, after all. She wanted the pendant I wore, whose power I did not begin to understand. It didn't matter how she had concluded that I carried it. What mattered was that, somehow, she knew. How foolish of me to have believed, even for an instant, that she had seen something special about me. About my person, rather than my pendant.

"You don't really want me," I growled.

Her face turned quizzical. "You think not?"

Before I could answer, Trouble's talons dug into my shoulder with sudden force. I winced with pain. It was all I could do to keep myself from swiping at the bird, but I knew that he might attack me as ferociously as he had attacked the killer rat by the stream. All I could do was try to tolerate the pain, while despairing that he had chosen me to be his perch. But why had he chosen me? What did he really want? I had absolutely no idea.

"Look!" Rhia pointed at a brilliant flash of iridescent red and purple disappearing into the trees. "The alleah bird!"

She started after it, then paused, glancing back at me. "Come!

Let's get closer. The alleah bird is a sign of good fortune! I have not seen one for years."

With that, she dashed after the bird. I noticed that the wind seemed to sweep through the trees at that very moment, causing the branches to chatter vigorously. Yet if they were truly saying something, Rhia was not paying any attention. I rushed after her.

Over fallen branches and through needled bracken we chased the bird. Each time we drew close enough to get a better look, it flew off in a burst of brilliant color, showing only enough of its plumed tail to make us want to see more.

Finally, the alleah bird settled on a low branch in a stand of dead trees. Most likely it had chosen this place to perch because the supple, living branches all around were swaying so wildly in the wind. For the first time, no leaves hid its bright feathers. Rhia and I, panting from the chase, held ourselves as still as possible, studying the flaming purple crest on the bird's head and the explosions of scarlet along its tail.

Rhia could hardly contain her excitement. "Let's see how near we can get." She started to creep closer, pushing past a dead limb.

Suddenly Trouble whistled sharply. As I cringed from the blast in my ear, the hawk took flight. My heart missed a beat when I realized that he meant to attack the beautiful bird.

"No!" I cried.

Rhia waved her arms wildly. "Stop! Stop!"

The merlin paid no attention. Releasing another wrathful whistle, he shot like an arrow straight into his prey. The alleah bird, taken unaware, shrieked in pain as Trouble sunk his talons deep into its soft neck and pecked at its eyes. Still, it fought back with surprising savagery. The branch snapped beneath them. Feathers flying, the two birds tumbled to the ground.

Rhia ran forward, with me right behind. Reaching the spot, we both froze.

Before us on the brown leaves, Trouble, his talons smeared with blood, stood atop the body of his motionless prey. I noticed that the alleah bird seemed to have only one leg. Probably the other one had been torn off in the attack. I felt sick at the sight of those crumpled feathers, those luminous wings that would never fly again.

Then, as we watched in amazement, the alleah bird began to metamorphose. As it changed, it pulled away from its former skin, much like a snake that is shedding. This left behind a brittle, almost transparent skin, marked with ridges where the feathers had been. Meanwhile the bird's wings evaporated, as the feathered tail transformed into a long, serpentine body covered by dull red scales. The head grew longer and sprouted massive jaws, filled with jagged teeth that could easily bite off a hand. Only the eyes, as red as the scales, remained unchanged. The serpentlike creature lay dead, the thin skin of its former body clinging to its side.

I took Rhia's arm. "What does this mean?"

Her face drained of color, she turned slowly toward me. "It means that your hawk has saved our lives."

"What is that . . . thing?"

"That is—or was—a shifting wraith. It can change into whatever shape it wants, so it is especially dangerous."

"Those jaws look dangerous enough."

Grimly, Rhia poked at the shed skin with a stick. "As I said, a shifting wraith can change into anything. But there is always a flaw, something that gives it away, if you look closely enough."

"The bird had only one leg."

Rhia motioned toward the still-whispering branches beyond the dead stand. "The trees tried to warn me, but I wasn't listening. A shifting wraith in the Druma! That has never happened before. Oh, Emrys . . . my dream is coming true before my eyes!"

I bent low and extended my hand toward the merlin, now preening his wings. Trouble cocked his head to one side, then the other, then hopped onto my waiting wrist. With quick, sideways steps, he climbed up my arm and sat once more on my shoulder. Yet this time his weight didn't feel so troublesome.

I faced Rhia, whose brow was wrinkled with foreboding. "All of us were wrong about this little fighter. Even Arbassa was wrong."

She shook her head. "Arbassa was not wrong."

"But—"

"When Arbassa closed the door, it was not to keep out the merlin." She drew a long breath. "It was to keep out *you.*"

I stepped backward. "The tree thinks I could be dangerous to you?"

"That's right."

"Do you believe that?"

"Yes. But I decided to let you in anyway."

"Why? That was before your dream."

She studied me curiously. "One day, perhaps, I will tell you."

XVIII

THE NAME OF
THE KING

My second sight moved from the skin of the shifting wraith, as brittle as a dried leaf, to the living, whispering boughs of the Druma. "Tell me what is happening to Fincayra."

Rhia frowned—such an unnatural expression for her. "I only know a little, what I've learned from the trees."

"Tell me what you know."

She reached toward me, wrapping one of her forefingers around one of mine. "It reminds me of a basket of sweet berries that turns sour. Too sour to eat." She gave a sigh. "Some years ago, strange things—evil things—started happening. The lands east of the river, once nearly as green and full of life as this forest, fell to the Blight. As the land darkened, so did the sky. But until today, the Druma has always been safe. Its power was so strong, no enemies dared to enter. Until now."

"How many wraiths are there?"

Trouble fluttered his wings, then grew quiet again.

"I don't know." Her frown deepened. "But the shifting wraiths are not even our worst enemies. There are warrior goblins. They used to stay underground, in their caves. But now they run free, and they kill just for pleasure. There are ghouliants—the deathless warriors who guard the Shrouded Castle. And there is Stangmar, the king who commands them all."

At the mention of that name, the living branches surrounding the stand of dead trees started shaking and clacking. When at last they grew still, I asked, "Who is this king?"

Rhia chewed her lip. "Stangmar is terrible—too terrible for words. It's hard to believe, but I've heard the trees say that when he first came to power, he wasn't so wicked. In those days, he sometimes rode through the Druma on his great black horse, even pausing to listen to the voices of the forest. Then something happened to him—no one knows what—that made him change. He destroyed his own castle, a place of music and friendship. And where it stood, he built the Shrouded Castle, a place of cruelty and terror."

She sat solemnly for a moment. "It lies far to the east, in the darkest of the Dark Hills, where the night never ends. I've heard of no one, other than the king's own servants, who has gone there and returned alive. No one! So the truth is difficult to know. Yet . . . it is said that the castle is always dark, and always spinning, so fast that no one could ever attack it."

I stiffened, remembering my dream at sea. Even now, that terrible castle felt all too real.

"Meanwhile, Stangmar has poisoned much of Fincayra. All the lands east of the Druma, and some to the south, have been *cleansed,* as those loyal to him would say. What that really means is that fear—cold, lifeless fear—has covered everything. It reminds me of snow, except snow is pretty. Villages are burned. Trees and rivers are silent. Animals and birds are dead. And the giants are gone."

"Giants?"

Her eyes burned angrily. "Our first and oldest people. Giants from every land call Fincayra their ancestral home. Even before the rivers began rolling down from the mountains, the footsteps of giants marked Fincayra. Long before Arbassa first sprouted as a seedling, their rumbling chants echoed over ridges and forests. Even now, the Lledra, their oldest chant, is the first song many babies ever hear."

The Lledra. Had I heard that name before? It seemed familiar somehow. But how could it be? Unless, perhaps, it was one of Branwen's chants.

"They can grow taller than a tree, our giants. Or even a hillside. Yet throughout the ages, they've stayed peaceful. Except for the Wars of Terror long ago—when goblins tried to overrun the giants' ancient city of Varigal. Usually, unless someone makes them angry, they are as gentle as butterflies."

She stamped her foot on the ground. "But some years ago, Stangmar issued a command—for some reason known only to him—to kill the giants wherever they were found. Since then, his soldiers have hunted them ruthlessly. Although it takes twenty or more soldiers to kill just one, they nearly always succeed. The city of Varigal, I've heard, is now just a ruin. It's possible that a few giants still survive, disguised as cliffs or crags, but they must always stay in hiding, afraid for their lives. In all my travels through the Druma, I've never seen a single one."

I gazed at the corpse of the shifting wraith. "Isn't there any way to stop this king?"

"If there is, no one has found it! His powers are vast. Besides his army, he has assembled almost all of the Treasures of Fincayra."

"What are they?"

"Magical. Powerful. The Treasures were always used to benefit the land and all its creatures, not just one person. But no more. Now they are his—the Orb of Fire, the Caller of Dreams, the Seven Wise Tools. The sword called Deepercut—a sword with two edges, one that can cut right into the soul, and one that can heal any wound. The most beautiful one, the Flowering Harp, whose music can bring springtime to any meadow or hillside. And the most hateful one, the Cauldron of Death."

Her voice fell to a whisper. "Only one of the legendary Treasures hasn't yet fallen into his hands. The one whose power is said to be greater than all the rest combined. The one called the Galator."

Beneath my tunic, my heart pulsed against the pendant.

Her finger wrapped tighter around mine. "I've heard the trees saying that Stangmar has given up searching for the Galator, that it disappeared from Fincayra some years ago. Yet I've also heard that he is still searching for something that will make his power complete—something he calls *the last Treasure*. That could only mean one thing."

"The Galator?"

Rhia nodded slowly. "Anyone who knows where it's hidden is in the gravest danger."

I could not miss the warning. "You know I have it."

"Yes," she replied calmly. "I know."

"And you think it could help save the Druma."

She pursed her lips in thought. "It might, or it might not. Only the Galator itself can say. But I still think *you* could help."

I stepped back, jabbing my neck on a broken limb. Trouble screeched at me reproachfully.

Yet the pain in my neck, like the pain in my ear, didn't distress me. For I had heard in her voice that certain something I had not allowed myself to hear before. She really did see something of value in me! I felt sure that she was mistaken. But her faith was a kind of treasure itself, as precious in its way as the one around my neck.

The words jumped out at me. *As precious as the one around my neck.* Suddenly I realized that I had my clue! The clue I'd been seeking!

Until now I had assumed that the Galator was simply known in Fincayra—not that it truly *belonged* in Fincayra. Now I knew better. It was the most powerful of this land's ancient Treasures. And it may have disappeared around the time Branwen and I washed ashore on Gwynedd. If only I could find out how the Galator had come into Branwen's hands, or at least learn some more of its secrets, then I might find some of my own secrets as well.

"The Galator," I said. "What else do you know about it?"

Rhia released my hand. "Nothing. And now I must go. With or without you."

"Where?"

She started to speak, then froze, listening. Trouble, clinging firmly to my left shoulder, also froze.

Rhia's loose brown hair stirred like the branches as yet another wind moved through the forest. As her features hardened with concentration, I wondered whether her laughter like bells would ever ring again among these trees. The sound swelled steadily, a chorus of swishing and creaking, drumming and moaning.

As the wind subsided, she leaned toward me. "Goblins have been seen in the forest! I have no time to lose." She caught a fold of my tunic. "Will you come? Will you help me find some way to save the Druma?"

I hesitated. "Rhia . . . I'm sorry. The Galator. I need to find out more about it! Can't you understand?"

Her eyes narrowed. Without saying good-bye, she turned to go.

I strode up to her and caught a vine from her sleeve. "I wish you well."

"And I wish you well," she said coldly.

A sudden crashing came from the underbrush behind us. We whirled around to see a young stag, with the beginning of a rack above its bronze-colored head. The stag leaped over some fallen timber, eager to get away from something. For a split second I caught a glimpse of one of its brown eyes, dark and deep, filled with fear.

I tensed, recalling the one time before when I had seen a stag. Yet that time the fear was in my own eyes. And that time the stag did everything in its power to help me.

Rhia pulled free, then started to go.

"Wait! I will come with you."

Her whole face brightened. "You will?"

"Yes . . . but only until our two paths diverge."

She nodded. "For a while, then."

"And where are we going?"

"To find the one creature in all the Druma who might know what to do. The one who is called the Grand Elusa."

For some reason, I wasn't sure I liked the sound of that name.

XIX

HONEY

As swiftly as the stag, Rhia bounded off. Although my legs still felt stiff, I tried my best to keep up with her through dense thickets and over moss-banked streams. Even so, she often needed to stop and wait for me.

Because the sun rode high above us, sending shafts of light to the forest floor, I could see obstacles much more easily than the night before. Even so, I stumbled often enough that Trouble finally took off from my shoulder. He stayed close by, flying from branch to branch. And while my shoulder felt grateful for the rest, I did not resent his watchful eye as I had only a while ago.

Animals of all kinds were on the move. Birds with small gray bodies or bright green wings or huge yellow bills, traveling sometimes in flocks and other times alone, flew overhead. Large-eyed squirrels, beavers, a doe with its fawn, and a golden snake also passed me. In the distance, wolves howled. At one point an enormous shape, black as night, ambled out of the trees. I froze, fearful, until two smaller shapes appeared just behind—and I knew that I had encountered a family of bears. All these creatures shared the same look of fear I had seen in the stag. And all of them, it seemed, were heading in the opposite direction from Rhia and myself.

Late in the morning, perspiration dripping from my brow, I stepped into a shadowed glade. Cedars, very old from the looks of them, stood arranged in a perfect circle. So shaggy was their bark that at first glance they might have been mistaken for an assembly of ancient men whose long manes and beards flowed down over their stooped bodies. Even the sound of their gently stirring branches seemed different from the whispers of other trees. More like people at a funeral, humming a solemn, mournful lament.

Then I noticed, in the center of the glade, a narrow earthen mound. No wider than my body, it stretched at least twice my own height in length. It was surrounded by round, polished stones, which glistened like blue ice. Cautiously, I moved closer.

Trouble flew back to my shoulder. But instead of perching himself as usual, he paced back and forth with sharp, agitated steps.

I caught my breath. *I have been here before.* The notion—the conviction—came to me in a fleeting instant. Like a scent of some flower that appears and then vanishes before you have time to find its source, some dim memory touched me briefly and then fled. Perhaps it was only a dream, or the memory of a dream. Yet I could not shake the feeling that, in some way I could not quite identify, this mound within the circle of cedars was familiar.

"Emrys! Come on!"

Rhia's call jarred me back to the present. With a final glance at the mound, and at the mournful cedars, I left the glade. Soon I could hear the strange humming no more. But it continued to haunt the darkest corners of my mind.

The terrain grew steadily wetter. Frogs piped and bellowed so loudly that sometimes I could not even hear my own breathing. Herons, cranes, and other water birds called to one another in eerie, echoing voices. The air began to reek of things rotting. At last I saw Rhia, standing by the tall grasses at the edge of a dark swath of land. A swamp.

Impatiently, she beckoned. "Let's go."

I viewed the swamp skeptically. "We have to cross that?"

"It's the quickest way."

"Are you sure?"

"No. But we are running out of time—did you see all the animals fleeing?—and if it works it could save us an hour or more. Just on the other side of the swamp are the hills of the Grand Elusa."

She turned to cross the swamp, but I caught her arm. "Just what *is* the Grand Elusa?"

She shook loose. "I don't really know! Her true identity is a secret, even to Arbassa. All I know is that the legends say she lives among the living stones of the Misted Hills. That she knows things no one else knows, including some things that haven't happened yet. And that she is old, very old. I've even heard that she was present when Dagda carved the very first giant from the side of a mountain."

"Did you say . . . living stones?"

"That's what they're called. I'm not sure why."

I glanced toward the murk, studded with dead trees and stagnant pools. A crane cried out in the distance. "Are you sure this creature will help us?"

"No . . . but she might. That is, if she doesn't eat us first."

I rocked back on my heels. "Eat us?"

"The legends say she is always hungry. And fiercer than a cornered giant."

Trouble cocked his head toward Rhia. He piped a long, low whistle.

She lifted her eyebrows.

"What's wrong?"

"Trouble promises to keep us safe. But this is the first time I've heard that note of worry in his voice."

I sniffed. "I feel sorry for the Grand Elusa if she should try to eat Trouble. This bird doesn't know the meaning of fear."

"That's why I'm not happy to hear him sounding worried."

With that, she turned again to the swamp. She stepped on a slab of caked mud, from which she leaped to a rock. As I followed, I noticed we had left our footprints in the mud, but dismissed any concern about leaving tracks. We were already so deep into the forest, it could not matter.

We hopped from rock to log to rock again, making our way slowly across the swamp. Snags reached out to us with long, withered arms. Strange voices, somehow different from birds or frogs, echoed across the murky water, joining the occasional whistle from Trouble. Often, as we struggled to keep to the shallower places, something would slap the surface of the water or seem to stir within its darkened depths. I could never quite tell what might be causing such disturbances. Nor did I really want to know.

At length, the swamp faded, even as gray mist began to thicken the air. We came to a wet field of tall grasses, which gradually lifted into solid ground. Ahead of us stood a steep, rock-strewn hill, where vaporous arms unfurled toward us.

Rhia halted. "The Misted Hills. If only I could find a cluster of sweet berries! We could use an extra dose of strength for the climb." She glanced at me uncertainly. "And for whatever else lies ahead."

As we started to ascend, Trouble lifted off from my shoulder. He flew in silence, making slow, stately circles in the air above our heads. Although I guessed that he was scanning the forest for any sign of danger, he also seemed to be enjoying himself, savoring the freedom of soaring on high.

Boulders, some as big as Rhia's whole house, appeared here and there among the trees. The trees themselves grew farther and farther apart, their gnarled roots grasping the hillside. Yet despite the greater distance between the trunks, the forest didn't seem any lighter. Maybe it was the shadows of the immense boulders. Or the curling mist surrounding them. Or something else. But the forest felt increasingly dark.

As we labored to climb the steep slope, doubts flowed over me like the mist. Whatever kind of being this Grand Elusa was, she certainly didn't pick such a place to live because she enjoyed having visitors. And what if the goblins in the forest found us first? I clutched the Galator beneath my tunic, but I did not feel any better.

Suddenly, a great gray stone loomed directly before me. I froze. Perhaps it was only a trick of the mist, confusing my second sight. But it looked less like a boulder than like a face, craggy and mysterious. A face staring straight at me. Then I heard, or thought I heard, a grinding sound, almost like someone clearing his throat. The boulder seemed to shift its weight ever so slightly.

I didn't wait to learn what happened next. Up the hill I raced, tripping over roots, rocks, and my own feet.

At last I topped the rise. Above my panting, I heard an angry, buzzing sound. Bees. Thousands of bees, swarming around the broken trunk of a dead tree. Although it was hard to be certain in the mist, it looked as if the tree had broken off, probably in a storm, not long ago. What was not hard to tell was that the bees were not pleased about it.

Rhia, hands on her hips, watched the furious buzzing with interest.

Reading her thoughts, I shook my head. "You're not thinking," I panted, "about going after their honey . . . are you?"

She grinned slyly. "A person can never get enough honey! It would take just a minute to fetch some. It wouldn't slow us down."

"You can't! Look at all those bees."

Just then Trouble dropped down, enjoying a final flying swoop before landing on my shoulder. This bird clearly loved to fly. As he settled in, he gave a satisfied chirp. I felt surprised at just how familiar, almost natural, it felt to have him there. So different from yesterday! He folded his banded wings upon his back, cocking his head toward me.

On a whim, I winked at him.

Trouble winked back.

Rhia continued to examine the broken trunk. "If only I could find some way to distract the bees, just for a few seconds. That would be enough."

With a sudden screech, Trouble took off again. He flew straight into the swarm. He swooped and dived among the bees, batting them with his wings, then raced away into the mist. The swarm sped after him.

"Madness! That bird likes a fight as much as you like . . ."

I didn't bother to finish, since Rhia was already scaling the severed trunk in search of the bees' stores of honey. I listened for any buzzing, but heard none. I ran to join her. As I pulled myself up on a low branch, the trunk cracked and wobbled unsteadily on its base.

"Careful, Rhia!" I called. "This whole thing could topple over anytime."

But she could not hear. Fully occupied, she was already leaning over the jagged top of the trunk.

Standing on the branch, I leaned over beside her. A golden pool of honey, surrounded by walls of honeycomb as thick as my chest, lay beneath us. Bits of broken branches, bark, and honeycomb floated in the heavy syrup. I plunged in my hand, scooped out a heaping handful, then drank the sweet, gooey liquid. I had never in my life tasted such satisfying honey. Rhia apparently agreed, since she was busy feasting with both hands at once, her cheeks and chin dripping.

"We should go," she declared at last. "Have your last swallow."

Seeing a large chunk of honeycomb floating just below me, I grabbed it. As I tugged, however, the honeycomb refused to budge. Bracing myself, I pinched it as hard as I could and yanked with all my might.

At that instant, the object rose out of the pool with a deafening howl. I suddenly realized that I had been holding not a honeycomb but the tip of a huge, bulbous nose. Rhia shrieked as I jerked sideways to get away from the head, covered with honey, that was lifting toward us. Just then the base of the thick trunk cracked, tilted, and split apart. It toppled over the side of the hill, taking both of us with it.

XX

SHIM

Rhia and I cascaded down the slope. Ahead of us the weighty log, loaded with honey and whatever had boiled up from its depths, rolled and bounced down the ridge, gathering speed as it descended. Finally it smashed into a gigantic boulder, splintering into bits.

When at last I stopped, the world around me kept spinning for some time. Half dazed, I made myself sit up. "Rhia."

"Over here." She lifted her head from the grass just below me, her brown wisps of hair matted with honey and twigs.

Simultaneously we turned to the moaning sound coming from the wreckage of the trunk. Rhia reached for me, wrapping her forefinger around mine. We stood and carefully crept closer.

What we saw was a little mound, completely covered with honey, sticks, and leaves, lying beneath the boulder. Then the mound rolled over, shook itself vigorously, and sat up.

"It's a man." My words were filled with awe. "A tiny little man."

"A dwarf," corrected Rhia. "I didn't know there were any dwarves left in Fincayra."

Two pink eyes popped open in the mask of honey. "You both is wrong. Totally, horribly, disgustingly wrong! I is no dwarf."

Rhia looked quite skeptical. "No? Then what are you?"

The little man blew a blast of honey out of his bulbous nose. As more honey dripped off his chin, he licked his fingers, palms, and wrists. Having cleaned his hands, he looked nervously from one side to the other. "You isn't a friend of the king's, is you?"

Rhia scowled. "Of course not."

"And what about your black-haired friend there, who pullses on other people's noses?"

"He's not either."

"Certainly, definitely, absolutely not?"

Rhia could not keep herself from grinning. "Certainly, definitely, absolutely not."

"All right then." The little man struggled to unstick himself from the ground so that he could stand. He strode up to Rhia. Although he came to only just above her knee, he threw his head back with pride.

"I is no dwarf. I is a giant."

"A what?" I exclaimed, starting to laugh.

The little man glared at me, pink eyes shining. "I is a giant." Then his pride seemed to melt away. His face fell, and his shoulders drooped. "I is just a very, very, very *small* giant. I wishes, I truly wishes, that I could be big. Like a giant should be."

"I don't believe it." I stooped lower to get a better view. "You don't look like a giant to me. Not even a small one."

"But I is!"

"Then I'm a fungus."

"And why is a fungus going around pullsing other people's noses?"

Rhia burst out laughing, shaking every leaf on her suit of vines. "Leave him alone, Emrys. If he says he's a giant, well then, I believe him."

Seeming vindicated, the tiny fellow patted his bulging belly. "I is having a nicely meal, too, bothering nobodies, until I is interrupted."

"My name is Rhia. What's yours?"

Glancing nervously over his shoulder, he muttered, "Can't be too careful these dayses." He took a tiny step closer. "My name is Shim."

I observed him suspiciously. "And tell us, Shim, do you always go swimming in your honey when you drink it?"

"Certainly, definitely, absolutely! If you would like not to get stingded by the bees, that is the best way to do it."

Amused, Rhia smiled. "You have a point. But getting out again must be difficult."

The little giant sputtered, "You is, you is, makings fun of me!"

"Not at all," I teased. "You're not funny in the least." I tried my best to hold back my laughter, but it spewed out of me all at once. I roared, clutching my side.

The tiny fellow darted up to me and kicked me as hard as he could in the foot. My mirth vanished. With a growl, I started after him.

"No, stops! Please, stops!" cried Shim, hiding behind Rhia's legs. "I doesn't mean to hurts you. Really, truly, honestly."

"You certainly did!" I tried to grab hold of the sticky mass behind Rhia. "When I catch you I'll pinch more than your nose."

"Wait," commanded Rhia. She held me by the shoulder. "We don't have time for this. We've dawdled long enough!"

Reluctantly, I backed away. "I suppose you're right. Anyway, those bees will be coming back any second, with their stingers ready for battle." I shot a glance at Shim. "If I were you, I'd take a good bath before they descend on you."

The pink eyes swelled in fright. "On me?"

"Certainly, definitely, absolutely."

The little giant gasped. "I truly hates to get stingded!"

With that, he tore off into the swirling mist behind the boulder. He had only just disappeared, however, when he screamed with terror. Rhia and I both ran to see what had happened.

A few seconds later, we too screamed. We fell, spinning head over heels, into a deep pit plunging straight into the ground. Eventually, we rolled to a stop. The world had gone totally dark.

"Ohhhh, my head," I grumbled.

Something wriggled beneath me. "Gets you off me, you fool!"

An arm or a leg, sticky and caked with dirt and leaves, struck me square in the face. "Ow! Watch out, you blundering ball of honey!"

"Stop it," cried Rhia. "We must find our way out of here."

"Where is here, anyway?" I asked. "We must have fallen into a hole. A deep one. So deep I can't even see any light up there. And feel the floor! It's all poky, not like normal rock."

"I caaan aaanswer yooour queeestion," boomed a thunderous voice from deeper in the darkness. "Youuu haaave fouuund my laaair."

"Whose lair?" we all asked at once.

A long pause ensued.

"The laaair of the Graaand Eluuusa."

XXI

THE GRAND
ELUSA

The chamber's walls seemed to shake with the force of the voice.

Rhia pressed against my side. I tried my hardest to see, but my second sight was useless in such total darkness. For an instant I considered breaking the promise made at Caer Myrddin and tapping whatever powers I might still possess. To protect us however I could. But the very thought rekindled all my old fears, and I sat frozen.

"Is you," whispered Shim into the darkness, "the creature who, who, who eatses everything?"

"I eeeat whaaatever I choose." The deep voice echoed, its vibrations continuing to pummel us. "Nooow teeell meee whooo youuu aaare, befooore I eeeat youuu."

Bravely, I cleared my throat. "I am called . . . Emrys."

"Emryyys of wheeere?"

This time my voice was weaker. "I don't know."

"And I am Rhia, of Druma Wood."

After a silence, the Grand Elusa boomed, "Whooo eeelse is heeere?"

No answer.

"Whooo eeelse is heeere?" So loud came the voice that flakes of dirt shook loose and fell on our heads.

No answer. Only a gasping sound that I assumed was the rapid panting of the frightened little giant.

"He is Shim," answered Rhia. "Also of the Druma." She drew in a deep breath. "Please don't eat us. We need your help."

"Fooor whaaat?"

"To save the Druma! My home!"

I added, "Your home as well."

For a moment, no one spoke.

Then, all of a sudden, light filled the chamber. We looked at one another, truly amazed. For we found ourselves in an enormous cavern cut from the rock. Although the walls around us fairly glowed, there was no clear source of the light. More mysterious yet, there was no sign at all of the Grand Elusa. But for ourselves, the radiant cavern looked empty.

"Where is she?" I scanned the glowing cavern walls.

Rhia's brow furrowed. "I have no idea."

Shim, meanwhile, sat with his face in his hands, shivering.

"And this light . . ." I reached a hand to the wall. "Look! It comes from the rocks themselves!"

"Crystals," said Rhia in wonderment. "A cave of glowing crystals."

Indeed, the walls, ceiling, and floor of this cave radiated a clear, dancing light. Crystals sparkled and flashed all around us, as if the sunlight shining on a rippling river had been poured into the very Earth. And I am quite sure that my own face glowed as well, for even in the days when I could see with my own eyes, when colors ran deeper and light shone brighter, I had never seen anything as beautiful as this crystal cave.

Then I felt a sudden surge of warmth against my chest. Peering into the neck of my tunic, I jumped. The Galator was glowing as bright as the walls! Vibrant green light flowed from the pendant's jeweled heart. I looked up to find Rhia watching me, smiling.

"You like my cave?" A new voice, airy and small, floated to us from one of the walls.

While Shim continued to shiver with fear, Rhia and I leaned closer to the source. There, amidst a massive curl of crystals, hung a delicate web. Its strands radiated out from the center like the light from a star. Upon this web dangled a single spider, the size of a thumbnail. Its tiny head and back were covered with minuscule hairs which glowed as white as the crystals themselves.

"I like it very much," I replied.

"It reminds me of all the stars I have ever seen," said Rhia.

I watched the spider, the round hump of her back jiggling as she climbed to a higher strand. "Are you—"

"I am," declared the spider, "the Grand Elusa."

"But your voice was so much . . . *larger* before."

Ignoring me, the white spider hooked a silken thread to the strand. Throwing a line over a torn section of the web, she leaped down to a lower level. With a quick motion, two of her eight arms tied off the line. Having completed her repair, she scurried back to the center.

"How could you have sounded so large?" I asked again.

"Oh, I can be large when I please." The spider waved at Shim. "Large enough to eat that shivering morsel over there with one bite."

The little giant, his face still in his hands, gave out a groan.

"If I am not in the mood to eat my guests," she continued in her airy little voice, "I make myself smaller for a while. My stomach shrinks, even if my appetite doesn't. Anyway, image and reality are rarely the same. As you surely know by now, Emrys, that is the first rule of magic."

I caught my breath. "I know nothing about magic! Except that it's dangerous, very dangerous."

"Then you do know something about magic."

"That is all I will ever know."

"Too bad. You might have found it useful in the future."

"Not me. There is no magic in my future. At least not of my own making."

The spider seemed to observe me for a moment. "If you say so."

Spying a beetle twice her size who had flown into the web, she rushed over, bit its neck, then waited for it to cease struggling. In a flash, she secured it tightly with a strand of silk. She plucked off one of its legs and started munching. "I do enjoy eating, though. That much of the image is reality."

"Can you help us?" pleaded Rhia. "The Druma . . . it's in trouble."

The Grand Elusa pulled off another leg from the beetle. "Of course it is in trouble! Like all the rest of Fincayra! As much trouble as this poor beetle, being consumed bit by bit. Have you only just realized that?"

Rhia hung her head. "I . . . didn't want to believe it."

"Until now, when the Blight is practically at your door! You have waited too long."

"I know! But maybe there's still time. Will you help?"

The spider took another bite, chewed avidly. "Just what do you expect me to do?"

"You could explain why it's happening."

"Why?" More chewing. "It would take too long to tell you everything. I will run out of food and then I will have to eat all of you."

"Just tell me if it can be stopped. By anything." Then Rhia added, with a glance in my direction, "Or anyone."

The spider reached a leg up and scratched the hump of her hairy back. "I will tell you this. Fincayra—and that includes the Druma—is doomed, unless the king you call Stangmar can be toppled."

"Toppled! Is that possible?"

"It all depends," declared the spider, "on what Stangmar calls *the last Treasure*. Something he once had, then lost long ago."

I looked down at my tunic, under which the Galator glowed. "Can you tell us its powers?"

The spider considered the question for a while before answering. "The last Treasure carries great powers, greater than you know." She grabbed another leg and bit off the bottom half. "Stangmar is convinced that when he finds it, his power will be complete."

Rhia sighed. "He is right."

"No! He is wrong. It is not his power that will be complete, but his servitude."

"Servitude?"

"To the most terrible spirit of all, the one known as Rhita Gawr."

I stiffened.

"To Rhita Gawr, your king is nothing but a tool for his greater goal." She nibbled on the beetle's knee, then gave a satisfied smack of her lips. "To dominate all of this world, the Earth, and the Otherworld. That is his true desire."

She smacked her lips again, before crunching into the joint. "His supreme adversary, Dagda, is battling him on many fronts, too many to name. Yet Rhita Gawr has already won over Stangmar, and he has used the king to gain control of much of Fincayra. Few things now stand in his way, and the most important of them is . . ."

Another smack, another crunch. "The last Treasure. If that too falls into his hands, he will certainly win Fincayra. Then Rhita Gawr will control the bridge between the Earth and the Otherworld. He will be within reach of winning the Earth itself. Tough, but tasty— this leg, I mean. And if that ever happens, all is lost."

Frowning, I tried to understand. "Doesn't the king know he's being used in this way?"

"He knows. But he was corrupted by Rhita Gawr long ago." She swallowed the last section of the last leg. Then she carefully wiped her mouth, using the two arms nearest to her head. "Stangmar has lost the ability to choose for himself."

"Yet if he could be toppled somehow, Rhita Gawr might still be stopped."

"Perhaps."

Rhia, looking discouraged, leaned against a wall of glowing crystals. "But how?"

The Grand Elusa bit into the beetle's belly. "Mmmm, tender as could be."

"How?" repeated Rhia.

The spider swallowed. "There is only one possibility left. No, no. It is not really a possibility at all."

"What is it?"

"The king's castle must be destroyed."

Rhia blinked. "The Shrouded Castle?"

"Yes. It is the creation of Rhita Gawr, and through its walls the evil spirit's power flows into Stangmar and his army. The ghouliants themselves are part of the castle they guard, you know." She took another bite of the belly. "*Mmmm.* Very good. What was I saying? Oh yes, the ghouliants. That is why they never venture outside the castle walls. If you can destroy the castle, you can also destroy them."

"It can't be done!" exclaimed Rhia. "The Shrouded Castle is always spinning, always dark. It would be impossible to attack, let alone destroy."

"There is a way." The spider, still chewing, turned toward me. "Just as there is a way for a man who is blind to see again."

I started. "How do you know that?"

"In the same way you can see things with your second sight that others cannot see with their eyes."

At that I faced Rhia. "The writing on the walls inside Arbassa! That's why it was invisible to you."

"And if you should survive," continued the Grand Elusa, "your second sight could improve further. One day you might not only see, but understand."

"You mean it could help me read the writing?"

"If you survive."

"Really?"

"Do not underestimate your second sight! One day, you might come to rely on it. To love it. Maybe even more than you once loved your own eyes." She paused long enough to nibble on the beetle's forehead. "Though I happen to love eyes myself."

Rhia addressed the spider. "You said there is a way."

Using three of her arms, the white creature grasped the remainder of the beetle and ate some more of the belly. She chewed slowly, savoring its flavor. "I may not have time to explain it to you. In fact, you ought to leave while you can. I will finish this morsel quite soon, and then, with my appetite, I am afraid it will be your turn next."

Again Shim groaned from behind his hands.

"What is the way?"

"Do you know about the Cauldron of Death?" asked the spider, cleaning one of her arms.

Grimly, Rhia nodded. "Just that anyone who is thrown into it is killed instantly."

"True enough. But it is also true that it bears a fatal flaw. If someone were to crawl into it willingly, not by force, then the cauldron itself would be destroyed."

"Crawl into it willingly? Who would ever do such a thing?"

"No one who wants to live to see another day." The spider munched some more, lips smacking. "Yet, in the same manner, the castle itself has a flaw. A tiny one, perhaps, but a flaw nonetheless."

"What is it?"

"There is an ancient prophecy, as ancient as the giants themselves."

At this, Shim spread his fingers just wide enough to peek through.

The spider swung to another strand, pulled free an old antenna that some victim had left behind, and gobbled it in one bite. Returning to the nearly eaten beetle, she chanted:

> *Where in the darkness a castle doth spin,*
> *Small will be large, ends will begin.*
> *Only when giants make dance in the hall*
> *Shall every barrier crumble and fall.*

"What does it mean?" demanded Rhia. "*Only when giants make dance in the hall . . .*"

"*Shall every barrier crumble and fall.*" I pushed some black hairs back from my face. "So the castle walls would crumble if giants ever danced there?"

Having finished off the beetle's belly, the spider tore off one of the wings. "So goes the prophecy."

Rhia's expression darkened. "So that's why Stangmar has been hunting down all the giants! He must have heard this prophecy, too. He's doing everything he can to make sure it never comes true."

The spider crunched on the remainder of the wing. "Including destroying Varigal, the most ancient city of all."

"Ohhh," moaned Shim. "I doesn't means it when I says I wishes to be big. I doesn't means it. Really, truly, honestly."

The Grand Elusa eyed the shivering mass of dirt, twigs, and honey. "I pity you, shrunken one. For though your parents came from the giants' race, you have not learned that bigness means more than the size of your bones."

"But I is happy being small! Just a foolish whim to gets big. Big and dead! I is happier small but alive."

"So be it," said the spider. "Now, I ought to warn all of you. This little morsel has only one wing left, and also part of the head." She pulled off the wing, crammed it into her mouth, and chewed for a few seconds. "*Hmmm.* Now just the head. I am still very hungry. And also tired of being this size. If you do not leave my crystal cave quite soon, I will be forced to sample a few of your arms and legs."

Rhia clutched my arm. "She's right. Let's get out of here."

"But how?"

"I am not certain," the spider answered, "but I think you might be able to climb out on the crystals."

"Of course!" exclaimed Rhia. "Let's go."

She began to scamper up the radiant wall, using the larger crystals as holds for her hands and feet. Shim pushed past her, scaling the steep wall as rapidly as his stubby arms and legs could manage. He left behind a trail of gooey syrup on the crystals.

Seeing me standing beneath her, Rhia called down. "Quick! Or you'll follow that beetle."

I hesitated, driven to ask the Grand Elusa one thing more.

"Come on!"

"Go ahead," I called back. "I'll be there right away."

"You had better do just that." The spider reached for the beetle's head, leaving nothing but an empty noose of silk. "On the other hand, you do look scrawny but edible."

"Please tell me one last thing," I begged. "About my home. My true home. Can you tell me where it is? The Galator—glowing right here—is my only clue."

"Ah, the Galator! Come closer and show it to me."

"I don't dare. You might . . ."

"My, but you *do* look more meaty than I thought."

"Please!" I cried. "Then can you tell me how to find my mother? My father? My true name?"

Swallowing the very last of the beetle, the spider answered, "I cannot say. That is for . . . I daresay, you do smell unusually interesting. Come closer, boy. Come closer. Yes! Leeet meee taaake a cloooser loook!"

As the spider's voice swelled in size, so did the spider. But I did not stay to watch the change. I scurried out of the cave with all the speed I could muster.

XXII

ENCOUNTER
IN THE MIST

I emerged from the cave into the swirling mist. I could barely make out Rhia, even though she was only a few paces away. Beside her stood Shim, so covered with sticks and dirt and leaves that he looked more like a miniature mountain than a miniature person. Glancing down at the Galator, I noticed that it no longer glowed.

Rhia sat in a small grove of elms, where five young saplings had sprouted around an elder. She watched me exit the cave, clearly relieved. Then she leaned close to the old elm tree in the center of the grove. She began talking with it, whispering in low, swishing tones. In response, the tree rocked slowly on its roots, creaking with a voice that seemed terribly sad.

In time, Rhia turned to me, her eyes clouded. "This tree has seen more than two hundred springs in Druma Wood. Yet now it's sure it has seen its very last. It weeps every day for the future of its children. I told it not to lose hope, but it said it has only one hope left. To live long enough to do at least some small thing to keep the Druma safe from warrior goblins. But it expects just to die of grief instead."

Shim, standing beside her, rubbed his dirt-caked nose and looked down.

I could only nod sadly and watch the streaming mist. All at once I picked up the sweet scent of apple blossoms.

"You sssseem sssso very glum," said a familiar voice.

"Cwen!" Rhia leaped to her feet. "What ever brings you here? You almost never go out walking anymore."

Passing a branched hand before her face, Cwen emerged from the mist. "I sssshouldn't have followed you." She hesitated, a touch of fear in her teardrop eyes. "Issss it possible you can sssstill forgive me?"

Rhia's eyes narrowed. "You have done something terrible."

At that instant, six huge warrior goblins stepped out of the mist. Swiftly they surrounded us. Their thin eyes glinted beneath pointed helmets, their muscular arms protruded from shoulder plates, their three-fingered hands grasped the hilts of broad swords. Beads of perspiration gathered on their gray-green skin.

One of them, wearing red armbands above his elbows, brandished his sword at Cwen. In a wheezing, rasping voice, he demanded, "Which one has it?"

Cwen glanced furtively at Rhia, who was glaring at her in astonishment. "They promisssed me I could usssse the Galator to make myssssself young again." She waved her shriveled fingers. "Don't you ssssee? My handssss will wither no more!"

Rhia winced with pain. "I can't believe you would do this, after all the years—"

"Which one?" rasped the goblin.

Cwen pointed a knobby finger at me.

The warrior goblin stepped into the grove of elms and aimed his sword at my chest. "Give it to me now. Or shall I make it very painful for you first?"

"Remember what you ssssaid," urged Cwen. "You promissssed not to harm them."

The goblin wheeled around to face the aging treeling. A thin smile curled his crooked mouth. "I forgot. But did I make any promise about you?"

Cwen's eyes widened in fright. She started to back away.

"No!" cried Rhia.

It was too late. The goblin's sword whizzed through the air, slicing off one of Cwen's arms.

She shrieked, grasping the open wound as brown blood gushed from it.

"There." The goblin's wheezing laughter filled the air. "Now you won't have to worry about that old hand any more!" He advanced at Cwen. "Now let's do the other one."

Screaming in terror, blood pouring from her stunted arm, Cwen stumbled off into the mist.

"Let her go," rasped the goblin. "We have more important work to do." He jabbed his sword, dripping with brown blood, at my throat. "Now, where were we?"

I swallowed. "If you kill me, you'll never know how it works."

A sinister look filled the goblin's face. "Now that you remind me, my master did tell me to keep alive the person who wears it. But he said nothing about keeping your friends alive."

I sucked in my breath.

"Perhaps if I agree to spare your friends, though, you will tell me how it works." He winked at another goblin. "Then my dear master and I will have some bargaining to do."

He pivoted to Shim, who was shaking in fear, and kicked him so hard he flew across the grove. "Shall I start our fun with this dirty little dwarf? No, I think not." He turned to Rhia, his thin eyes gleaming. "A girl of the forest! What an unexpected pleasure."

Rhia stepped backward.

The goblin nodded, and two members of his band lunged at her. Each of them seized one of her leaf-draped arms.

"Give it to me," ordered the goblin.

I glanced at Rhia, then back at him. How could I possibly give up the Galator?

"Right now!"

I did not move.

"All right then. We'll amuse ourselves while you make up your mind." He flicked his wrist at Rhia. "To start with, break both of her arms."

Instantly the goblins wrenched Rhia's arms behind her back. At the same time, she cried out, "Don't do it, Emrys! Don't—"

She shrieked with pain.

"No!" I pleaded. I pulled the Galator out of my tunic. The jewels glinted darkly in the mist. "Spare her."

The goblin smiled savagely. "Give it to me first."

Rhia's captors twisted her arms harder, almost lifting her off the ground. She shrieked again.

I removed the cord from my neck. The grove was silent, except for the sad creaking of the old elm. I hefted the precious pendant, then handed it over.

The goblin snatched it from me. As he gazed into the jeweled object, he wheezed excitedly. Meanwhile, his greenish tongue danced around his lips. Then he smirked at me. "I have changed my mind. First I will kill your friends, and then I will ask you how it works."

"No!"

All the goblins wheezed in laughter. Their immense chests shook at their leader's joke, while Rhia winced painfully.

"All right," rasped the goblin. "Maybe I will be merciful. Show me how it works. Now!"

I hesitated, not knowing what to do. If there was ever a moment to break my vow and call upon my powers, this was it. Did I dare? Yet even as I asked myself the question, my mind filled with surging, searing flames. The screams of Dinatius. The smell of my own burning flesh.

Try, you coward! a voice within me cried. *You must try!* Yet, just as urgently, another voice answered: *Never again! Last time you destroyed your eyes. This time you will destroy your very soul. Never again!*

"Show me!" commanded the goblin. Even through the thickening mist, I saw his muscles tighten. Raising his sword, he aimed the blade at Rhia's neck.

Still I hesitated.

Just then a strange wind, wilder by the second, shook the branches of the old elm in the center of the grove. Its creaking rose to a scream. As the goblin looked up, the tree snapped free of its roots and toppled over. He had only enough time to howl in agony as the tree crashed down on top of him.

I reached for the Galator, which had dropped to the ground. I slung the leather cord over my neck. With my other hand, I grabbed the fallen goblin's sword and started slashing at another member of the band. The goblin, far stronger than I, quickly backed me against the trunk of the downed tree.

The goblin reared back to strike me down. Suddenly, he froze.

A look of sheer horror came over his face—horror that I had seen only once before, in Dinatius when the flames swallowed him.

I whirled around. Then I, too, froze. The sword fell from my hand. For out of the swirling mist came a gargantuan white spider, her jaws slavering.

"Huuungry," bellowed the great spider in a blood-curdling voice. "I aaam huuungry."

Before I knew what was happening, Rhia grabbed me by the wrist and pulled me out of the path of the Grand Elusa. To the shrieks of the cornered goblin, we ran down the hill, closely pursued by Shim. The little giant sprinted almost as fast as we did ourselves, his feet kicking up a cloud of dirt and leaves.

Two of the warrior goblins dodged the monster, leaving their companions to fend for themselves, and chased after us. Wheezing and cursing, waving their swords in the air, they pursued us through the mist-shrouded boulders. Though we charged with all our speed down the hillside, they gained on us steadily. Soon they were almost on top of Shim.

Suddenly a river appeared out of the mist. Rhia cried out, "The water! Jump in the water!"

With no time to ask questions, Shim and I obeyed. We hurled ourselves into the fast-flowing water. The goblins plunged in after us, thrashing their swords in the current.

"Help us!" Rhia shouted, although I had no idea to whom. Then she slapped her hands wildly against the water's surface.

At once, a wave began to crest in the middle of the river. A great, glistening arm of water rose up, bearing Rhia, Shim, and myself in the palm of its hand. The liquid fingers curled over us like a waterfall, as the hand lifted us high above the river's cascading surface. Spray, sparkling with rainbows, surrounded us. The arm of water whisked us downstream, leaving our pursuers far behind.

Minutes later, the arm melted back into the river itself, dumping us on a sandbar. We climbed out of the water, bedraggled but safe. And, in the case of Shim, considerably cleaner as well.

XXIII

GREAT LOSSES

Rhia collapsed on the bank, her garb of leaves wet and glistening in the sun. As the surface of the river returned to normal, a thin finger of water splashed across her hand. It clung there for an instant before dissolving into the sand.

But she did not seem to notice. Morosely, she kicked at the emerald reeds by the river's edge.

I sat down beside her. "Thank you for saving us."

"Thank the river, not me. The River Unceasing is one of my oldest friends in the forest. He bathed me as an infant, watered me as a child. Now he has saved us all."

I glanced at the waterway, then at Shim, who had flopped down on his back in the sun. For the first time, no dirt and honey covered his clothing, and I noticed that his baggy shirt was woven of some sort of yellowish bark.

Suddenly, I remembered the yellow-rimmed eye of Trouble. Had the brave hawk eluded that swarm of bees? If he had not, had he survived their wrath? And if he had, would he ever be able to find me again? My shoulder felt strangely bereft without him sitting there.

I turned back to Rhia, who looked more glum than I. "You don't seem very glad."

"How can I be glad? I lost two friends today—one old, one new." Her eyes wandered across my face. "Cwen I've known ever since she found me abandoned so long ago. The old elm I met only a few minutes before she felled herself to spare us harm. They couldn't be more different—one crooked and bent, the other straight and tall. One stole my loyalty, the other gave me life. But I grieve for both."

I heaved a sigh. "That elm won't see its saplings ever again."

She lifted her chin a bit. "Arbassa wouldn't agree. Arbassa would say that they'll meet again in the Otherworld. That we all will, someday."

"Do you really believe that?"

She drew a deep breath. "I'm . . . not sure. I know I *want* to believe it. But whether we really will meet after the Long Journey, I don't know."

"What Long Journey?"

"It's the voyage to the Otherworld, after a Fincayran dies. Arbassa says the more a person needs to learn when she dies, then the longer her Long Journey must be."

"In that case, even if the Otherworld is real, it would take me *forever* to get there."

"Maybe not." She glanced at the rushing river, then back at me. "Arbassa also told me that, sometimes, the bravest and truest souls are spared the Long Journey completely. Their sacrifice is so great that they are brought right to the Otherworld, at the very instant of death."

I scoffed at this. "So instead of dying, they just . . . disappear? One second they're here, writhing in pain, and the next second they're in the Otherworld, dancing merrily? I don't think so."

Rhia lowered her head. "It does sound hard to believe."

"It's impossible! Especially if they're not capable of such a sacrifice anyway."

"What do you mean by that?"

"If they're too cowardly!" I bit my lip. "Rhia, I . . . could have done more, much more, to help you."

She looked at me sympathetically. "What more could you have done?"

"I have some, well, powers. Nothing to do with the Galator. I don't begin to understand them. Except that they are strong—too strong."

"Powers like your second sight?"

"Yes, but stronger. Fiercer. Wilder." For a moment I listened to the churning water of the River Unceasing. "I never asked for such powers! They just came to me. Once, in a rage, I used them badly, and they cost me my eyes. They cost another boy much more. They weren't meant for mortals, these powers! I promised never to use them again."

"Who did you promise?"

"God. The Great Healer of Branwen's prayers. I promised that, if only I might somehow see again, I would give up my powers forever. And God heard my plea! But still . . . I should have used them back there. To save you! Promise or no promise."

She peered at me through her tangle of curls. "Something tells me that this promise isn't the only reason you didn't want to use your powers."

My mouth went dry. "The truth is, I fear them. With all my heart I fear them." I pulled a reed out of the shallow water and twisted it roughly with my fingers. "Branwen once told me that God gave me those powers to use, if I could only learn to master them. To use them *well*, she said, with wisdom and love. But how can you use wisely something that you fear to touch? How can you use lovingly something that could destroy your eyes, your life, your very soul? It's impossible!"

She waited quite a while before responding. Then she waved toward the white-capped waters. "The River Unceasing appears to be just a line of water, flowing from here to there. Yet he is more. Much more. He is all that he is—including whatever hides beneath the surface."

"What does that have to do with me?"

"Everything. I think Branwen was right. If someone—God, Dagda, or whoever—gave you special powers, they are for you to use. Just as the River Unceasing has his own powers to use. You are all that you are."

I shook my head. "So I should ignore my promise?"

"Don't ignore it, but ask yourself if that is really what this God wanted you to do."

"He gave me back my sight."

"He gave you back your *powers*."

"That's insane!" I exclaimed. "You have no idea—"

A loud snort from somewhere nearby cut me off. I jumped, thinking it came from a wild boar. Then came the snort again, and I realized that it was not a boar after all. It was Shim. He had fallen asleep on the sandbar.

Rhia watched the tiny figure. "He snores loud enough to be a true giant."

"At least, with him, you can see what he really is with just one look. With me, it's not so simple."

She turned back to me. "You worry about who you are too much. Just be yourself, and you'll find out eventually."

"Eventually!" I stood angrily. "Don't try to tell me about my life. Stick to your own life, if you please."

She stood to face me. "It might help you to think about somebody's life besides your own! I've never met anybody more wrapped up in himself. You're the most selfish person I've ever met! Even if you are—" She stopped herself. "Forget it. Just go away and worry about yourself some more."

"I think I'll do just that."

I stomped off into the thick forest by the River Unceasing. Too angry to watch where I was going, I crashed through the underbrush, bruising my shins and scraping my thighs. This made me all the angrier, and I cursed loudly. Finally, I sat down on a rotting trunk that was already mostly a mound of soil.

Suddenly I heard a gruff voice shout, "Get him!"

Two warrior goblins, the same ones we had eluded upstream, jumped from the underbrush and threw me to the ground. One of them pointed a sword at my chest. The other produced a large sack made of roughly stitched brown cloth.

"None of your tricks this time," growled the goblin with the sword. He beckoned to the other with a burly, gray-green hand. "Get him in the sack."

At that instant, a piercing whistle shot from the sky. The goblin with the sword cried out and fell back, his arm bleeding from the gouges of talons.

"Trouble!" I rolled out of the fray and jumped to my feet.

The merlin, talons slashing and wings flapping in the face of the goblin, drove him back several paces. Every time the goblin slashed with his sword, Trouble dived into his face, ripping at the eyes beneath the pointed helmet. Despite the huge size advantage of the goblin, the small hawk's ferocity was proving too much.

But Trouble did not count on the other goblin joining the battle. Before I could shout any warning, the second warrior whipped his powerful hand through the air. He caught the hawk in mid-dive. Trouble slammed into the trunk of a tree and fell stunned to the ground. He lay there, utterly still, his wings spread wide.

The last thing I saw was the first goblin raising his sword to chop the merlin into pieces. Then something smashed me on the head and day turned into night.

XXIV

THE SWITCH

Conscious again, I sat bolt upright. Though my head still swam, I could make out the massive boughs of trees all around me. I inhaled the rich, moist air. I listened to the quiet whispering of the branches, which sounded strangely somber. And I knew that I must still be in Druma Wood.

No sign anywhere of the goblins. Or of Trouble. Was it all a bad dream? Then why did my head hurt so much?

"You is awake, I sees."

Startled, I turned. "Shim! What happened?"

The little giant examined me warily. "You is never very nicely to me. Is you going to hurts me if I tells you?"

"No, no. You can be sure of that. I won't hurt you. Just tell me what happened."

Still reticent, Shim rubbed his pear-shaped nose thoughtfully.

"I won't hurt you. Certainly, definitely, absolutely."

"All rights." Keeping his distance, he paced back and forth on the mossy soil. "The girl, the nicely one, she hears you fightsing. She is upset the goblinses capture you. She wants to finds you, but I tells her this is madness. I do try, I do try!"

At this point he sniffed. His eyes, more pink than usual, squinted at me. A tear rolled down his cheek, making a wide curve around his nose.

"But she does not listen to Shim. I comes with her, but I is scared. Very, very, very scared. We comes through the woods and finds the place where you fights the goblinses."

I grabbed him by the arm. Small though it was, it felt as muscled as a sailor's. "Did you see a hawk? A little one?"

The little giant pulled away. "She finds some feathers, all bloody, by a tree. But no hawk. She is sad, Shim can tell. This hawk, he is your friend?"

Friend. The word surprised me as much as it saddened me. Yes, the bird I would have given anything to lose just a day ago had, indeed, become my friend. Just in time to leave me. Once again I knew the pain of losing what I had only just found.

"You is sad, too."

"Yes," I said quietly.

"Then you is not going to like the rest. It isn't nicely, not at all."

"Tell me."

Shim stepped over to a hefty hemlock root and sat down dejectedly. "She follows your trail. Shim comes, too, but I is more and more scared. We finds the place where goblinses camp. They is fightsing. Pushing and shouting. Then . . . she makes the switch."

I gasped. "The switch?"

Another tear rolled down his cheek, rounding the edge of his nose. "I tells her not to do it! I tells her! But she shushes me quietly and sneaks up to the sack holding you. She unties it, pulls you out, over to these bushes. She tries, we both tries, to wakens you. But you is like dead. So she climbs into the sack herself! I tries to stop her, but she says . . ."

"What? Tell me!"

"She says that she must do it, for you is the Druma's only hope."

My heart turned into lead.

"Then the goblinses stop fightsing. Without looksing into the sack, they carries her off."

"No! No! She shouldn't have done that!"

Shim cringed. "I knows you is not going to like it."

"As soon as they find her, they'll . . . oh, it's too horrible!"

"It is horrible, it is."

Images of Rhia crowded my mind. Feasting beneath the fruity boughs of the shomorra. Showing me constellations in the darkest parts of the night sky. Greeting Arbassa with a shower of dew on her face. Wrapping her finger around my own. Watching me, and the glowing Galator, within the crystal cave.

"My only two friends, gone in the same day." I slammed my fist against the moss-covered turf. "It's always the same for me! Whatever I find, I lose."

Shim's tiny shoulders drooped. "And there's nothing we can do to stops it."

I swung my face toward his. "Oh, yes there is." Wobbly though I was, I forced myself to stand. "I'm going after her."

Shim recoiled, and nearly fell backward off the root. "You is full of madness!"

"Maybe so, but I'm not going to lose the one friend I have left without a fight. I'm going after them, wherever they took her. Even if it means going all the way to the Shrouded Castle itself."

"Madness," repeated Shim. "You is full of madness."

"Which way did they go?"

"Down the river. They is marching fast."

"Then I will, too. Good-bye."

"Wait." Shim grabbed hold of my knee. "I is full of madness myself."

Though touched by the little giant's intention, I shook my head. "No. I can't take you, Shim. You'll just get in the way."

"I is not any fighter. That is truly. I is scared of almost everything. But I is full of madness."

I sighed, knowing I was not much of a fighter myself. "No."

"I asks you, please."

"No."

"That girl. She is sweet to me, sweet like honey! I only wants to help her."

For several seconds, I studied the upturned face by my knee.

"All right," I said at last. "You may come."

■ PART THREE ■

A STAFF AND
A SHOVEL

For hours, we followed the River Unceasing, clambering over smooth stones and low branches. Finally the river curled to the south, and we reached the eastern edge of Druma Wood. Through the thinning trees, I viewed the bright line of the river and, beyond that, the shadowed plains of the Blighted Lands. From this vantage point, there could be no doubt that the River Unceasing had been the sparkling waterway that I had glimpsed from the dune on my first day on Fincayra.

Downriver some distance, I could make out a group of egg-shaped boulders. They straddled both sides, and at least one sat in the middle of the waterway. The channel looked wider and shallower in that area. If so, it would make a good place to cross. On the opposite bank, a stand of trees had been planted in parallel rows, like an orchard. Yet if indeed it was an orchard, it was the most scraggly one I had ever come across.

Twigs snapped behind me. I whirled around to see Shim, struggling to get through some ferns. Several green arms wrapped around his stubby legs. As he twisted and jumped in the ferns, his floppy yellow shirt, hairy feet, and prominent nose combined to make him look more like a poorly dressed puppet than a person. But his coarse brown hair (still wadded with honey, dirt, and sticks), not to mention his fiery pink eyes, made it clear that he was alive. And angry.

"Madness," he muttered as he finally broke free of the ferns. "This is madness!"

"Turn back if you like," I suggested.

Shim scrunched his bulbous nose. "I knows your thinking! You wants me not to goes!" He drew himself up, which still made him only a bit taller than my knee. "Well, I goes. I goes to rescue her."

"It won't be easy, you know."

The little giant folded his arms and frowned at me.

I turned my second sight once more toward the lands across the river. It struck me that everything, including the trees in the orchard, wore blander colors than I had seen in the Druma. Whatever vividness the rest of Fincayra had added to my vision would vanish as soon as we crossed the river. I had grown accustomed to seeing brighter colors in the forest, and even dared to hope that my second sight had improved. But now I knew the truth. My second sight was just as faded as before, as faded as the landscape in front of me.

And, as before, the strange reddish brown color painted the plains beyond. All the eastern lands, but for the black ridges in the distance, showed the color Rhia had described as *dried blood*.

I drew a deep breath of fragrant forest air. I listened, perhaps for the last time, to the continuous whispering of the boughs. I had only barely begun to sense the variety and complexity of this language of the trees, sometimes subtle, sometimes overwhelming. I wondered what they might be saying to me even now, if only I could understand their voices. Silently, I promised myself that if I should ever return to this forest, I would learn its ways, and cherish its secrets.

Just above my head, a hemlock branch quivered, filling the air with spicy scent. Reaching up, I rubbed some of its flat needles between my thumb and forefinger, half hoping that this would make my hand smell forever of the forest. On an impulse, I wrapped my fingers around the middle of the limb. I squeezed tight as if I were clasping another person's hand. I pulled, just enough to feel the branch sway.

Suddenly the branch broke off. Still clasping it, I tumbled into the ferns—and onto Shim.

"You stupidly fool!" The miniature fellow regained his feet, took a swipe at my arm, missed, and fell back into the ferns. "What is you doings?" he cried from the tangle of green fronds. "You almost crushes me."

"Sorry," I replied, trying hard to keep a serious face. "The branch broke."

From behind the mountainous nose, two pink eyes glared at me. "Shim almost broke!"

"I said I'm sorry."

He stood again, growling furiously. "I makes you sorrier." Clenching his fist, he prepared for another swipe.

Just then, I noticed the branch in my hand. To my astonishment, its bark started to peel away. At the same time, the smaller branches attached to the main stem began snapping off, one by one, dropping their needles on my lap. The peeling bark rolled into large curls, then fell away, as if shaved by an invisible knife.

Catching sight of this, Shim lowered his fist. A look of wonder filled his face.

By now the branch in my lap was no longer a branch. It was a sturdy, straight stick, thick and gnarled at the top, tapered at the bottom. Lifting it higher, I could see it stretched a full head taller than myself. I twirled it in my hands, feeling the smooth wooden skin. In a flash, I understood.

Using the stick as support, I lifted myself from the ferns. Standing before the fragrant hemlock tree, I recalled my clumsy attempt to find a staff when I had first entered this forest. I bowed my head to the tree in thanks. Now I held my staff. And more precious by far, I held a small piece of the Druma that would travel with me beyond its borders.

"You isn't going to hit me with that stick, I hopes," said Shim rather meekly.

I looked at him sternly. "If you won't hit me, I won't hit you."

The little figure stiffened. "I didn't want to hurts you."

I raised an eyebrow, but said nothing. Hefting my new staff in my hand, I started striding toward the egg-shaped boulders downriver. Shim followed behind, fighting through the brush, grumbling as much as before but not quite so loudly.

A few moments later we reached the spot. Here the river widened considerably, flowing over a bed of white stones. As I had hoped, the water, while still fast flowing, looked quite shallow. Beneath the boulders, the mud on both banks showed tracks of large, heavy boots.

"Goblinses," said Shim, observing the tracks.

"I'm sure the River Unceasing did not make it easy for them to cross."

Shim glanced up at me. "Myself, I hates to cross rivers. Really, truly, honestly."

I leaned against my staff, grasping the gnarled top. "You don't have to do it. It's your choice."

"How far will you goes?"

"To wherever Rhia is! Since those goblins think they have the Galator in their sack, they are probably heading to Stangmar's castle. I don't know if we can catch them before they get there, but we must try. It's our only hope, and Rhia's."

My second sight scanned the shadowed hills in the distance. A wall of clouds, blacker than any storm clouds that I had ever seen, rose above them, plunging the easternmost hills in total darkness. Rhia's own description of the location of the Shrouded Castle came back to me. *In the darkest of the Dark Hills, where the night never ends.* I must find her before she reached those hills! *Where the night never ends.* For in such darkness I would have no vision. And almost no hope.

Shim swallowed. "All right. I goes. Maybe not alls the way to the castle, but I goes."

"Are you sure? We won't find much honey over there."

He answered by starting to wade into the river. He made his way for a few paces, struggling against the water. As he neared the partly submerged boulder, though, he stumbled. Suddenly he found himself in much deeper water. He shouted, thrashing his little arms. I leaped to his aid just before he went under. Hauling him onto my shoulders, I began to cross.

"Thanks you," panted Shim. He shook himself, spraying water all over my face. "This water is muchly wet."

Carefully, I stepped through the surging water, using my staff for support. "I'd be grateful if you'd keep your hands away from my nose."

"But I needs a handle to holds on to."

"Then hold on to your own nose!" I exclaimed, certain now that I had made a mistake to let him come along.

"All right," he replied with such a nasal voice that I knew he was holding tight to his own nose.

With every step through the rapidly flowing river, I felt something pulling backward against my leather boots, tugging me back toward the forest. It was not the current itself. Rather, it seemed that hundreds of invisible hands were trying to restrain me from leaving the Druma. Whether these hands were in the water, or in myself, I could not tell. But my feet grew increasingly heavy as I neared the opposite bank.

A feeling of foreboding swelled in me. At the same time, I felt an image forming in my mind, an image from some source other than my second sight. I saw strange lights, dozens of them, moving toward me. Suddenly I realized that my hidden powers were at work. This was going to be an image of the future!

"No!" I cried, shaking my head so violently that Shim had to grab my hair to avoid falling off.

The image disappeared. The powers receded. Yet the feeling of foreboding remained, deeper than before.

As I crossed onto the eastern bank, Shim wriggled down from my shoulder. Not without punching me in the ear, however.

"Ow! What was that for?"

"For makings me holds my nose all that way."

The thought of throwing him back into the river crossed my mind, but somehow I resisted. And my anger was swiftly crowded out by the closer view of the orchard. The trees, thin and tormented, looked considerably more frail than even the oldest trees in the Druma. Indeed, those farthest away from the river seemed positively sickly, mere ghosts of living things. We had arrived in the Blighted Lands.

I approached one of the sturdier trees, whose branches draped over the river. Reaching up, I plucked a small, withered fruit. Turning it in my hand, I puzzled at the leathery toughness, the rusty brown color, the wrinkled skin. Sniffing it, I confirmed my suspicion. It was an apple. The scrawniest apple I had ever encountered.

I tossed it to Shim. "Your supper."

The little giant caught it. He looked unsure as he brought the fruit to his lips. Finally, he took a bite. The bitter expression on his face said it all.

"Bleh! You wishes to poison me!"

I smirked. "No. I didn't think you'd take a bite."

"Then you wishes to trick me."

"That I cannot deny."

Shim placed his hands on his hips. "I wishes the girl is here!"

Grimly, I nodded. "I do, too."

At that instant I saw in the distance, beyond the last row of trees, a band of six figures marching out of the eastern plains. They seemed to be heading straight for the orchard. Warrior goblins! Their swords, breastplates and pointed helmets gleamed in the late afternoon sun. I watched them disappear behind a rise. Although the slope hid them, their gruff voices grew steadily louder.

Shim, who had seen them too, stood petrified. "What is we goings to do?"

"Hide someplace."

But where? From where we stood, I could not find even a single rock to crouch behind. The withered vegetation offered no protection. The slope along the bank ran low and smooth, with not so much as a gully.

The goblins neared the top of the rise. Their voices grew louder, as did the heavy stamping of their boots. My heart raced. I scanned the terrain to find any possible hiding place.

"You!" whispered a voice. "Over here!"

I turned to see a head poking out from among the roots of the

202 · THE LOST YEARS OF MERLIN

trees at the far end of the orchard. Shim and I dashed to the spot. We found a deep, newly dug ditch that had not yet been connected with the river. In the ditch stood a broad-shouldered, sunburned man with a strong chin and brown hair, the more so because it was flecked with dirt. Below his bare chest, he wore loose leggings of brown cloth. He gripped his shovel as effortlessly and securely as a practiced soldier grips his sword.

He waved at us with his shovel. "Get in here, lads. Quick."

We did not hesitate to follow the command. I tossed aside my staff and dived into the ditch. Even as Shim dived in behind me, the goblins marched over the rise and entered the orchard. Quickly, the man covered us with dirt and leaves. He left only a small hole where each of us could breathe.

"You there!" called a goblin's voice. From beneath the blanket of dirt, it sounded a bit higher, though no less grating, than the voice of the goblin who had led the band in the Druma.

"Yes?" answered the ditch digger. He sounded perturbed at being interrupted in his work.

"We're searching for a dangerous prisoner. Escaped this morning."

"From who?" asked the man.

"From guards, you buffoon! Former guards, that is. Lost their prisoner, then their heads." He gave a high, wheezing laugh. "Have you seen anybody cross this river? Speak up, man!"

The laborer paused for some time before speaking. I started to wonder whether he might yet give us away.

"Well," he said at last, "I did see somebody."

Beneath the dirt, my stomach clenched.

"Who?"

"It was . . . a young man."

Sweat, mixed with dirt, stung my lips. My heart pounded.

"Where and when?" barked the goblin.

Again the man paused. I debated whether I should try to bolt, hoping to outrun the warriors.

"A few hours ago," answered the laborer. "Heading downstream. Toward the ocean."

"You'd better be right," rasped the goblin.

"I'm right, but I'm also late. Got to finish this irrigation ditch before nightfall."

"Ha! This old orchard needs a lot more than a ditch to save it."

Another goblin voice, slower and deeper than the other, joined in. "Why don't we chop down a few of these trees to lighten this poor fellow's load?"

The whole band wheezed in laughter.

"No," declared the first goblin. "If we're going to catch the prisoner by nightfall, we have no time to lose."

"What did they do with that fool girl?" rasped another goblin as the band marched off, boots pounding on the soil.

I pushed my head out of the dirt too late to hear the full reply. All I caught were the words *of the king* and, a bit later, *better off dead*.

I shook the dirt off my tunic. As the gruff goblin voices faded away, finally swallowed by the sound of the churning river, I crawled out of the ditch and faced the man. "I am grateful. Most grateful."

He planted his shovel in the loose dirt, then extended a burly hand. "Honn is my name, lad. I may be just a common ditch digger, but I know who I like and who I don't. Anyone who is an enemy of those overgrown toads is surely a friend of mine."

I took the hand, which nearly swallowed my own. "I am called Emrys." I nudged the pile of dirt beside my foot. "And my brave companion here is Shim."

Shim popped out, spat some dirt from his mouth, and glared at me.

"We must go now," I said. "We have a long journey ahead of us."

"And where are you bound for?"

I drew a deep breath. "For the castle of the king."

"Not the Shrouded Castle, lad?"

"Yes."

Honn shook his head in disbelief. The gesture revealed his ears, somewhat triangular in shape and pointed at the top, beneath the mat of brown hair. "The Shrouded Castle," he muttered. "Where the Seven Wise Tools, hewn ages and ages ago, are kept. I remember when they belonged to the people. Now they belong just to the king! The plow that tills its own field . . . the hoe that nurtures its seeds . . . the saw that cuts only as much wood as is needed . . ."

He caught himself. "Why do you want to go there?"

"To find someone. A friend."

He stared at me as if I had lost my mind.

"Can you tell me where the castle sits?"

Raising his shovel, he jabbed it at the air in the direction of the Dark Hills. "That way. I can tell you no more, lad, except that you would be wise to change your plans."

"That I can't do."

He grimaced, studying me with care. "You are a stranger to me, Emrys. But I wish you whatever luck there is left in Fincayra."

Honn reached for his shirt beside the ditch. He pulled out a worn dagger with a narrow blade. He twirled it once in his hand, then handed it to me. "Here. You will need this more than I."

XXVI

THE TOWN OF
THE BARDS

I strode across the tundra, trekking toward the rising waves of the Dark Hills. My satchel of herbs felt heavier, now that it also carried Honn's dagger. As my boots crunched on the dry, crusty soil, my staff clicked against the ground. Every so often my shoulder rubbed against the staff's knotty top and I caught a faint scent of hemlock.

Shim, grumbling to himself about madness, struggled to keep pace with me. But I would not slow down for him. We had no time to lose. Over and over the goblin's words *better off dead* echoed in my mind.

Despite the blades of grass, clumps of bracken, and groves of scraggly trees that managed to survive on this tundra, the dominant colors of this plain, stretching to the dark horizon, were dull grays and browns, tinged with rust. Several times I looked over my shoulder at the fading green hills of Druma Wood, trying to recall the lushness of that land. As the sun sank lower against our backs, our shadows grew longer and darker.

I noticed in the distance a stand of dark, leafless trees. Then, drawing nearer, I realized the truth. What had looked like trunks and limbs were really the skeletons of houses and stables—all that remained of a village about the size of Caer Vedwyd. No people or animals were left. The buildings had been burned to the ground. The stone walls had been torn apart. By the side of the ash-strewn road through the village, a wooden cradle, once the bed of a child, lay in splinters. Why this village had been destroyed, no one remained to tell.

We pushed on toward the Dark Hills. Although I stretched both my ears and my second sight for any sign of goblins, I found none. But that was no cause to relax. The first hint of sunset already streaked the sky. In another hour, night would fall. I could only imagine what creatures might prowl this terrain after dark.

Meanwhile, Shim fell farther behind. He kept stopping to rest, I kept urging him to move. His strength was ebbing, just like my vision. Reluctantly, I concluded that we would need to find some sort of shelter before the day ended. Where, though? This desolate plain didn't offer many choices.

We continued to trek over the long, gradual rises and depressions of the land. As our shadows grew, so did my fears. Strange howling sounds, half wolf and half wind, reached our ears. Despite my pleas, Shim lagged ever more.

At last, as I topped a rise, I glimpsed a village below. Warm yellow torches blazed in the streets, while fires burned in the hearths of low houses made of mud brick. My mouth watered when I realized that the smell of burning wood mingled with roasting grain.

Shim approached and traded glances with me. With a joyful cry, he started running down to the village gates. Clumsily, but full of hope, I ran after him.

A man, sitting on the ground by the gates, suddenly leaped to his feet as we came near. He was tall and gaunt, and he held a spear. He wore a simple tunic. A thick black beard covered most of his face. But his unusually large, dark eyes were his most striking feature. Even in the dwindling light, his eyes shone eerily. Yet I could not shake the feeling that their light came less from intelligence than from fear. Indeed, his eyes seemed nearly crazed, like the eyes of an animal frightened to the very edge of death.

Bracing himself, the man pointed his spear at my chest. Though he said nothing, his expression was grim.

"We come in peace," I declared. "We are strangers in this land and seek only some shelter for the night."

The man's large eyes opened still wider, but he said nothing. Instead, he thrust his spear closer, nicking the wood of my staff and barely missing my hand.

"We is hungry," moaned Shim. "Hungry and sleepily."

Again the silent man thrust his spear at us. Only then did I notice the sign behind him, hanging at an angle from one of the gate posts. Carved into a weathered slab of wood, it read, *Welcome to Caer Neithan, Town of the Bards.* Below that were inscribed the words *Here song is ever,* but the phrases that followed had been damaged somehow. I could not be sure, but they seemed to have been scraped away.

Through the gates, I watched a woman, tall and dark like the man, scurry across the town square. Before she slipped into one of the houses, she paused to beckon to two children, perhaps four or five years old, their black hair falling over their shoulders. They darted up to her and the door closed with a slam. It struck me as odd that we heard the padding of their bare feet, but not their voices. The woman, as well as the children, were as silent as the man with the spear.

Then I realized that, in this entire village, not a single voice could be heard. No babies crying. No friends laughing. No neighbors arguing over the price of wheat, the cause of lice, or the likelihood of rain. No sounds of rage, or joy, or sorrow.

No voices at all.

The man jabbed again with his spear, nearly brushing the folds of my tunic. I backed slowly away, still pondering the eerie glow of his eyes. Through my frown, I said to him, "Whatever happened to you and your village, I am sorry."

The spear slashed the air again near my chest.

"Come, Shim. We are not welcome here."

The little giant whimpered, but turned to follow me. We trudged across the tundra, as wordless as the Town of the Bards. In time we left its flickering torches far behind, though its sorrowful silence continued to cling to us.

Behind us, sunset draped a curtain of rich purple over Druma Wood. Before us, the dark night swiftly deepened. I reluctantly gave up hope of finding any shelter on this featureless plain. Yet I knew that I must keep searching, right up to the moment I could no longer see my own staff. Otherwise, like whatever creatures howled hungrily in the distance, Shim and I would have to spend the night in the open.

At that moment I spotted a shape of some sort ahead. It appeared to be a rock—and on the rock, a person.

As we approached, I saw to my surprise that it was a girl. She looked a few years younger than Rhia. Swinging her bare feet, she sat on the rock, watching the purples and blues streak the darkening sky. She did not seem at all afraid to see approaching travelers.

"Hello." She tossed her brown curls that reached almost to her waist. A playful smile illuminated her face.

Cautiously, I drew closer. "Hello."

"Would you like to watch the sunset with me?"

"Thank you, but no." I studied her bright, exuberant eyes, so different from the eyes of the man we had just left. "Shouldn't you be getting back to your home? It's rather late."

"Oh no," she chirped. "I love watching the sunset from here."

I stepped nearer. "Where is your home?"

The girl giggled shyly. "I'll tell you if you'll tell me where you're going."

Perhaps because of her friendly manner, or because she reminded me a little of Rhia, I felt drawn toward this spirited girl. I wanted to speak with her, if only for a moment. I could pretend, in some remote corner of my heart, that I was once more speaking with Rhia herself. And if her village was somewhere nearby, we might yet find shelter for the night.

"Where are you going?" she repeated.

I smiled. "Oh, wherever my shadow may lead me."

Once more she giggled. "Your shadow will disappear fairly soon."

"As will yours. You should go home before it gets any darker."

"Don't worry. My village lies just over that rise there."

While we spoke, Shim edged nearer to the rock on which she sat. Perhaps he too felt drawn to her, for the same reasons as I. For her part, she did not seem to notice his approach. Then, for whatever reason, he halted and started slowly backing away.

Thinking nothing of Shim's movements, I asked the girl, "Do you think it might be possible for us to stay in your village tonight?"

She threw back her head with a hearty laugh. "Of course."

My spirits lifted. We had found shelter after all.

Just then Shim tugged on the bottom of my tunic. As I bent down, the little giant whispered, "I isn't sure, but I think something is strangely about her hands."

"What?"

"Her hands."

Not expecting to find anything, I glanced quickly at the girl's hands. At first, I saw nothing strange. And yet . . . they did seem somehow different. In a way I couldn't quite define. Suddenly, I knew.

Her fingers. Her fingers are webbed.

The alleah bird! Rhia's warning that shifting wraiths always show a flaw of some kind! I reached for the dagger Honn had given to me.

Too late. The girl had already begun to metamorphose into the shape of a serpent. Her brown eyes transformed to red, her skin to scales, her mouth to ruthless jaws. Even as the wraith leaped at my face, a thin veil of discarded skin crackled as it floated to the ground.

I drew the knife barely in time to lash out as the serpent bowled me over backward. Shim shrieked. We rolled on the tundra, a knot of teeth and tail, arms and legs. I could feel the wraith's claws digging into the flesh of my right arm.

Then, almost as swiftly as it had started, the battle stopped. Our two entwined bodies lay utterly still on the ground.

"Emrys?" asked Shim meekly. "Is you dead?"

Slowly, I stirred. I extracted myself from the grasp of the serpent, whose throat had been slashed open by the dagger. Rancid-smelling blood poured out of the gash and down the scaled belly. Weakly, I staggered over to the rock and propped myself against it, clutching my wounded arm.

Shim looked at me admiringly. "You has saved us."

I shook my head. "Plain luck saved us. That . . . and one observant little giant."

CAIRPRÉ

The little light remaining fled swiftly. We settled for the night by a barely trickling stream a few hundred paces from the remains of the shifting wraith. Each consumed by his own thoughts, neither of us spoke. While Shim stared hard at the eroded banks to make sure that no deadly creatures hid there, I mixed a poultice from my satchel of herbs.

The herbs smelled vaguely of thyme. And beech root. And Branwen. Gingerly, I patted the poultice on the claw marks on my arm, knowing full well that she would have done much better. I tried to hum to myself one of her soothing chants, but couldn't remember more than a few notes.

I knew, as the darkness submerged us, that my second sight would soon be no help at all. I laid down my staff and leaned back against a rotting tree stump, the dagger clutched in my hand. I hefted the narrow blade that had slain the wraith. Had Honn used it in his labors? Or had he carried it just for protection? Either way, I was now twice indebted to him.

A few faint stars began to appear overhead. I tried to search for some of Rhia's constellations, made not from the stars but from the spaces between them. I thought about the shomorra tree, heavy with fruit. The writing on Arbassa's walls. The crystal cave, all aglow. Yet all that seemed so long ago, so far away.

To my disappointment, the stars were so few and so scattered that I found no patterns at all. Then I realized that even those stars were not growing brighter as the sky darkened. They seemed shrouded somehow. And not by clouds, at least not by ordinary clouds. Something held them back, kept them from lighting this land.

At that moment, I sensed a faint smoky smell in the air, as if a fire burned nearby. I sat up straight, straining my second sight. But I found no flame anywhere.

Stranger still, I noticed that a vague circle of light brightened the area where we lay upon the ground. It came not from the dimly lit stars, but from somewhere else. What else could be shining down on us? Puzzled, I looked closer.

Suddenly I understood. The gentle illumination came not from above, but from below. It came, in fact, from the rotting tree stump!

I rolled away. Cautiously, I took a closer look. I noticed a glowing circle in the top of the stump, as though a door had been cut in the wood, allowing the ring of light to shine through.

"Look here, Shim."

My companion strode over. Seeing the glowing stump, he sucked in his breath. "Now I is sure we camps in the wrong place."

"I know. But this light feels good somehow."

Shim frowned. "The snakely girl feels good at first, too."

Then, without warning, the door popped open. From it emerged a shaggy head with a tall brow and dark, observant eyes. The head of a man.

The eyes, deeper than pools, gazed at me, then at Shim, for a long moment.

"All right," said the stranger in a low, resonant voice. "You can come in. But I don't have any time for stories."

The head disappeared down into the trunk. Shim and I exchanged looks of bewilderment. Stories? What could he mean?

At length, I announced, "I'm going down there. Come with me or stay here, as you choose."

"I stays!" answered Shim decisively. "And you should forgets this foolery and stays, too."

"It's worth the risk if it means we won't have to camp out in the open."

As if to emphasize my point, the distant howling resumed.

"Supposing this man becomes another snakely snake? Supposing you is trapped down in his hole?"

I did not answer. I peered through the door and into a narrow tunnel. Although it was well lighted, which restored my second sight, all I could see from this position was a rough-hewn ladder leading downward. I hesitated, pondering Shim's warning.

The howling swelled in volume.

Clutching my dagger in one hand, I put my feet into the entrance and began to climb down. I noticed as I descended that the wooden rungs were heavily worn, as if many hundreds of hands and feet had entered by them. And, I hoped, left by them.

Down I climbed, one rung after another. Soon a leathery, musty smell drifted up the tunnel. It was a smell that excited me, for I had encountered it only one place before, in the Church of Saint Peter at Caer Myrddin. The farther I descended, the stronger it became.

It was the smell of books.

When at last I reached the bottom, I stared in astonishment. For hundreds and hundreds of volumes surrounded me. They covered the walls and floor of this underground room from end to end and top to bottom.

Books everywhere! Books of all thicknesses, colors, heights, and also languages—judging from the varied scripts and symbols on the covers. Some bound in leather. Some so tattered that they wore no covers at all. Some formed of papyrus scrolls from the Nile. Some, made of pergamentium from the land the Greeks called Anatolia and the Romans called Lesser Asia, with the feel of sheepskin.

Books sat in rows on the sagging shelves that lined the walls. They lay stacked in piles on the floor, so many that only a narrow path remained from one side of the room to the other. They huddled in a mound beneath the heavy wooden table, itself cluttered with papers and writing supplies. They even covered most of the bed of sheepskins in the corner.

Across from the bed, a small but adequate pantry held shelves of fruits and grains, breads and cheeses. Two low stools sat to one side, and a hearth to the other. The hearth crackled with a flame bright enough to light the living space as well as the tunnel leading to the stump above. Next to the fire sat a cauldron made of iron. Bowls, grimy with leftover food, lay stacked beside the cauldron, perhaps in the hope that given enough time they might eventually wash themselves.

Sitting in a high-backed chair by the far wall, the long-haired man sat reading. His tangled brows, streaked with gray, sprouted like brambles above his eyes. He wore a flowing white tunic, with a high collar that nearly touched his chin. For a moment or two, he did not seem to notice that I had joined him.

I put the dagger back into my satchel. The man did not move. Feeling uncomfortable, I cleared my throat.

Still the man did not look up from his book.

"Thank you for inviting me."

At this the man stirred. "You are most welcome. Now would you mind shutting the hatch to my front door? Drafts, you know. Not to mention the unmentionable beasts who like to prowl at night. You'll see the lock."

He paused, noticing something. "And tell your diminutive friend that he is under no obligation at all to join us. He need not feel awkward in the least. Of course, it is too bad that he will miss out on my fresh clover honey."

Suddenly, I heard a slam up the tunnel. Seconds later, Shim stood beside me.

"I changes my mind," he said sheepishly.

The man closed the book, replaced it on the shelf behind his chair. "Nothing like a good read to finish a day of good reads."

Despite myself, I grinned. "I have never seen so many books."

The man nodded. "Stories help me. To live. To work. To find the meaning hidden in every dream, every leaf, every drop of dew."

I blanched. Had not Branwen said almost the same thing to me once?

"I only wish," continued the man, "that I had more time to enjoy them. These days, as you surely know, we have other distractions."

"You mean goblins and the like."

"Yes. But it is *the like* that I most dislike." He shook his head gravely, pulling down another book. "That is why I have so little time for my favorite stories right now. I am trying to find some sort of answer in the books, so that Fincayra's own story does not have to end before its time."

I nodded. "The Blight is spreading."

Without looking up from his book, he replied, "So it is! Sophocles—do you know the Greek playwrights?—had a stunning phrase. In *Oedipus*, as I recall. *A rust consumes the buds.* And that is indeed what has been happening to our land. Rust. Consuming the buds. Consuming everything."

He pulled down another book and placed it on top of the first one, still on his lap. "Yet we mustn't lose hope. The answer just might lie hidden in some forgotten volume. *It's worth a look in every book.*" He raised his head, looking slightly embarrassed. "Forgive the rhyme. They just slip out, it seems. Even if I try to stop making them, I can't. As I was saying, *There are sages in these pages.*"

He cleared his throat. "But enough of that now." He waved toward the pantry. "Are you hungry? Do help yourselves. Honey is on the left, by the plums. Breads of many kinds are there, twice-baked in the manner of the Slantos to the north."

"I've not heard of them," I confessed.

"Not surprising." The man went back to flipping through pages. "Most of those northerly reaches are unexplored and uncharted. And consider the Lost Lands! There may be people there, most unusual people, who have never been visited by anyone."

He bent closer to the book, pondering a particular page. "And may I ask your names?"

"I am called Emrys."

The man lifted his head, eyeing me in an odd sort of way. "Called? You say it as if you were not sure it is your true name."

I bit my lip.

"What about your companion?"

I glanced at the small figure who was already at the pantry, devouring some bread slathered with fresh clover honey. "That is Shim."

"And I am Cairpré, a humble poet. Forgive me for being too preoccupied to be a good host. But I am always glad to welcome a visitor."

He closed the book, still observing me. "Especially a visitor who reminds me so much of a dear friend."

I felt a strange surge of fear as I asked, "What friend might that be?"

"I was a close friend . . . of your mother."

The words fell on me with the weight of anvils. "My—my mother?"

Cairpré dropped the books on his lap onto the chair. He stepped over to me and placed a hand on my shoulder. "Come. We have much to discuss."

A SIMPLE
QUESTION

Cairpré led me to the twin stools by the pantry. After removing some leather-bound books from the seats, we sat down. Shim, for his part, had already climbed onto the pantry's bottom shelf and seemed very comfortable, surrounded by ample supplies for his supper.

The poet observed me silently for several seconds. "You have changed since I last saw you. Quite a lot! So much I didn't even recognize you at first. Though you could, I suppose, say the same about me. It has been five or six years, after all."

I could not contain my excitement. "You have met me before? And my mother as well?"

His eyes darkened. "You don't remember?"

"I don't remember any of my childhood! Up to the day I washed ashore, it's all a mystery." I grasped the sleeve of his white tunic. "But you can help me! You can answer my questions! Tell me everything you can. First—about my mother. Who is she? Where is she? Why did you say she *was* a friend?"

Cairpré leaned back on his stool, clasping his knee with both hands. "It seems as though I will be telling you a story, after all."

After a pause, he began. "There came a day when a woman, a

human woman, arrived on the shores of this island. She came from
the land of the Celts, from a place called Gwynedd."

A sudden pang of doubt struck me. Had I been wrong all along
about Branwen? Hesitantly, I asked, "What was her name?"

"Elen."

I breathed a sigh of relief.

"Now, Elen looked very different from us Fincayrans. Her skin
was lighter than most, more creamy than ruddy. Her ears were
shaped differently, too—more round than triangular. Truly, she was
beautiful. But her most striking feature was her eyes. They glowed
with a color unlike any ever seen on this island. Pure blue, untinted
with gray or brown. Blue as a sapphire. So she was called Elen of
the Sapphire Eyes."

I shuddered.

"She came here," he continued, "because of her love for a man
of Fincayran blood. A man from this world, not her own. And soon
after she arrived, she discovered yet another love." He glanced
around the room. "Books! She loved books, from all lands and all
languages. In fact, we met over a book, when she came here to
collect one I had borrowed that was slightly overdue—a decade or
so. After that, she came here often to read and talk. She sat in the
very chair where you sit now! Especially, she was interested in the
art of healing, as it has been practiced through the ages. She herself
had a gift for healing others."

Again I shuddered.

Remembering something, Cairpré smiled to himself. "But her
favorite books of all, I think, were the stories of the Greeks."

"Is this true?" I demanded. "Do you swear this is true?"

"It is."

"She told me so little. Not even her name! She only called herself Branwen."

Cairpré turned toward a high shelf of books. "How like her to choose a name from legend. Yet it grieves me to hear that she chose such a tragic one."

"Alas that I was ever born," I quoted.

The poet gazed at me. "So you know the legend?"

"I know it." My lower lip trembled. "But I didn't know *her*. Not at all. She said so little about herself that I refused . . ."

A knot filled my throat, and I started to sob quietly. The poet watched me with the compassion of someone feeling the same stab of pain. Yet he did not try to comfort me. He merely let me shed the tears that I needed to shed.

Finally, in a hoarse whisper, I finished the sentence. "I refused . . . to call her Mother."

Cairpré said nothing for some time. When at last he spoke, he asked a simple question.

"Did she love you?"

Raising my head, I nodded slowly. "Yes."

"Did she care for you when you needed help?"

"Yes."

"Then you did know her. You knew her down to her soul."

I wiped my cheeks with my tunic. "Perhaps. But it doesn't feel that way. Can you tell me some . . . about my father?"

A strange, faraway look came into Cairpré's eyes. "Your father was an impressive youth. Strong, willful, passionate. *Full of zest, the ardent quest.* No, the rhythm's all wrong. Let me try again. *Awake! Alive! A startling drive.* There, that's better. In our most ancient tongue, his name means Tree Climber, because as a boy he so enjoyed climbing trees. Sometimes he would even climb to the top of a tall tree and stay there just for the experience of riding out a fierce storm."

I laughed out loud, understanding more fully than the poet knew.

"Yet Tree Climber's childhood, I believe, was far from joyous. His mother, Olwen, was a daughter of the sea, one of those beings the Earth folk call *mer people*, though Fincayrans prefer *people of the mer*. So he—like you—was born with the strange depths of the sea in his bones. Yet Olwen's Long Journey came too soon."

"I've heard about this Long Journey."

Cairpré sighed. "And long it is. Arduous, too, according to *The Glories of Dagda*. Unless, of course, you happen to be one of the few who are taken to the Otherworld right in the moment of death. But that is rare, extremely rare."

"You were talking about my father."

"Oh, yes. Your father. Since Olwen died when he was but an infant, your father was reared by his own father, a Fincayran known as Tuatha, son of Finvarra. Now Tuatha was a masterful wizard and a powerful man. It is said that even the great spirit Dagda would sometimes come to his home to confer on high matters. But alas, this wizard had very little time for his own son's needs. And Tuatha had even less time when he discovered—when your father was about the age you are now—that the boy lacked the gift of making magic. *The powers*, as Tuatha called them."

I swallowed hard, knowing that such powers were not a gift, but a curse. I recalled the prophecy of my grandfather, as told to me by Branwen—Elen—my mother. That she would one day have a son who would possess powers even greater than his own. *Whose magic would spring from the very deepest sources*. Such folly! He might have been a great wizard, but he could not have been more wrong.

"Your father's life changed, however, when he first met Elen during one of his travels to Earth. They fell deeply in love. Although it is rarely done, and still more rarely done with success, this man and woman of different worlds were married. Elen came to live in Fincayra. And because of her love, a new strength came into his heart, a new calm into his eye. *The loving bond may reach beyond.* Their happiness was great, for a time, though I am afraid that time was all too brief."

Grasping the edge of the stool where my own mother had sat long ago, I leaned forward. "What happened?"

Cairpré's face, so serious already, grew still more serious. "Your father," he began, then paused to clear his throat. "Your father was part of the royal circle of Stangmar. When the evil spirit Rhita Gawr, who has long had designs on Fincayra, began courting the king, your father was present. And your father—like the rest of the circle—slipped gradually into trouble. The same trouble that eventually corrupted the king, as well as the whole of Fincayra."

"Didn't my father try to resist Rhita Gawr? Didn't he try to keep the king from listening to him?"

"If he tried, he failed." The poet sighed. "You must understand. Many good people have been fooled by Rhita Gawr's treachery. Your father was only one of them."

I felt heavier than a boulder. "So my father helped to bring the Blight to Fincayra."

"That is true. But all of us bear some of the blame."

"What do you mean?"

Cairpré winced, so painful was the memory. "It all happened gradually, you see. So gradually that no one quite understood what was happening—until it was too late. No one but Stangmar himself understands just how it started. All anyone else knows is that, somehow, Rhita Gawr offered to protect the king in a time of need. To have refused this help would have placed the king, and therefore Fincayra, in some sort of danger. Rhita Gawr must have planned it out very carefully, because he made it almost impossible for the king not to accept his help. And Stangmar did just that."

He paused to lift a small brown moth off his white collar and place it gently on top of a pile of books by his stool. "That one little decision has led to a cascade of tragedies, one after another. When Rhita Gawr convinced Stangmar that his enemies were plotting to overthrow him, the king forged a questionable alliance with the warrior goblins and the shifting wraiths. Out of their dark crevasses they crawled! Then came the rumors that the giants, Fincayra's most ancient people, had suddenly become dangerous. Not only to the king, but to the rest of us, as well. So not many objected when Stangmar ordered the giants hunted down. Giants always seemed so . . . *different* to most people. Those of us who did object were either ridiculed or battered into silence. Next Stangmar heeded Rhita Gawr's warnings and began a campaign to cleanse the land of all the king's enemies—and to confiscate the Treasures of Fincayra because they might somehow fall into enemy hands."

"Didn't anyone try to stop this?"

"Some brave souls tried, but they were too few and too late. Stangmar stamped out any opposition, burning whole villages to the ground on the slightest suspicion of treason. Yet even that was preferable to what he did to the village of Caer Neithan."

I jumped. "You mean . . . the Town of the Bards?"

"You know of it? Oh, what a loss, to our world and all the others! For ages beyond memory, that town has been a fountain of music and song, home of our most inspired storytellers, nurturer of generations of bards. Laon the Lame was born there! Pwyll wrote her first poem there! *The Vessel of Illusion* was composed there! I could go on and on. *Here song is ever in the air, while story climbs the spiral stair.*"

With a nod, I observed, "The words on the sign."

"Quite so. They were written in truth, though now they are but a mockery. I should know, since I wrote them myself." He sighed. "Caer Neithan was my birthplace, as well."

"What happened there?"

Cairpré studied me sadly for a while. "Of all the fabled Treasures stolen by Stangmar—the sword Deepercut that can slice to the soul, the Flowering Harp that can call forth the spring, the Cauldron of Death that can end any life—the one most celebrated by bards throughout time was the Caller of Dreams. It was a horn with the power to bring wondrous dreams to life, and for centuries it was used only sparingly and wisely. But with the help of Rhita Gawr, Stangmar used it to punish Caer Neithan for harboring some who dared to oppose his policies. He called to life the most horrible dream ever beheld by any bard—and inflicted it upon the entire town."

Remembering the half-crazed eyes of the man with the spear, I was almost afraid to ask, "What dream was that?"

The poet's eyes grew cloudy. "That every man, woman, and child in that village would never speak, nor sing, nor write again. That the instruments of their souls—their very voices—would be silenced forever."

His voice a mere whisper, he continued. "By this time, no one was left to protest when Rhita Gawr urged Stangmar to destroy his own castle, the grandest yet most welcoming home any king or queen could ever ask for, including its library of books, a library more vast than my own by a thousandfold. And why? On the grounds that it was not safe enough from attack! So Rhita Gawr, calling it a gesture of friendship no doubt, built a new castle for Stangmar, a castle infused with his own evil power. Thus arose the Shrouded Castle, ever spinning on its foundation, from which spreads the impenetrable cloud that now darkens our sky and the terrible Blight that now strangles our soil."

He rubbed his chin. "The castle is guarded by Rhita Gawr's own deathless warriors, the ghouliants. Their lives, if you can call them lives—for they are actually men whose bodies were raised from the dead by Rhita Gawr—will never end, at least not by mortal blows. For their lives are sustained by the very turning of the Shrouded Castle! So as long as the castle keeps turning, they will remain there, performing deeds even darker than the Shroud itself."

I ached for Rhia. If she was still alive, she was probably in the bowels of that very castle! She would be at the mercy of the ghouliants, and of Stangmar himself. What would become of her when he concluded that she neither could nor would help him obtain the Galator, the last Treasure? I shuddered at the thought. And I despaired at the Grand Elusa's belief that the only way to topple Stangmar was to destroy the Shrouded Castle. I might as well wish to sprout wings!

"Now you can see," Cairpré added, "That Stangmar is truly the prisoner of Rhita Gawr. And as Stangmar is imprisoned, so are we all."

"Why hasn't Dagda intervened to stop all this? He is battling Rhita Gawr on other fronts, isn't he?"

"That he is. In the Otherworld as well as in this world. But Dagda believes, as Rhita Gawr does not, that to win ultimately he must respect people's free will. Dagda allows us to make our own choices, for good or ill. So if Fincayra is to be saved, it must be saved by the Fincayrans."

LOST WINGS

Cairpré reached around Shim, who had managed to spread himself (as well as clover honey) across the pantry shelf. The long-haired man tore off a slab of dark, grainy bread and ripped it in half. Keeping one piece, he handed me the other.

"Here. Before your little friend eats it all."

Shim did not seem to notice and continued stuffing himself.

I half grinned and took a bite of the crusty bread. It felt hard, almost like wood, until some vigorous chewing softened it up a bit. Then, to my surprise, it swiftly dissolved into liquid, filling my mouth with a tangy, minty flavor. Almost as soon as I swallowed, a wave of nourishment flowed through me. I straightened my back. Even the usual pain between my shoulder blades eased a little. I took another bite.

"You like ambrosia bread, I can see," said Cairpré through a mouthful. "One of the Slantos' finest achievements, without doubt. Still, it is said that no one from other parts of Fincayra has ever tasted any of the Slantos' most special breads, and that they guard those precious recipes with their lives."

I scanned the walls and floor of the room, so densely jammed with volumes. Being here felt like being in the hold of a ship whose cargo consisted of nothing but books. I remembered Branwen's wistful look when she had spoken about being in a room full of books—this very one, no doubt. Even with the spreading Blight, it must have been difficult for her to leave this room, this land, forever.

I turned back to Cairpré. "Bran—I mean, my mother—must have loved being here, with all your books."

"Indeed she did. She wanted to read the teachings of the Fincayrans, the Druids, the Celts, the Jews, the Christians, the Greeks. She called herself my student, but it was really more the other way around. I learned so much from her."

He glanced at a mound of books at the base of the ladder. On the leather cover of the book on top, a gold-leaf portrait, showing a figure driving a blazing chariot, gleamed in the light of the hearth fire.

"I remember once," he said in a distant voice, "when we talked the whole night through about those remarkable places where beings of mortal flesh and beings of immortal spirit live side by side. Where time flows both in a line and in a circle. Where sacred time and historical time exist together. *In between places,* she called them."

"Like Mount Olympus."

The poet nodded. "Or like Fincayra."

"Was it all the mounting troubles that made her want to leave Fincayra? Or was there something more?"

He eyed me strangely. "Your suspicion is correct. There was something more."

"What?"

"You, my boy."

My brow furrowed. "I don't understand."

"Let me explain. Do you know about the Greek Isle of Delos?"

"Apollo's birthplace. But what does that have to do with me?"

"It was another *in between place,* both sacred and historical at once. That is why the Greeks never allowed anyone to give birth on Delos. They didn't want any mere mortal to be able to claim a birthright to soil that belonged first to the gods. And they killed or banished anyone foolish enough to disobey."

"I still don't see what this has to do with me."

At this moment, Shim released an immense belch, far bigger than one would expect from a person so small. Yet the little giant did not seem aware of it, just as he seemed to have forgotten about Cairpré and myself. He merely patted his belly and returned to the serious matter of fresh clover honey.

Cairpré's shaggy eyebrows lifted in amusement, then his expression darkened. "In the same manner as Delos, it is strictly forbidden that anyone with human blood should ever be born on the island of Fincayra. This is a land not of the Earth, nor of the Otherworld, though it is a bridge between them both. Visitors come here from either world, and they sometimes stay for years. Yet they cannot call this place home."

I leaned closer. "I have been searching for my own home. So help me understand this. If my mother had to leave Fincayra to give birth to me, where did she go? Do you know where I was born?"

"I know," replied the poet, his tone grave. "It was not where you should have been born."

I caught my breath. "Are you saying that I was born on Fincayra, even though I have human blood?"

His face told me everything.

"Does that mean I am in danger?"

"More danger than you know."

"How did that happen? You said it is forbidden."

"I can explain what, but not why." Cairpré scratched the top of his head. "It happened this way. Your parents, aware of Fincayra's ancient law, knew that Elen must sail to another land to give birth. But they also knew that no one can be sure, when setting sail from Fincayra, whether or not he or she will ever return. The passage here is a strange one, as you are well aware. Sometimes the door is open; sometimes it is not. Many who have left this island, hoping desperately to return, have found only a shred of mist upon the waters. Others have met their deaths in the stormy seas. *Nothing is known but we sail alone.*"

He shook his head. "Your mother and father loved each other deeply, and did not want to part. If Tuatha had not commanded your father to stay, I believe he would have sailed with her. Moreover, I suspect that Elen could sense trouble brewing, and did not want to leave him. So they lingered long before parting. Too long. Your mother was already in her ninth month when at last she set sail."

Feeling something warm against my chest, I looked down at my tunic. Beneath the folds, the Galator was glowing faintly, making a circle of green light over my heart. Swiftly, I covered the place with my hand, hoping that Cairpré would not notice and interrupt his tale.

"Soon after the ship had launched, a terrible storm arose on the waves. It was the kind of storm that few sailors since Odysseus have survived. The ship was battered, nearly drowned, and forced back to shore. That very night, huddled in the wreckage of the ship, your mother gave birth." He paused, thinking. "And she named the boy Emrys, a Celtic name from her homeland."

"So that is my true name?"

"Not necessarily! Your true name may not be your given name."

I gave a nod of understanding. "Emrys has never felt right to me. But how do I find my true name?"

The deep-set eyes pondered me. "Life will find it for you."

"I don't know what you mean."

"With luck, you will in time."

"Well, my true name is a mystery, but at least now I know I belong in Fincayra."

Cairpré shook his gray head. "You do, and you do not."

"But you said I was born here!"

"Your place of birth may not be where you belong."

Feeling a surge of frustration, I pulled the Galator out of my tunic. Its jeweled center, still glowing faintly, flared in the light of the fire. "She gave me this! Does this not prove I belong here?"

A new depth of sadness filled the pools beneath Cairpré's brows. "The Galator belongs here, yes. Whether or not you belong here, I do not know."

Exasperated, I demanded, "Must I destroy the castle and the king and all his army, before you will tell me I belong here?"

"I may tell you that one day," answered the poet calmly. "If you tell me the same."

His demeanor, if not his words, soothed me somewhat. I replaced the pendant under my tunic. Feeling again the pain between my shoulder blades, I stretched my arms out wide.

Cairpré observed me knowingly. "So you too feel the pain. In that way you are certainly a son of Fincayra."

"This pain in my shoulders? How should that make any difference?"

"It has made all the difference in the world." Seeing the confusion in my face, he once again leaned back on his stool, clasped his knee, and began to tell a story.

"In the far, far reaches of time, the people of Fincayra walked upon the land, as they do now. Yet they also could do something else. They also could fly."

My eyes widened.

"The gift of flight was theirs. They had lovely white wings, the old legends say, sprouting from between their shoulder blades. So they could soar with the eagles and sail with the clouds. *Wings of white to endless height.* They could venture high above the lands of Fincayra, or even to lands beyond."

For an instant, I could almost feel the flutter of the feisty hawk who would swoop through the air before landing on my shoulder. Trouble had so enjoyed the gift of flight! I missed him, almost as much as I missed Rhia.

I smiled sadly at Cairpré. "So the Fincayrans had both the ears of demons and the wings of angels."

He looked amused. "That's a poetic way to put it."

"What happened to their wings?"

"They lost them, though it's not clear how. That is one story that has not survived, though I would gladly give away half of my books just to hear it. Whatever happened, it took place so long ago that many Fincayrans have never even heard that their ancestors could fly. Or if they have, they simply dismiss it as untrue."

I watched the poet. "But you believe it's true."

"I do."

"I know someone else who would believe it. My friend Rhia. She would love to be able to fly." I bit my lip. "First, though, I must save her! If she still lives."

"What happened to her?"

"Carried off by goblins! She tricked them into taking her instead of me, though what they really wanted was the Galator. She is probably at the Shrouded Castle by now."

Cairpré tilted his head, frowning. From that angle his face looked like a stern statue, made of stone rather than flesh. At last he spoke, his resonant voice filling the room so crowded with books.

"Do you know the prophecy of the giants' dance?"

I tried to recall it. *"Only when giants make dance in the hall, Shall every . . ."*

"Barrier."

"Shall every barrier crumble and fall. But I don't have any hope of destroying the castle! All I can hope to do is save my friend."

"And what if that requires destroying the Shrouded Castle?"

"Then all is lost."

"No doubt you are correct. Destroying the castle would destroy Rhita Gawr's presence in Fincayra. And neither he nor Stangmar is about to let that happen! A warrior as great as Hercules would find it impossible. Even if he carried some weapon of enormous power."

Suddenly an idea struck me. "Perhaps the Galator is the key! It is, after all, the last Treasure, the one that Stangmar has been searching for."

Cairpré's shaggy mane wagged from side to side. "We know very little about the Galator."

"Can you at least tell me what its powers are?"

"No. Except that they are described in the ancient texts as *vast beyond knowing.*"

"You're no help at all."

"Too true." Cairpré's sad face brightened only a little. "I can, however, give you my own theory about the Galator."

"Tell me!"

"I believe that its powers, whatever they are, respond to love."

"Love?"

"Yes." The poet's gaze rambled over his shelves of books. "You shouldn't be so surprised! Stories about the power of love abound." He stroked his chin. "As a start, I believe the Galator glows in the presence of love. Do you recall what we were talking about when it started shining under your tunic?"

I hesitated. "Was it . . . my mother?"

"Yes. Elen of the Sapphire Eyes. The woman who loved you enough to give up everything in her life in order to save yours! That, if you really want to know the truth, is why she left Fincayra."

For a long while, I could find no words to speak. Finally, I said regretfully, "What an ass I was! Never calling her my mother, never putting her pain ahead of my own. I wish I could tell her how sorry I am."

Cairpré lowered his eyes. "As long as you stay in Fincayra, you will never have that chance. When she left, she swore she would never come back."

"She should never have given me the Galator. I know absolutely nothing about how it works or what it can do."

"I just told you my theory."

"Your theory is mad! You say it glows in the presence of love. Well, you should know that I've seen it glow once before since I came back to Fincayra. In the presence of a bloodthirsty spider!"

Cairpré froze. "Not . . . the Grand Elusa?"

"Yes."

He almost smiled. "That strengthens my theory all the more! Do not be fooled by the Grand Elusa's alarming appearance. The truth is, her love is as great as her appetite."

I shrugged. "Even if your theory is correct, what good does it do? It doesn't help me save Rhia."

"Are you determined to go after her?"

"I am."

He scowled. "Do you know what the odds are against you?"

"I have some idea."

"But you don't!"

Cairpré stood up and started pacing down the narrow path between the stacks of books. His thigh brushed against one large, illuminated volume, and it fell to the floor in an explosion of dust. As he bent to retrieve it, stuffing loose pages back between the covers, he looked my way. "You remind me of Prometheus, so certain he could steal the fire of the gods."

"I'm not that certain. I just know I must try. Besides, Prometheus finally succeeded, didn't he?"

"Yes!" exclaimed the poet. "At the price of eternal torture, being chained to a rock where an eagle would gnaw forever upon his liver."

"Until Hercules rescued him."

Cairpré's face reddened. "I can see that I taught your mother too well! You are right that Prometheus found freedom in the end. But you are wrong if you think for a minute that you will be so fortunate. Out there, in the lands controlled by Stangmar, people are at risk just by showing themselves! You must understand me. All your mother's sacrifices will have been wasted if you go to the Shrouded Castle."

I folded my arms. While I certainly did not feel courageous, I did feel resolved. "I must try to save Rhia."

He stopped pacing. "You are no less stubborn than your mother!"

"That sounds to me like a compliment."

He shook his head in defeat. "All right, then. You ignore my warnings. *Thou withered breath, approaching Death.* I suppose then I should at least give you some advice that might conceivably help."

I slid off my stool. "What is it?"

"More likely, though, it will only hasten your death."

"Please tell me."

"There is one person in all of Fincayra who might have the power to help you enter the castle, though I doubt that even she can help you beyond that point. Her powers are old, very old, springing from the same ancient sources that brought the very first giants into being. That is why Stangmar fears to crush her. Even Rhita Gawr himself prefers to leave her alone."

Cairpré stepped closer, wading through the sea of books. "Whether or not she will choose to help you, I cannot say. No one can! For her ways are mysterious and unpredictable. She is neither good nor evil, friend nor foe. She simply *is*. In legend, she is called Domnu, which means Dark Fate. Her true name, if it ever was known, has been lost to time."

He glanced at Shim, now sleeping soundly on the pantry shelf, his hand inside the empty jar of honey. "You and your little friend may not have the pleasure of meeting her, however. Getting into her lair will be very dangerous." He added under his breath, "Though not as dangerous as getting out again."

I shivered slightly.

"To find her you must start before sunrise. Although the light of dawn is now only a pale glow through the spreading darkness, it will be your best guide. For just to the north of the sunrise, you will see a notch, cut deep into the ridge of the highest row of hills."

"I should head for the notch?"

Cairpré nodded in assent. "And you will miss it at your peril. If you cross the ridge to the north of the notch, you will find yourself in the middle of Stangmar's largest encampment of goblins."

I sucked in my breath. "No risk of that."

"And if you cross the ridge to the south of the notch, you will be even worse off, for you will enter the Haunted Marsh."

"No risk of that, either."

At that moment, Shim released a loud, prolonged snort. The books lining the shelves seemed to jump in surprise, as did Cairpré and I.

The poet frowned, but continued. "Passing through the notch itself will not be easy. It is guarded by warrior goblins. How many, I don't know. But even one can mean trouble enough. Your best hope is that these days they are unused to travelers, for reasons you can well understand. It is just possible they will not be paying much attention. There is at least a chance you could slip past them."

"Then what?"

"You must proceed straight down the ridge, being careful not to veer to one side or the other, until you reach a steep canyon. Eagles once soared among its cliffs, but no more, since now the canyon is always darker than night. Turn south, following the canyon to the very edge of the Haunted Marsh. If you make it that far, you will encounter the lair of Domnu. But not before you have met some other creatures almost as strange as she is."

Feeling weak, I leaned against my stool. "What does her lair look like?"

"I have no idea. You see, no one who has ventured there has ever returned to describe it. All I can tell you is that, according to legend, Domnu has a passion for games of chance and wagers—and dearly hates to lose."

Cairpré bent down to the floor and pushed a pile of books aside. He threw a sheepskin on the spot. With deep sadness, he said, "If you mean to pursue this idea of yours, you had better try to rest now. Sunrise will come before long."

He pondered my face. "I can see by the scars on your cheeks and the strange distance in your eyes that this is not the first time you have shown bravery. Perhaps I have underestimated you. Perhaps you possess all the hidden strengths of your forebears and more."

I waved away the comment. "If you knew me better, you would know that I am no credit to my forebears! I have no special powers, at least none that I can use. All I have is a stubborn head, and the Galator around my neck."

He rubbed his chin thoughtfully. "Time will tell. But I will say this. When first you entered my home, I was looking for an answer in some forgotten volume. Now I am wondering whether I should be looking for that answer in some forgotten person."

Wearily, I stretched myself out on the sheepskin. For some time I lay awake, watching the firelight dance on the walls of books, the scrolls of papyrus, the piles of manuscripts. Cairpré had returned to his high-backed chair, absorbed in his reading.

So this is where my mother learned her stories. I felt a swell of desire to stay many days in this room filled with books, to travel wherever their pages might carry me. Perhaps one day I would do just that. But I knew that I must travel somewhere else first. And that I must depart before dawn.

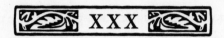# XXX

T'EILEAN AND
GARLATHA

Shim scrunched his pear-shaped nose in puzzlement. "Why is she called Dumb Now? That is muchly strange."

"Domnu," I replied, pushing myself up from the sheepskin. "I've told you everything I know, which isn't much." I glanced at Cairpré, fast asleep in his chair with three open books in his lap. His long gray hair fell over his face like a waterfall. "Now it is time to go."

Shim's gaze moved to the pantry, whose bottom shelf glistened from spilled honey. "I is not gladly to leave this place."

"You don't have to come, you know. I will understand if you want to stay."

The pink eyes kindled. "Really, truly, honestly?"

"Yes. I am sure Cairpré will make you welcome, although he probably doesn't have much food left."

The little giant smacked his lips. Then, glancing toward the wooden ladder up the tunnel, his expression clouded. "But you is going?"

"I am going. Now." For a few seconds, I studied the little face at my knee. Shim had turned out to be not such a bad companion after all. I took one of his tiny hands in my own. "Wherever you go, may you find plenty of honey there."

Shim scowled. "I is not happy about going."

"I know. Farewell."

I moved to the ladder and grasped a worn rung.

Shim ran over and pulled on my tunic. "But I is not happy about staying, either."

"You should stay."

"Is you not wantsing me?"

"This will be too dangerous for you."

Shim growled with resentment. "You is not saying that if I is a real giant, big and strong. Then you begs me to come."

Sadly, I smiled. "Maybe so, but I still like you the way you are."

The little fellow grimaced. "I don't! I still wishes I am big. Big as the highlyest tree."

"You know, when Rhia was irked at me once, she told me *Just be yourself.* I've thought about it now and then. It's much easier to say than to do, but she had a point."

"Bah! Not if you don't likes the self you are being."

"Listen, Shim. I understand. Believe me, I do. Just try being at home with who you are." I paused, a little surprised to hear myself say such a thing. Then, with a final look around Cairpré's crowded walls of books, I began climbing up the tunnel.

As I squeezed through the door in the stump, I scanned the eastern horizon. Dry, reddish soil stretched as far as I could see, broken only by the occasional scrawny tree or cluster of thorned bracken. Although no birds were around to announce the dawn, a faint line of light was already appearing above the Dark Hills, which stood blacker than coal. To the north of the glow, I made out two sharp knobs, divided by a narrow gap. The notch.

Standing beside the stump, I concentrated on the formation, trying to memorize its position. I did not want to miss the notch, even by a small margin. And I couldn't be certain it would remain visible as the day progressed.

Seeing my staff on the ground, I stooped to pick it up. Dew frosted its twisted top, making the wood slippery and cold to the touch. Suddenly I noticed several deep gashes along the shaft. Teeth marks. I had no way to tell what kind of beast had made them. I only knew that they had not been there when I climbed down into Cairpré's tunnel last night.

I reached to close the door, when Shim's bulbous nose emerged. The little body followed, clambering through the opening.

"I is coming."

"Are you sure?" I showed him the staff. "Whatever chewed on this last night could still be near."

Shim swallowed, but said nothing.

I waved toward the dimly glowing horizon. "And to find Domnu, we have to make it through that notch in the Dark Hills. No room for error, either. To one side lies an army of goblins, to the other lies the Haunted Marsh."

The little giant planted his feet firmly. "You is not leaving me."

"All right then. Come."

Hopping over the trickling stream by the stump, I strode off in the direction of the notch. Shim, hustling to keep up, followed.

For the rest of that morning—if such grim, lightless hours could be called morning—we trekked across the open tundra. The soil crackled under the weight of our feet. Heading toward the notched ridge, we followed no roads or trails, though we crossed several. Yet the roads were as empty as the village that had been burned to the ground.

Conversation was just as sparse as the surrounding vegetation, and almost as brittle, for both of us knew how easily we could be spotted by anyone loyal to Stangmar. Even when Shim reached into the pocket of his shirt and offered to share a hunk of ambrosia bread from Cairpré's pantry, he did so without speaking. I merely nodded in thanks, and we pressed on.

As the land gradually lifted toward the Dark Hills, I did my best to guide us. Although the notch no longer stood out against the sky, as it did during the brief glow that had passed for sunrise, it remained barely visible. Yet it seemed to me less a sign of the route than a sign of foreboding. Suppose we somehow passed through the notch, and even made it to Stangmar's castle, only to find that Rhia was not there? Or worse, that she was there but no longer alive?

Every so often, we encountered sparse signs of habitation. An old house here, a dilapidated pen there. Yet these structures seemed as lifeless as the landscape. They sat there, rotting, like bones on a beach. If anyone still lived there, they lived in hiding. And they existed somehow without trees or gardens or greenery of any kind.

Then, to my surprise, I sensed a subtle splash of green ahead. Thinking it might be just a mistake of my weak vision, I concentrated on the spot. Yet the color seemed real enough, contrasting with the rusty browns and grays on all sides. As I drew nearer, the green deepened. At the same time, I detected the outlines of trees, arranged in regular rows, with some sort of fruit clinging to their boughs.

"An orchard! Can you believe it?"

Shim rubbed his nose. "Looks dangerously to me."

"And see?" I pointed at a boxy shape behind the trees. "There's some sort of hut in the cleft of the hill."

"I thinks we better stays away. Really, truly, absolutely."

Whether because the green trees reminded me of the Druma, or because the hut reminded me of my days with the woman I now knew to be my mother, I felt curious to learn more. I looked down. "You can wait here for me if you want. I'm going closer."

Shim watched me depart, swearing under his breath. A few seconds later, he trotted to catch up to me.

As he approached, I stopped and turned to him. "Smelled some honey, did you?"

He growled. "Goblinses, more likely." Nervously, he glanced over his shoulder. "But even if no goblinses are there, they is not far away."

"You can be sure of that. We won't stop long, I promise. Just long enough to see who lives there."

As we neared the orchard, I discerned a rough stone wall bordering the trees. It was made of the same gray rock, splotched with rust-colored lichen, as the hut. Judging from the gaps and toppled portions of both, neither hut nor wall had been repaired in quite some time. Just as the crumbling wall embraced the trees, the trees themselves embraced the hut, flowing over its roof and sides with leafy branches. Beneath the boughs, several beds of green, speckled with brighter colors, thatched the ground.

I crouched, as did Shim. Cautiously, we crept closer. A fresh aroma wafted over us, the scent of wet leaves and newborn blossoms. It struck me how long it had been since I smelled the fragrance of living, growing plants. And then it struck me that this was not just an orchard. This was a garden.

Just then a pair of shapes, as gray as the stones in the wall, emerged from the hut. Taking wobbly steps, the pair slowly advanced toward the nearest bed of plants. They moved with an odd, disjointed rhythm, one back straightening as the other curved, one head lifting as the other drooped. As different as their motions were, however, they seemed unalterably connected.

As they came nearer, I could tell that these two people were old. Very old. White hair, streaked with gray, fell about both of their shoulders, while their sleeveless brown robes hung worn and faded. Had their backs not been so bent, they would have stood quite tall. Only their arms, muscular and brown, seemed younger than their years.

The pair reached the first bed of plants, then separated. One of them, a woman whose strong cheekbones reminded me of my mother, stooped to retrieve a sack of seeds and started working them into the soil on one side of the hut. At the same time the other, a man with a long banner of whiskers waving from his chin, picked up a basket and hobbled toward a tree laden with the same spiral fruit that I had tasted at the shomorra tree. Abruptly, the old man halted. He turned slowly toward the spot where we crouched behind the wall.

Without taking his eyes off us, he spoke in a low, crusty voice. "Garlatha, we have visitors."

The old woman looked up. Though her face creased with concern, she answered calmly, in a voice that creaked with age. "Then let them show themselves, for they have nothing to fear."

"I am T'eilean," declared the man. "If you come in peace, you are welcome here."

Slowly, we lifted our heads. I stood up and planted my staff on the ground. As my hand brushed over the place that had been raked by teeth only hours before, a chill passed through me. Meanwhile, Shim rose beside me and squared his shoulders, although only his eyes and frantic hair poked above the top of the wall.

"We come in peace."

"And what are your names?"

Feeling cautious, I hesitated.

"Our names is secret," declared Shim. "Nobody knows them." For good measure, he added, "Not even us."

One corner of T'eilean's mouth curled upward. "You are right to be cautious, little traveler. But as my wife has said, you have nothing to fear from us. We are simple gardeners, that is all."

I stepped across the wall, trying not to crush the slender yellow vegetables growing from a vine on the other side. I offered a hand to Shim, who pushed it aside and climbed over the jumble of rocks unaided.

T'eilean's expression became serious again. "These are dangerous times to travel in Fincayra. You must be either very brave or very foolish."

I nodded. "Time will tell which we are. But may I ask about you? If it's dangerous to travel here, it must be more so to live here."

"Too true." T'eilean beckoned to Garlatha to join him. "But where could we go? My wife and I have lived here together for sixty-eight years. Our roots are deep, as deep as these trees." With a wave at their unadorned home, he added, "Besides, we have no treasure."

"Not that could be stolen, that is." Garlatha took his arm, smiling at him. "Our treasure is too big for any chest, and more precious than any jewels."

T'eilean nodded. "You are right, my lady." Leaning toward me, he grinned mischievously. "She is always right. Even when she is wrong."

Garlatha kicked him hard in the shin.

"*Owww,*" he howled, rubbing the spot. "After sixty-eight years, you should have learned some manners!"

"After sixty-eight years, I have learned to see right through you."

Garlatha looked at him full in the face. Slowly, she grinned. "Yet, somehow, I still like what I see."

The old man's dark eyes glittered. "Come now, what of our guests? Can we offer you a place to sit? Anything to eat?"

I shook my head. "We have no time for sitting, I'm afraid." I pointed toward the spiral-shaped fruits dangling from the branch. "I would take one of those, though. I had that kind once before and it was wonderful."

T'eilean reached up and, with surprising dexterity, plucked one of the fruits with his large, wrinkled hand. As he gave it to me, he said, "You may certainly have this, but you have not had its kind, the larkon, before."

Puzzled, I shook my head.

"These grow nowhere else in Fincayra," explained the gardener, his voice solemn. "Years ago, long before you were born, trees bearing them dotted the hills east of the River Unceasing. But they have succumbed to the Blight that has afflicted the rest of our land. All but this one."

I took a bite of the fruit. The flavor like purple sunshine burst inside my mouth. "There is one other place this fruit still grows, and there I have eaten it before."

In unison, T'eilean and Garlatha asked, "Where?"

"In Druma Wood, at the shomorra tree."

"The shomorra?" sputtered Garlatha. "You have truly been there, to the rarest of trees?"

"A friend who knows it well took me there."

T'eilean stroked his wispy beard. "If that is true, you have a remarkable friend."

My face tightened. "I do."

A slight breeze stirred the branch above me, rustling the living leaves. I listened for a moment. I felt like a man, deprived of water for days, who finally heard the sound of a burbling stream. Suddenly, Shim reached up and yanked the spiral fruit from my hand. Before I could protest, he took two large bites.

I glared at him. "Don't you know how to ask?"

"*Mmmpppff*," said the little giant through a mouthful of fruit.

Garlatha's eyes shone with amusement. Turning to her husband, she said, "It appears that I am not the only one without manners."

"You are right," he answered. Hobbling a few steps away, he added with equal amusement, "As always."

Garlatha grinned. Her strong arm reached up to the branch, picked another spiral fruit, and handed it to me. "Here. You can start again."

"You are most generous, especially if this is the last tree of this kind east of the Druma." I sniffed the larkon's zesty fragrance, then took a bite. Once again, my tongue exploded with sunny flavor. Savoring the taste, I asked, "How has your garden survived so well in the midst of this Blight? It's a miracle."

The couple traded glances.

T'eilean's face hardened. "It is no more of a miracle than all of these lands once were. But our wicked king has changed all that."

"It has broken our hearts to watch," said Garlatha, her voice cracking.

"Stangmar's Shroud blocks out the sun," continued the old man. "More with each passing month. For as the Shrouded Castle grows in power, the sky grows ever darker. Meanwhile, his armies have sown death across the land. Whole villages have been destroyed. People have fled to the mountains far to the west, or left Fincayra altogether. A vast forest, as remarkable as Druma Wood, once grew on those hills to the east. No more! What trees have not been slaughtered or burned have retreated into slumber, never to speak again. Here on the plains, what soil has not been soaked with blood has taken on its very color. And the Flowering Harp, that could perhaps coax the land back to life, has been stolen from us."

He looked down at his weathered hands. "I carried the Harp only once, when I was just a boy. But after all these years, I still cannot forget the feel of its strings. Nor the thrill of its melody."

He grimaced. "All that and more is lost." He motioned toward the cleft in the hill behind the hut. "See our once joyous spring! Hardly a trickle. As the land has withered, so has the water that nourished it. Half of my day I now spend hauling water from afar."

Garlatha took his hand. "As I spend half of mine searching the dry prairie for seeds that still may be revived."

Awkwardly, Shim offered to her the remains of his fruit. "I is sorry for you."

Garlatha patted his unruly head. "Keep the fruit now. And do not feel sorry for us. We are far more fortunate than most."

"That we are," agreed her husband. "We have been granted a long life together, and a chance to grow a few trees. That is all anyone could ask for." He glanced at her. "That and our one remaining wish, that one day we might die together."

"Like Baucis and Philemon," I observed.

"Who?"

"Baucis and Philemon. They are characters in a story from the Greeks, a story I learned from . . . my mother, long ago. They had but one wish, to die together. And in the end the gods turned them into a pair of trees whose leafy branches would wrap around each other for all time."

"How beautiful," Garlatha sighed, looking at her husband.

T'eilean said nothing, though he studied me closely.

"But you have not told me," I continued, "how your garden has survived in this terrible time."

T'eilean released Garlatha's hand and opened his sinewy arms to the greenery, the roots, the blossoms surrounding them. "We have loved our garden, that is all."

I nodded, thinking how wondrous this region must have been before the Blight. If the garden where Shim and I now stood was only a small sampling of its riches, the landscape would have been as beautiful—though not as wild and mysterious—as the Druma itself. The kind of place where I would have felt alive. And free. And possibly even at home.

Garlatha observed us worriedly. "Are you certain you cannot rest here for a while?"

"No. We cannot."

"Then you must be extremely careful," warned T'eilean. "Goblins are everywhere these days. Only yesterday, at sunset, when I was coming back with water, I saw a pair of them. They were dragging away a helpless girl."

My heart stopped. "A girl? What did she look like?"

The white-bearded man looked pained. "I could not get very close, or they would have seen me. Yet, while I watched, part of me wanted to attack them with all my strength."

"I am glad you did not," declared his wife.

T'eilean pointed at me. "The girl was about your age. Long, curly brown hair. And she wore a suit that seemed to be made of woven vines."

Shim and I gasped.

"Rhia," I whispered hoarsely. "Where were they going?"

"There can be no doubt," the old man answered dismally. "They were traveling east. And since the girl was alive at all, she must be someone Stangmar wants to deal with personally."

Garlatha moaned. "I cannot bear the thought of a young girl at that terrible castle."

I felt for the dagger in my satchel. "We must go now."

T'eilean extended his hand to me, clasping my own with unexpected firmness. "I do not know who you are, young man, nor where you are going. But I suspect that, like one of our seeds, you hold much more within than you show without."

Garlatha touched Shim's head again. "The same, I think, could be said for this little fellow."

I did not reply, although I wondered whether they would have spoken so kindly to us if they had known us better. Even so, as I crossed over the crumbling wall, I found myself hoping that I might one day see them again. I turned to wave to the elderly couple. They waved back, then resumed their work.

I noticed that the Galator felt warm against my chest. Peeking under my tunic, I saw that its jeweled center was glowing ever so slightly. And I knew that Cairpré's theory about the Galator was true.

THEN CAME
A SCREAM

For several hours, we trekked toward the notch in the ridge, my staff rhythmically punching the dry soil and dead grass. A cold wind out of the Dark Hills blew down on us. Its bitter gusts slapped our faces. Despite the wind, Shim did his best to stay by my side. Even so, I had to stop several times to help him through some thorny bracken or up a steep pitch.

As the land sloped increasingly upward, the wind blew ever more fiercely. Soon it smacked with such piercing cold that my hand holding my staff no longer pulsed with pain, but started to go numb. It felt as wooden as the staff itself. Flying bits of ice began to whip against us. I lifted my free arm to protect my cheeks and sightless eyes.

The bits of ice turned into needles, then shards, then daggers. As the icy blades rained down on us, Shim, who had resisted complaining since leaving the garden, whined piteously. But I could only hear him in the lulls between gusts, for the howling of the wind grew fiercer.

Although it remained light enough for my second sight to help, the swirling ice and blowing dirt confused my sense of direction. Suddenly I stumbled against a low, flat outcropping of some sort. With a cry, I crumpled to the ground, dropping my staff.

Shivering, I crawled over to the outcropping, hoping to use it as a slight shelter against the storm. Shim tucked himself into the folds of my tunic. We sat there, our teeth chattering from the cold, for minutes that seemed like weeks.

In time, the ice storm abated. The howling wind hurled itself at us a few last times, then finally retreated. Although the air seemed no warmer, our bodies slowly revived. I opened and closed my hands, which made my palms and fingertips sting. Hesitantly, Shim poked his head out of my tunic, his wild hair embedded with icicles.

All at once, I realized that the outcropping that had partially shielded us was nothing more than an immense tree stump. All around us, thousands of such stumps littered the hills, separated by a vast web of eroded gullies. Though frosted with a glaze of ice, the stumps did not sparkle or gleam. They merely sat there, as lifeless as burial mounds.

In a flash, I understood. This was all that remained of the vast forest that T'eilean had described. *Stangmar's armies have sown death across the land.* The old man's words lifted like ghosts out of the rotting stumps, the blood red soil, the broken hills.

Shim and I looked at each other. Without a word, we stood up on the frosted ground. I picked up my staff, knocking a chunk of ice off the top. Then I located the notch again, stepped over the brittle remains of a branch, and started up the slippery terrain. Shim scrambled to stay with me, muttering under his breath.

As the day wore on, we continued to climb, over hills scarred with countless stumps and dry streambeds. All the while, the sky grew darker. Soon the notch disappeared, swallowed in the deepening darkness. I could only trust my memory of where I had last glimpsed its two sharp knobs, though that memory itself was fading with the light.

Slowly, we gained elevation. Despite the dim light, I detected a few thin trees rising amidst the stumps and dead branches. Their twisted forms resembled people writhing in pain. Seeing one tree wearing the bark of a beech, I approached it. Laying my hand on the trunk, I made the swishing, rustling sound that Rhia had taught me in Druma Wood.

The tree did not respond.

I tried again. This time, as I made the swishes, I imagined the living, breathing presence of a healthy tree before me. The powerful roots thrusting into the soil. The arching branches lifting toward the sky. The deep-throated song rising through the trunk, thrilling each and every leaf.

Perhaps it was just my imagination, but I thought I could sense the barest beginnings of a quiver in the uppermost branches. Yet if they had actually moved, they quickly fell still again.

Giving up, I trudged on. Shim huffed at my heels. As we climbed the rising slope, the ground grew more rocky. With each passing minute, the light dimmed further. The sky blackened, while the stumps and rocks around us melted into shadows.

Although my second sight was swiftly fading, I fought to see whatever I still could. And with all my concentration, I listened. I knew that any movement, no matter how slight, could provide our only warning of attack. As I tried to avoid tripping on rocks and snapping dead branches, my steps grew less certain.

Ahead, I discerned a barely visible gap, where twin knobs of dark rock lifted into the still darker sky. Might it be the notch? I edged closer, as quietly as I could.

Abruptly, I stopped. I stood as still as one of the twisted trees, listening.

Shim crept to my side. "You hears something?"

"Not sure," I whispered. "I thought I did, somewhere ahead of us."

Minutes passed. I heard no sound apart from our breathing and the thumping of my own heart.

Eventually, I touched the little giant's arm. "Let's go," I whispered. "But keep quiet. Goblins are near."

"Oooh," moaned Shim. "I is scared. Certainly, definitely, abs—"

"Quiet!"

Out of the shadows ahead of us came a raspy cry and a sudden pounding of feet. Torches flared, searing the darkness.

"Goblins!"

Across the rocky ridge we fled. Dead branches snapped under our feet. Thorns ripped at our shins. I could hear, just behind, the heaving of the goblins' chests, the clanking of their armor, the sputtering of their torches.

Shim and I tore across the rocks, trying not to stumble. Darkness pressed closer. We did not know where we were going, nor did we care. We only knew that the goblins were gaining on us.

In a desperate effort to lose them, I veered sharply to one side. Shim followed closely, and we crossed over the ridge. The vista before us could not have been more chilling. Against the darkened sky, more hills loomed even darker. Worse yet, the valley below us looked utterly black, but for the glint of hundreds of tiny lights. Despite the goblins at our backs, we hesitated for an instant.

A spear whizzed past, passing between my head and the top of my staff. Even as the spear clattered against the ground, to a chorus of raspy curses, we plunged down the slope. My foot struck a rock and I fell, sprawling. Shim waited long enough for me to roll back to my feet, grab my staff, and resume running. We charged downward into the black valley.

Total darkness swept over us like a wave. The ground became wet and mushy under our feet. The air turned rancid. Before long we splashed through something like an enormous puddle, covering a bed of oozing murk.

All at once I halted, causing Shim to run straight into my back. "What is you stopping for?" he demanded angrily.

"Listen."

"I hears nothing, except the throbbings of my tenderly nose."

"That's just it. The goblins stopped. Somewhere back there."

"You is right." The little giant shifted nervously in the murk. "Do you think they is scared to goes here?"

I felt something cold oozing into my leather boots. "We may be in . . . the Haunted Marsh."

As if in answer, a faint, wavering light appeared some distance away. It hovered in the darkness, seeming to examine us. Then another appeared, followed by another. Soon more than twenty of the eerie lights swam around us, moving slowly closer.

Shim squeezed my hand.

A reeking smell, like festering flesh, drifted over us. I gagged, my lungs rebelling. As the lights drew nearer, the smell grew stronger.

Then came a thin, unsteady wailing. An ancient dirge pulsing with anguish, with undying pain. The wailing made me cringe, as it welled out of the ground, the lights, the rotting air. It came from one side. It came from the other. It came from every direction at once.

Shim released a terrified shriek. Letting go of my hand, he dashed away from the cluster of floating lights.

"Wait!"

I hurled myself after him. I had only gone a few steps, however, when something caught my foot. I tumbled headlong into a puddle of slimy liquid. Pulling myself and my staff free, I shook the murk from my arms. They stunk of mold and decay.

The ominous lights circled, gathering again. The wailing swelled. The stench of death flooded over me.

"Shim!"

No answer.

"Shim!"

Then came a scream.

The lights pressed closer, staring down on me like so many eyes. So this was how my quest would end! I would have rather drowned in the sea off the coast of Gwynedd than die like this, wretched and alone.

Yet the loss of my own quest pained me less than the loss of Rhia. She, like the brave merlin, had given her life for me. I did not deserve such friendship. Yet she did not deserve to die. She was so full of life, so full of wisdom that I did not begin to comprehend. The pain of losing her made my heart sting, as if it were on fire.

Suddenly I realized that the Galator was blazing with heat against my chest. I tore it out of my tunic and held it high. The jeweled center sparkled with its own green light, pushing back the darkness just enough that I could see my own hand and arm.

The eerie lights faltered, stopped their advance. The wailing ceased. A touch of freshness wafted on the air. At the same time, the Galator's glow started to expand. In a few seconds, the circle of green illuminated my entire body as well as my staff.

"Shim! Where are you?"

"Here!" Soaked in murk, he staggered to my side. His chest, legs, arms, and one side of his face dripped with black ooze.

As the glowing circle expanded, the floating lights wavered, then slowly drew back into the darkness. The wailing resumed, but transformed into an angry murmur.

Heartened by the retreat of the lights, I pressed ahead. I would find some way out of this swamp, whatever it took.

Holding the Galator above my head with one hand, grasping my staff with the other, I made sure Shim held tight to my tunic. Then I started to trudge through the marshy pools. The mud was soft and sticky, sucking at my boots. Suddenly I stepped into a shallow pit. I fell forward with a splash, almost dropping the pendant. Instantly the eyes of light crowded closer and the murmur swelled louder.

As I regained my balance, the menacing lights pulled back a little. It took me a moment to extract my staff from the grasping mud of the pit, though it finally came free with a loud slurp. We slogged onward. I could tell, however, that Shim could not travel very far in this terrain. Although he was struggling to stay with me, the water was up to his waist, and the work of pushing through it was tiring him fast.

My own legs, as well as the arm holding the Galator, began to feel increasingly heavy. Nevertheless, I helped Shim climb up to the shoulder of my arm holding the staff. It was the same shoulder that Trouble had once claimed as his perch. But this load felt much heavier than the hawk ever did.

Each step grew more difficult, each breath more labored. I felt weaker and weaker, as if the marsh itself was sapping my strength. My shoulder ached. The murk from Shim's legs dripped onto my face, while the rancid taste burned my tongue.

As my stamina faded, the lights pressed ever closer. The murmur swelled, like a pack of wolves howling in my ears. The marsh seemed endless, stretching far beyond the limits of my flagging endurance.

My powers! Should I try to use them? I needed them so much. Yet I feared them so much. The flames rose again in my mind, snapping at my face, searing my flesh, scorching my eyes.

Suddenly I stumbled. I fell to my knees, barely hanging on to both my staff and the Galator. Shim gave a shout and clung to my neck, sobbing. Again the lights crowded around, waiting to see if I would rise again.

With all my remaining strength, I pushed myself out of the slime. I tried to lift the Galator, but could not bring it higher than my chest. I took another exhausted step—and stumbled again.

I heard the Galator smack against something hard, like stone. I heard Shim scream as the murmur grew almost deafening.

Then I heard no more.

DARK FATE

Is you alive?"

"Not sure," was my only answer. I sat up and shook the fog from my second sight. Shim sat on one side while my staff, caked with rancid-smelling mud, lay on the other.

Shim, his small face lined with worry, pulled on my tunic. "Where is we?"

Surveying our surroundings, I took in the strangest room I had ever seen. Polished stone walls, floor, and ceiling enclosed us, without even a slit for a window. Yet a quivering blue light filled the room, like the light from a candle just before it burns out. But no candle could be seen.

I shivered, though not from cold. I could not be certain why, but a feeling of foreboding hung in the air. As if Shim and I were about to be sliced up for someone's supper.

Shim slid closer. "This place is frighteningly. Like a dungeon."

"I agree."

Suddenly he pointed. "Bones!"

With a start, I viewed the shadowy pile next to us. It was indeed a mass of bones, picked perfectly clean. In the quivering light I could make out ribs, leg bones, and more than a few skulls. People's skulls.

I swallowed, wondering whether our own remains would soon rest there.

Then I noticed that several other piles, though not of bones, surrounded us. One held thin slabs of gray stone, stacked almost as tall as my staff. Another contained polished balls of wood, carved in varied sizes and etched with strange signs. Some smaller than fingernails and others larger than heads, the balls seemed to have been carefully arranged for some purpose. Still another pile contained bundles of sticks, sorted by size as well as number. In the far corner of the room, I noticed strange white cubes marked with black dots on their sides. Spools of black and white yarn were piled here, bizarre shells from the sea there. Iron bowls overflowed with pebbles and seeds of many shapes.

In the middle of the floor sat a thick, square rug that was divided into smaller red and black squares. On many of these squares stood carved wooden pieces, each of them about as high as my waist. Attacking dragons, galloping horses, howling wolves, warring goblins, kings and queens, plus others I could not begin to recognize. Back in Caer Vedwyd, I had heard of the game called *esches,* sometimes shortened to *chess,* but that game was played on a board, not a rug. And in any event, chess pieces did not include dragons. Or goblins.

On the stone wall opposite us, a dense jumble of blue markings wavered in the light. Columns of slashes, dots, and squiggles, running in several directions, covered much of the surface. There were thousands of squares, triangles, and meshes of crossed lines, as well as circles divided into sections, much as a round loaf of bread is sliced. There were runes, letters, numbers, and symbols squeezed over and under, inside and outside, the rest of the markings.

"Too bad," growled a deep voice behind us.

We spun around to see a pale, hairless head poking through the crack of a door. Slowly, the door swung open, revealing a body as round as the head, wearing a robe resembling a cloth sack with several pockets, a necklace of rough stones, and bare feet. I froze, fearful that this was another shifting wraith. Or perhaps something worse.

The hairless head, with rows of wrinkles gathering about two triangular ears, leaned toward us. One large, shriveled wart sprouted like a horn from the middle of the forehead. Eyes even blacker than my own watched us, unblinking, for several seconds. Then the mouth full of misshapen teeth opened again. "Definitely too bad."

Reaching for my staff, I scrambled to my feet, which was made more difficult by Shim's clinging to my leg. "Who are you?"

"Almost no chance they'll live out the day," muttered the strange figure, entering the room. "Definitely too bad."

Though my voice quaked, I repeated my question. "Who are you?"

The black eyes, seeming terribly old, observed me for a moment. "That's a difficult question, my pet."

Something about the words *my pet* made me cringe.

"Who am I?" continued the creature, pacing slowly around us like a vulture examining its carrion. "Hard to tell. Even for me. Today I'm someone, tomorrow someone else." The wrinkled face bent toward me, showing more crooked teeth. "And who are you?"

I gave a sigh. "The truth is, I'm not really sure."

"At least, my pet, you are honest." The circling continued, the bare feet slapping on the stone floor. "Perhaps I can tell you a bit about who you are. Though I should warn you, it's rather disappointing. For starters, you are too skinny to provide more than a mouthful or two, even with your little friend thrown in."

Shim squeezed my leg harder.

"Worse still, my pet, you look far too weak to be of any help to my wager. And I do *so* detest losing."

An icy finger ran down my spine. "I know who you are. You are Domnu."

"Very clever, my pet." The hairless hag stopped circling. She ran a hand across the top of her head, ruminating. "But cleverness won't be enough to win my wager."

"What wager are you talking about?"

"Oh, nothing of any importance. I merely made a little wager with someone who expects you not to survive until tomorrow." She shrugged. "Die today. Die tomorrow. What difference does it make? I should not have bet on you, but I could not resist the odds."

I shuddered, remembering what Cairpré had said about this being whose name means Dark Fate. *Neither good nor evil, friend nor foe. She simply is.* "Who did you wager against?"

Domnu's bare feet slapped across the stone floor as she moved to the wall covered with strange markings, still trembling in the unsteady light. She spat on the index finger of her left hand, which immediately turned blue. Then, using the finger as a paintbrush, she stretched to reach as high as she could and drew a squiggly line through one of the circles.

"Time to start using a new wall," she grumbled. With a glance in our direction, she added, "Must keep score, my pets. I do dislike losing a wager, but I must keep score. And it certainly does look like I will lose this one."

"You mean," piped Shim, "that we is going to die?"

Domnu shrugged again. "It certainly looks that way."

I demanded, "Who did you wager against?"

"No one you know. Although he does seem to have developed a genuine dislike for you."

"Who?"

She scratched the back of her bald head. "That fool Rhita Gawr, of course."

"Rhita Gawr? The spirit battling Dagda?"

Domnu grunted carelessly. "I suppose so. At least it was so a few thousand years ago when last I checked. But as to who is winning and who is losing, my pet, I have no idea. They must keep their own tallies."

"But it's not a game! It's serious."

Domnu stiffened. "Games *are* serious, my pet. As serious as life itself, for that too is just a game."

"You don't understand." I stepped closer, with Shim still holding tight to my leg. "Their battle is for all of Fincayra. As well as the Earth. And more beyond that."

"Yes, yes," said the hag, yawning. "They have an ongoing wager."

"No! It's more than that."

She stared at me, dumbfounded. "More than that? How can anything be more than that? A wager is the purest chance of all! Make your choice, place your bet. Then whatever happens, happens. Up or down. Life or death. It doesn't matter, as long as you collect your winnings in the end."

I shook my head. "It *does* matter. Whether Dagda or Rhita Gawr wins will determine—"

"What the odds will be on their next wager. Yes, I know."

Domnu's feet slapped over to the rug of red and white squares. She bent low to face one of the pieces, the figure of a red dragon. Nonchalantly, she tickled under its scaly chin. In the quivering light, I could not be sure, but it almost seemed that the dragon's head jerked slightly, and that two thin trails of smoke drifted out of its nostrils.

"Their little game is of no interest to me," she concluded, even as she gave the dragon's ear a tweak. "I have enough trouble keeping track of my own."

Shim clutched tighter. "I is scared. Very, very, very scared."

"I don't know why you should be," replied Domnu with a crooked grin. "Dying isn't so bad after the first time."

She placed her foot on the back of the dragon piece, reached for the figure of the black king, and grabbed it roughly by the neck. I could have been mistaken, but as she lifted the king off the rug, I thought I heard a faint, anguished squeal. Still grasping the neck, she began polishing the king's crown on her sacklike robe. "I suppose we should play a game of some kind before I send you on your way, my pets. It will take our minds off your impending deaths and my impending loss. Do you prefer dice or sticks?"

"We need your help," I pleaded.

She replaced the black king, dropping the piece with a thud. Then, feet slapping on the floor, she ambled over to the pile of sticks. She plucked a small bundle from the pile and contemplated it. "I think threes would be better than thirteens today, don't you? I have the feeling in my bones that this is a low number day. Bones! Perhaps you would rather play bones?"

"Please! We need to get to the Shrouded Castle."

"The Shrouded Castle?" She pulled a stick from the bundle and spat on it. "Why ever would you want to go there?"

"A goodly question," muttered Shim, hugging my shin.

"Besides," Domnu continued, all the while examining the stick, "if I send you there, then you will *certainly* die and I will lose my wager."

"Won't you please help us?"

"I am afraid not, my pet." She twirled the stick in the palm of her hand.

I scowled. "If you're not going to help us, then why don't you just put us back in the Haunted Marsh and get it over with?"

Shim looked up at me with amazement.

"I may well, my pet. After all, I did promise Rhita Gawr that I would not keep you safe here all day. Rules of the wager, you understand. And I never break the rules." She lowered her voice. "Besides, he would notice if I did."

She inserted the stick back into the bundle, then tossed it carelessly onto the pile. "But why the hurry? We still have time for a game or two."

"We do not have time!" I exclaimed. "Isn't there any way we can convince you?"

"The only question," she went on, scanning the room, "is which game to choose. Of course! Chess! Though I don't suppose you know anything about the rules, young as you are. No matter. Just come over here and I will teach you a bit. And bring that brave warrior there. The one clinging to your leg."

She walked back over to the rug and glanced around at the chess pieces. "Too tall, I think."

With an expression of concentration, she placed the palm of her hand on the crown of the red queen. She muttered a phrase softly, then began to press slowly downward. To my astonishment, the red queen—as well as all the other chess pieces—grew steadily smaller, until they were only half of their original size. Now the tallest pieces were about the same height as Shim.

Proudly, Domnu waved at the chess pieces. "It really is one of my better inventions, this game. A great success wherever it goes. Even the humans, with their limited powers of concentration, have adopted it. Though it grieves me to see how they try to oversimplify the rules of the game. The only drawback is that it is best played with two people. And finding the right partner can be very difficult indeed."

Raising her thin eyebrows, she sent waves of wrinkles across the top of her scalp. "Especially if you have as few visitors as I do. By the way, most of my visitors come by the front door. What ever possessed you to use the back door? I might never have found you, if you hadn't knocked on the doorstep."

"I didn't knock."

"Of course you did! Though I almost didn't hear you with that awful din outside."

"But I didn't knock."

"My pet, you are forgetful! You knocked with something hard. It must have been your head. Or perhaps that unattractive little pendant of yours."

Suddenly remembering the Galator, I clutched it tightly. It was no longer glowing. Swiftly I replaced it under my tunic.

"I might have left you there, but I haven't had any company for games in so long. Two centuries at least! Then, after I brought you in, I realized you must be the ones Rhita Gawr had wagered would not survive the day, if you should ever turn up here." Her ancient eyes narrowed. "I only wish I had seen you before I agreed to the wager."

Domnu started pacing around the rug, inspecting each of the

chess pieces carefully. Although the wavering light made the whole room seem to vibrate, it struck me that each of the chess pieces trembled slightly as she approached. Then, when she passed in back of a gallant looking black stallion, the horse seemed to shift its hind leg ever so slightly. Instantly, Domnu whirled around.

"You wouldn't be wanting to kick me, now, would you?" The black eyes flashed, as she ran her finger slowly down the horse's mane. "No, your manners are better than that. Much better. You must be wanting a bit more weight on your back. Yes, I am certain that's it."

The barest whinny seemed to come from the stallion. Its carved muscles almost tensed.

Domnu bent over it and blew a long, gentle breath. Out of nowhere, a rough black stone, half the size of the horse itself, appeared on the middle of its back. While the stallion seemed to sag under the weight, it continued to hold its head high.

"There now," declared Domnu. "That's much better."

She spun to face me. "Time for a little game of chess," she said in a voice more threatening than inviting. "Before I return you to your, shall we say, friends waiting outside. You make the first move."

THE WAGER

My heart pounded. I could not bring myself to step onto the rug with Domnu.

"Come, my pet. I don't have all day." She smirked, baring her uneven teeth. "Neither do you."

"Don't goes near her," whispered Shim frantically.

"I am waiting," growled Domnu.

Perspiration beaded on my brow. What was I to do? Maybe, if I humored her, I could still find some way to win her help. Yet no sooner had I formed this thought than I knew it was impossible. Domnu would never send us to the castle, for she believed that to do so would guarantee that we would lose our lives—and she her wager. And, I admitted grimly to myself, she was probably right.

Even so, dragging a whimpering Shim with me, I moved toward the edge of the rug. I had no idea what to do next, either about Domnu's game or my own quest to help Rhia. I only knew that we had traveled too far, survived too much, to give up before trying every possibility.

When I reached the edge of the rug, Domnu pointed to the black horse weighed down by the stone. "Make your move," she commanded.

"But—but," I stammered, "I don't know the rules."

"That has not stopped you before, I'll wager."

Unsure of her meaning, I tried again. "Can you tell me the rules?"

"The way I play, you can make up your own rules. Until you break one of mine, that is."

I faltered. "I don't know how to begin."

"In the game of chess, unlike the game of life, you get to choose how you begin."

"But what if I choose poorly?"

"Ah," she said, wrinkling her scalp. "In that way the two games are quite alike. One way or another, your choice will make all the difference."

Drawing a deep breath, I stepped onto the rug of red and black squares. Hesitantly, I laid down my staff. Then, with effort, I lifted the black stallion and carried it all the way over to the other side of the rug. I placed it on a square directly in front of the red king.

"Hmmm," observed Domnu. "You chose a very risky move, my pet." She eyed me curiously. "Though no more risky than storming the Shrouded Castle without an army."

She shoved the red king to a square where he could hide behind a pair of goblins. "You must have some sort of reason."

"I do. It is—"

"A terrible shame you are so eager to die. Especially when you are just learning how to play the game. Normally, I would be quite happy to help you die sooner. But a wager is a wager."

"What if I made you a wager myself?"

Domnu scratched her hairless head. "What kind of wager?"

"Well," I replied, my mind racing, "If you can get me to the castle—"

"Us," corrected Shim. Although his whole body was quaking, he let go of my leg and stood on his own beside me. "We goes together. I is still feeling the same old madness."

I nodded at him, then turned back to Domnu. "If you can get us to the castle, then I will wager you that . . . that we will *still* survive this day. Even with Stangmar and all his goblins and ghouliants there to greet us. You could wager the opposite, that we won't succeed."

Domnu pulled thoughtfully on one of her ears. "Ah, so you are raising the stakes, are you?"

"That's right."

"And what happens if you don't survive the day?"

"Well, then you would have lost one wager, against Rhita Gawr, but you will have won another, against me. So at the end of the day, you will be no worse off. Whereas if you *don't* wager me, you will finish the day merely having lost."

She frowned. "Not a chance! What sort of a novice wagerer do you take me for, boy? I am giving you something of value by sending you to the castle. Whether or not you win, you get that much. And what do I get? Nothing."

My face fell. "But I have nothing to give you."

"Too bad." Her head wrinkled. "Time for your next move."

"Wait." I pulled out the dagger from Honn. "You could take this."

Domnu frowned again, waving it away. "A weapon? Why would I ever need that?"

"Then what about this?" I removed the satchel that Branwen had given to me. "These herbs are good for healing."

Domnu hissed. "What use would I have for such a thing?"

As I picked up my staff, she declared, "I have no need of that, either."

I knew well that my one truly valuable possession was the Galator. I suspected that Domnu knew it also. Yet . . . if I parted with that, my quest would be ruined.

"Here," said Shim, starting to peel off his baggy shirt of woven bark. "You can keeps this. Made by my own mother, when I is a babesy." He sighed. "A shame I never outgrows it."

Domnu scowled. "Keep it yourself." The black eyes probed me. "If you have nothing more to offer, then we have nothing more to discuss. Except, of course, the game of chess."

My head was whirling. While I knew almost nothing about the Galator's powers, they were clearly extraordinary. *Vast beyond knowing,* Cairpré had said. I could not possibly part with this, the last Treasure! It had already saved our lives once. It might well do so again. Besides, if Stangmar wanted it so badly, I might somehow be able to use it to bargain for Rhia's life. Though I had no way of knowing if she was still alive, I could be sure that, without the Galator, I could never save her. Moreover, this jeweled pendant had been worn by my own mother. She had given it to me to keep, to protect. To give it away would also be to give away some of her love for me.

And yet . . . if I did not offer it to Domnu, she would never help me. And I could not possibly reach the castle without her help! So I, in turn, could not help Rhia. Then again, what good was it to reach the castle without the Galator?

"Your move." She nudged me impatiently. "Make your move."

"All right, I will." Slowly, I removed the Galator from my neck. "You know this pendant, don't you?"

Domnu yawned, showing all her unruly teeth. "I have seen it a few times over the ages, yes. What about it?"

"Then you also know its value."

The hag remained dispassionate. "I have heard rumors."

Shim tugged hard on my tunic. "Don't do this! This is foolishly!"

Ignoring him, I declared, "I will wager you . . . with the Galator. If you can get us to the castle of Stangmar, I will . . ." I choked on the words. "I will give it to you."

The black eyes swelled.

"No!" cried Shim. "We needs it!"

I took a step toward her. "But if either Shim or I should ever return to you alive, no matter how much time has passed, then you must give the Galator back." Grasping the leather cord, I held up the pendant. Its jewels gleamed darkly in the shifting light. "Those are the terms of my wager."

Domnu clucked, as if she were about to swallow something tasty. "And if you should ever return—which I doubt, my pet—you would trust me to give it back to you?"

"No!" protested Shim.

I regarded her sternly. "You said you never break the rules."

"That is true." Then she added in passing, "With minor exceptions here and there, of course." All of a sudden her hand shot out and snatched the pendant. "You have a wager."

My heart sank. The Galator was gone.

Domnu gazed briefly into the Galator, her eyes reflecting its green hue. She plunged it into one of the sagging pockets in her robe. Then she smiled the smile of someone who has just won a grand wager.

For my part, I felt sure that I had just given away my last, best hope. "You wanted that all the time," I said bitterly.

"I suppose that is true, my pet."

"Why didn't you just take it from me, then? Why did you drag it out like this?"

Domnu looked offended. "Me? Take something that does not belong to me? Never!" She patted the pocket with the Galator. "Besides, the Galator must be given freely. Not stolen. Or else its powers are useless. Did no one ever tell you that?"

I shook my head.

"Too bad." She released an extended yawn. "Definitely too bad."

"Let's get on with your part," I said grimly. "How are you going to get us to the castle?"

"You wouldn't mind a slight delay, would you?" she asked. "I am feeling quite tired at the moment."

"Delay!"

"Yes." She yawned again. "Just until tomorrow sometime."

"No! You promised!"

"That's dishonestly!"

She scrutinized us for a moment. "Well, all right. I suppose I can get you there today. But you should be ashamed for denying a poor old woman her much needed rest." Her bald head wrinkled in thought. "The only question is how to do it."

She patted the top of her head, her dark eyes roaming around the room. "Ah, that's it. Wings. You will need wings. Perhaps even a pair you are accustomed to."

My heart leaped, as I wondered whether she might be referring to the legendary wings that Cairpré had told me about. Was Domnu about to restore to me what all Fincayrans had lost long ago? I flexed my shoulders in anticipation.

Her feet slapped across the floor to the doorway. She opened the heavy door, reached into the darkness, and pulled out a compact iron cage. It contained a small, tattered hawk. A merlin.

"Trouble!"

I rushed at the cage. The bird flapped and whistled enthusiastically, ripping at the iron bars with his talons.

"Let him out," I pleaded, my fingers stroking the warm feathers through the bars.

"Careful," warned Domnu. "He is feisty, this one. A real fighter. Small in body, large in spirit. He could rip you to shreds if he chose."

"Not me he won't."

She shrugged. "If you insist."

She tapped the cage lightly and it instantly disappeared. Trouble found himself falling, but caught himself just before he hit the floor. With two flaps and a whistle, he landed on the top of my staff, before hopping down to my left shoulder. With his feathered neck, he nuzzled my ear. Then he turned to Domnu and raked the air angrily with his talons.

"How did you find him?" I asked.

She scratched the wart on her forehead. "He found me, though I have no idea how. He looked, well, rather feeble when he arrived. Like someone had tried to make him into mincemeat. How the little wretch could fly at all is a miracle. I fixed him up a bit, hoping I might be able to teach him to play dice. But the ungrateful savage refused to cooperate."

At this, Trouble whistled sharply and clawed the air again.

"Yes, yes, I threw him in the cage against his will. But it was for his own good."

Trouble whistled another reprimand.

"And for my own protection! When I told him I had no interest in finding his friend, he flew at me. Tried to attack me! I could have turned him into a worm right then and there, but I decided to keep him around in case his manners improved. At any rate, he should prove useful to us now."

Puzzled, Trouble and I cocked our heads in unison.

"I should warn you," Domnu continued, "that while I can get you to the castle, I cannot get you *into* the castle. That much you will have to do on your own. Not to mention getting out again."

She peeked inside the pocket holding the Galator. "Since I will not be seeing you again, allow me to thank you for giving me this."

I sighed, but the familiar weight on my shoulder tempered my sadness. I indicated the bird. "And thank you for giving me this."

Domnu slid toward us. As Trouble eyed her warily, she placed her hands on both my head and Shim's. With the same look of concentration she had shown when shrinking the chess pieces, she started muttering.

All at once, I felt myself growing smaller. Beyond Shim's shriek, I heard Domnu calling some sort of instructions to Trouble. In a flash, the hawk was no longer riding on my shoulder. Instead, it was I who was riding on Trouble's feathery shoulder, flying high above the Dark Hills.

XXXIV

FLIGHT

Flying through the darkness, I wrapped my arms tightly around Trouble's neck. By the angle of the bird's back, I could tell that we were steadily gaining altitude. In one hand I held my staff, now almost as small as myself. I wondered where Shim might be at this moment, hoping that he was at least safe.

Chilled air flowed over us, so strongly that my sightless eyes began to water, sending thin streams of tears across my cheeks and over my ears. Neck feathers quivered with every gust, brushing against my face and hands. Being no larger than Trouble's own head, I realized that the hawk's feathers were much more than the soft, fluffy plumage they had once seemed. Each quill combined the flexibility of a branch with the sturdiness of a bone.

Gradually, the motions of the body bearing me became my own. With every upstroke of the powerful wings, I inhaled. With every downstroke, I exhaled. I could feel Trouble's shoulder and back muscles tense before each beat, then spring into action with startling strength.

As we flew, I listened with all my concentration to hear whatever I could in the blackness. I felt surprised to realize how little sound the beating wings themselves made. Only a quiet *whoosh* of air accompanied every downstroke, the barest creak of shoulder bones every upstroke.

For the first time in my life, I tasted the freedom of flight. The surrounding darkness only enhanced my sensation of soaring without limits, without boundaries. Wind in my face, I caught at least a hint of the sublime experience that the people of Fincayra had once known, then lost—an experience that I recalled not in my mind, but in my bones.

The wind shifted, and I heard a faint whimpering coming from below the talons. I realized that Trouble was also carrying another passenger, just as on a different day the hawk might carry a field mouse. And I knew that Shim, now littler than little, must be just as distraught as a mouse about to be eaten.

I tried to stretch my second sight to the limit and beyond. To push back the darkness that seemed to thicken as we progressed. Yet I felt the limits of my vision more than its gifts. The castle's Shroud poured over the Dark Hills. It enveloped them just as it did the three of us. For we were flying into the land, as Rhia had once put it, *where the night never ends.*

With effort, I sensed some of the contours of the hills rising below. No trees dotted this terrain, no rivers creased its slopes. At one point I felt the land fall away into a steep but narrow canyon, and I heard the faint cry of what might have been an eagle. To the north, a dense group of flaming torches mingled with the raspy shouts of goblins. And to the south, eerie lights flickered that chilled me deeper than the wind.

On the slopes above the canyon, I detected a few clusters of buildings, which once had been villages. A strange, uncertain yearning arose in me. Might I, as a young child, have lived in one of those villages? If I could somehow view this land in the light, would it bring back at least a little of my lost memory? But the villages below were as dark and silent as my own childhood. No fires burned in any hearths; no voices lifted in any squares.

I doubted that any laborers like Honn still toiled away in this terrain, as their ancestors had for centuries before the rise of Stangmar and the onset of never-ending darkness. It was even less likely that any gardeners could have survived in such a place. For the land of T'eilean and Garlatha at least still clung to twilight, while the lands below existed in permanent eclipse.

The darkness deepened, pressing against us like a heavy blanket. I felt Trouble's rapid heartbeat, pulsing through the veins of the bird's neck. At the same time, the beating of the wings slowed down just a notch, as if the darkness inhibited flight in the same way that it inhibited vision.

The merlin leveled off. More and more, his wings faltered, sometimes not completing a stroke, other times missing a stroke entirely. As the cold winds gusted, he weaved unsteadily. His head cocked to one side and then the other. He seemed confused, trying to see what could not be seen. He struggled to stay on course.

I clutched my feathered steed. If Trouble was having such difficulty seeing, how could he possibly guide us safely into the ever-spinning castle? Perhaps that was the point of Domnu's final warning, that getting near the castle would be less difficult than getting inside it.

With a slap of fear, I realized that our only hope now lay in my own second sight. I, whose own eyes were blind, must somehow see for the hawk! Although my second sight had always grown weaker as the light around me faded, I could not let that happen this time.

Perhaps second sight did not require light after all. Perhaps I could see despite the dark. I summoned all of my energy. I must try to pierce the darkness.

Minutes passed. I could sense nothing different. And why should I? I had never before been able to see at night, even when my eyes functioned. What made me think I could change that now?

Yet I continued to try. To probe with my mind's eye. To see beyond the grays, beyond the shadows. To fill in the swaths of darkness, just as Rhia showed me how to fill in the empty places between the stars.

Meanwhile, Trouble's flight grew more erratic and uneven. His wings labored as the fierce winds buffeted us. The bird hesitated, changed direction, hesitated again.

So very gradually that I myself did not at first notice the shift, I began to sense wispy images through the thickening darkness. A curve in a ridge. A depression that might once have been a lake. A twisting road. An uneven line that could only be a wall of stone.

Then, in the deep distance, I detected something odd. A vague, throbbing glimmer on a far ridge. It seemed both moving and stationary, both light and dark. I was not even certain that it really existed. Firmly, sinking my arms deep into his feathery neck, I turned Trouble's head toward the spot. The bird resisted at first, then started to shift the angle of his wings. Slowly, he changed direction.

In time I detected a structure of some kind, mammoth in size. It rose from a high hill like a black ghost of the night. I thought I could see strange rings of light on its sides, and some sort of pinnacles at its top. As foreboding as Domnu's lair had felt, this structure felt a hundred times worse. Still, pushing firmly on Trouble's neck, I guided us closer. By now Trouble not only accepted my steering, but also seemed heartened by it. The wings beat with renewed strength.

I reached farther and farther with my second sight. Now I could see the flat hilltop, scattered with stones, where the strange structure sat. Yet even as the land surrounding it became clearer, the structure itself remained blurred. A low, rumbling sound swelled as we approached, a sound like stone grinding against stone.

At once I understood: The structure was slowly turning on its foundation. We had found the Shrouded Castle.

Biting my lip in concentration, I steered the hawk to fly in a circle around the revolving castle. The blurred outlines immediately sharpened. The pinnacles revealed themselves as towers, the rings of light as torches seen through the spinning windows and archways. Every so often, within the torch-lit rooms, I glimpsed soldiers wearing the same pointed helmets as the warrior goblins.

I focused my vision on one lower window where no soldiers seemed to be present. Then I guided Trouble into a dive. We aimed straight at the window. The battlements, the towers, the archways drew near. Suddenly, I realized that we were flying too slow, dropping too far. We were going to hit the wall! Across my mind flashed the terrifying dream I had experienced at sea.

I pulled with all my might, forcing the hawk to veer sharply upward. Shim, clasped in the talons, screamed. We whizzed past the battlements, barely above the stones. In another split second, we would have crashed.

Refocusing, I brought Trouble around again. This time, as we circled the castle, I tried to gauge our relative speeds more closely. Yet I faltered. The truth was, I had no eyes, no real vision. Did I dare try again, guided only by my second sight?

I sucked in my breath, then urged the hawk into another dive. We shot down toward the same open window as before. Wind tore at me, screaming in my ears.

As the window neared, my stomach tightened like a fist. Even the slightest error would send us smashing into the wall. Our speed accelerated. We could not turn back now.

We tore through the window. In the same instant, I saw a stone column straight ahead. Leaning hard, I caused Trouble to swing left. We brushed past the column, slid across the floor, and slammed into a wall somewhere in the bowels of the Shrouded Castle.

XXXV

THE SHROUDED
CASTLE

When I regained consciousness, the first thing I noticed was how small Trouble had become. The valiant bird sat on top of my chest, poking at me with one wing and then the other. At once I realized the truth. It was I, not the bird, who had changed size. I had grown large again.

Seeing me wake up, the merlin hopped down to the stone floor. He released a low, quiet whistle, much like a sigh of relief.

A similar sound came from the far corner of the bare, shadowy room, beneath a sputtering torch fixed to the wall with a black iron stand. Shim sat up, looked at Trouble, patted himself from hairy head to hairy toes, blinked, and patted himself again.

The little giant turned to me, his nose cradled by a bright smile. "I is gladly to be big and tall again."

I raised an eyebrow, but kept myself from smirking. "Yes, we are both big again. Domnu must have worked her magic so that it would wear off if we entered the castle."

Shim scowled. "How kindly of her."

"I am grateful to her for that much." I reached to stroke the hawk's banded wings. "And more."

Trouble gave a resolute chirp. The yellow rims of his eyes shone in the torchlight. He scratched his talons on the stone floor, telling me that once again he was ready for battle.

Yet the hawk's feistiness buoyed my spirits for only an instant. I scanned the rough, imposing stones surrounding us. The walls, floor, and ceiling of this room showed no adornment, no craftsmanship whatsoever. The Shrouded Castle had been built not out of love but out of fear. If there had been any love at all during its construction, it was merely the love of cold stone and sturdy defenses. As a result, unless this room was an exception, the castle would hold no beauty, no wonder. But it would in all likelihood outlast the Dark Hills themselves. I felt sure it would outlast me.

Only then did I notice the continuous rumbling around us. The rumbling swelled, faded, and repeated, as incessantly as ocean waves. The sound of the castle turning on its foundation! As I clambered to my feet, I felt thrown off balance, both by the continuous shaking of the floor and the steady pull toward the outside wall of the room. I stooped to pick up my staff. Even with its support, I needed a moment to stand firmly.

I turned to Shim. "I would feel a lot better if I still had the Galator."

"Look," he replied, standing on his tiptoes by the open window. "It's all so darkly out there! And feels the floor moving and shaking all the time. I doesn't likes this place."

"Neither do I."

"I is scared. Very, very, very scared."

"I am, too." I nodded in his direction. "But it gives me courage to be with friends."

A new gleam appeared in Shim's tiny eyes. "Courage," he said softly to himself. "I gives him courage."

"Come." Carefully, I crept to the doorway. It led to a dark corridor, lit only by a hissing torch at the far end. "We must try to find Rhia! If she is alive, she is probably below in the dungeon."

Shim's small chest inflated. "Such a terribly place! I will fights anybody who is hurtsing her."

"No you won't," I countered. "The castle is guarded by warrior goblins and ghouliants."

"Oooh." He swiftly deflated. "We should not fights them."

"Right. We must outfox them, if we can. Not fight them."

Trouble fluttered up to my shoulder, and we set off. Down the dimly lit corridor we stole, keeping as quiet as possible. Fortunately, the steady rumbling of the revolving castle covered most of our sounds, but for the slightest clacking of my staff against the stones. I reasoned that as long as we could keep ourselves from being discovered, the castle guards were probably not alert for intruders. On the other hand, I vividly recalled expecting the same thing of the goblins patrolling the notch near the Haunted Marsh.

When we reached the hissing torch, crudely jammed into a niche in the stones, the corridor turned sharply to the right. Arched doorways lined both sides of the next section, while only one narrow window slit opened to the outside. As we approached the window, I tensed as I saw shafts of darkness streaming through it, as shafts of light would pour through a window in any land not choked by the Shroud.

Gingerly, I placed my hand in the path of one of the shafts. Its coldness nipped at my fingers. My skin felt withered, half alive.

With a shiver, I withdrew my hand and moved on. Shim's bare feet padded softly by my side, as Trouble's talons hugged my shoulder securely. One corridor led to another, one sputtering torch to the next. All the rooms that we encountered were empty except for the writhing shadows of torchlight. I could only imagine how many such empty floors lay within this vast castle. Yet, for all our wandering, we did not discover any stairs.

Cautiously, we prowled the maze of corridors, turning left then right, right then left. I began to wonder whether we were traveling in circles, whether we would ever find any stairs to the lower levels. Then, as we approached one doorway, Trouble fluttered against my neck. Suddenly I heard several raspy voices trading rough remarks.

Goblins. Several of them, from the sound of it.

We waited outside the arched door, unsure how to get past without being seen. Trouble paced agitatedly on my shoulder. Then an idea struck me. I tapped the merlin on the beak, while pointing inside the doorway.

The hawk seemed to understand instantly. Soundlessly, he floated down to the floor. Keeping to the shadows by the wall, he slipped into the room. Just outside the doorway, Shim and I traded nervous glances.

A few seconds later, one of the goblins yelped in pain. "You stabbed me, you fool!"

"I did not," another retorted, over the crash of something metallic.

"Liar!"

Something heavy thudded against the stone floor. A sword slashed through the air.

"I'll show you who's a liar."

A brawl began. Swords clanged, fists struck, curses flew. In the commotion, Shim and I sneaked past the doorway. Pausing only long enough for Trouble to swoop back to his perch on my shoulder, we scuttled down the corridor. As we turned a corner, we found ourselves facing a stairwell.

Faintly lit by a flickering torch on the landing, the stone stairs wound downward in near darkness. I led the way, with Trouble riding close to my cheek, both of us trying to sense whatever might lurk in the shadows. Shim, whispering nervously to himself, stayed close behind.

The stairs spiraled down to another landing, sinister in the torch-light. Swaying shadows crawled across the walls. As we descended, the rumbling and groaning of the turning foundation increased, as did the stale odor in the air. We followed the stairs down to another level, gloomier than the last. And to another level, still gloomier. Here the stairs ended, opening into a high stone archway. Beyond that lay a dark cellar that reeked of putrid air.

"The dungeon," I whispered above the constant rumbling.

Shim made no reply except to open his eyes to their widest.

From the darkened entrance to the dungeon came a long, painful moan. A moan of sheer agony. The voice sounded almost human, though not quite. As the moan came again, louder than before, Shim froze as stiff as stone. Cautiously, I moved forward without him, poking at the blackest shadows with my staff.

Passing under the archway, I peered into the dungeon. To the left, beneath one of the few torches in the cavernous room, I viewed a man. He lay on his back on a bench of stone. From his slow, regular breathing, he appeared to be asleep. Although a sword and a dagger hung from his belt, he wore no armor except for a narrow red breastplate over his leather shirt, and a pointed helmet on his head.

Yet the strangest thing about this man was his face. It looked like paper, it was so pale. Or like a mask without any expression. Whatever the reason, the face seemed alive—and yet not alive.

The man suddenly started moaning and wailing. As the sound echoed in the dungeon, I realized that he must be dreaming, recalling in his sleep some moment of pain. Though I felt tempted to wake him, to spare him such torment, I dared not take the risk. As I spun around to tell Shim, I gasped. The little giant was gone.

Quickly, I darted back to the stairwell. I called his name, loud enough to be heard over the rumbling of the castle, but not so loud as to wake the sleeping soldier. Looking frantically, I could see no sign of him. I called again. No answer.

How could Shim have vanished? Where could he have gone? Maybe he had, at last, lost his nerve completely. He might be hiding somewhere, quaking. In any case, I had no time to look for him now.

With Trouble riding tensely on my shoulder, I turned around and crept past the sleeping soldier under the sizzling torch. Deeper into the dungeon I pushed. Where chains hung from the walls, the stones beneath were darkened with dried blood. I passed cell after cell, some with their heavy doors wide open, some still locked tight. Scanning through the slit in each of the locked doors, I found bones and rotting flesh still on the floor. I could not imagine Rhia, with all her zest for life, imprisoned in such a gruesome place. Yet, given the alternative, I desperately hoped that she was.

Since the day the sea returned me to Fincayra, I had discovered a little, but only a little, about my past. And I had learned even less about my true name. Yet those unfinished quests now pulled on me far less strongly than my desire to find Rhia. I was willing to put aside my own unanswered questions, perhaps forever, if only I could somehow reach her in time.

I found a cell with a skull crushed beneath a heavy rock. Then one in which two skeletons, one the size of an adult and the other no bigger than a baby, embraced each other for eternity. Then one that was completely empty but for the pile of leaves in one corner.

More despairing with every step, I trudged on. Had I come all this way to find nothing more than scattered bones and a pile of leaves?

I halted. *A pile of leaves.*

I sprinted back to the cell. My heart pounding, I peered again into the narrow slit. Just loud enough to be heard above the rumbling, I made the sound that Rhia had shown me to make a beech tree come to life.

The pile of leaves stirred.

"Rhia," I whispered excitedly.

"Emrys?"

She leaped to her feet and bounded to the door. Her garb of vines was tattered and filthy, but she was alive. "Oh, Emrys," she said in disbelief. "Is it you or your ghost?"

In answer, I slipped my forefinger through the slit. Tentatively, she wrapped her own around it, as she had so many times before.

"It is you."

"It is."

"Let me out."

"First I must find the key."

Rhia's face fell. "The guard. By the entrance. He has the key." She squeezed my finger fearfully. "But he is——"

"A soundly sleeper," finished another voice.

I whirled around to see Shim gazing up at me, an unmistakable look of pride on his small face. The little giant held out his hand. In it sat a large key wrought of iron.

I stared at him in amazement. "You stole this from the guard?"

Shim blushed, his bulbous nose turning almost as pink as his eyes. "He is a soundly sleeper, so it isn't hard."

Trouble, seated on my shoulder, whistled in admiration.

I grinned. It struck me that Shim might not be so small as he seemed after all.

With a rattle of the key, I unlocked the door. Rhia emerged, her face haggard but relieved. She embraced me, Trouble, and finally Shim, whose nose blushed more vividly than before.

Turning to me, she asked, "How do we get out of here?"

"I haven't figured out that part yet."

"Well, then, let's begin."

"I only wish I still had the Galator."

Rhia's jaw dropped. "You lost it?"

"I . . . gave it up. To get here."

Even in the dungeon, her eyes glowed. She hooked her finger around my own again. "You still have us."

Together, we started walking toward the entrance. Trouble fluttered against my neck. Even without the Galator against my chest, my heart felt a bit warmer.

But only a bit. As we passed the cell with the crushed skull, I told Rhia, "Getting in here was difficult, but getting out will be even more difficult. That is . . . getting out alive."

"I know." She stood as straight as a young beech. "In that case, all we can do is hope that Arbassa was right."

Trouble, who had started to pace across my shoulder, stopped. He cocked his head as if he were listening.

"About meeting again in the Otherworld?"

Rhia gave an uncertain nod. "After the Long Journey."

I could only frown. I was sure that, if we died today, there would be no more journeys for us—long or short.

Shim tugged on my tunic. "Let's get goings! Before that snoringly guard wakes—"

Suddenly the soldier stepped out of the shadows. His face, deathly pale under his helmet, showed no expression at all. Slowly, he slid his sword out of its scabbard. Then he lunged at me.

XXXVI

THE LAST
TREASURE

Look out!" cried Rhia.

I threw up my staff, deflecting the blow with its gnarled top. As chips of wood flew, I pulled out my dagger. At the same time, the soldier drew back his sword. He prepared to make another thrust.

Screeching, talons gouging, Trouble flew straight into his face. One talon slashed his cheek. Without even a cry of pain, he swatted at the attacking bird. I seized the moment to bury my dagger deep in the soldier's chest, just below the breastplate.

I stepped back, expecting to see him fall. Trouble flitted back to his customary perch on my shoulder.

Astonishingly, the soldier merely stood there, his emotionless gaze fixed on the hilt of the dagger. Dropping his sword, which clattered on the stone floor, he grasped the dagger with both hands. With a sharp tug, he pulled it from his body and cast it aside. Not so much as a single drop of blood trickled from the wound.

Before he could retrieve his sword, Rhia grabbed me by the arm. "Flee!" she cried. "He is a ghouliant! He cannot die!"

We dashed through the dungeon's entrance and ran up the stairs. Not far behind, the deathless soldier bounded after us. Rhia led the way, trailing torn vines from her leggings, followed closely by me and Shim.

Up the spiraling stairs we raced, nearly tripping over the stone steps in our frenzy. Past the next landing, with its sputtering torch. And the next. And the next. The stairwell grew narrower as we climbed higher. Rhia, her legs as strong as ever, pulled farther ahead of me, while Shim fell farther behind. Panting, I glanced over my shoulder. The ghouliant had drawn within a few steps of him.

Seeing Shim's danger, Trouble took off, his wing slapping the side of my neck. His angry screech echoed in the stairwell as he flew again into the face of our pursuer.

The ghouliant fell back a few steps, trying to fight off the bird. As they battled, so did their shadows on the dimly lit stone walls. I hesitated. Should I follow Rhia, or go back to assist Trouble?

I heard a scream from up the stairwell.

"Rhia!"

I practically flew up the stairs, taking them two at a time. The stairwell curled tighter and tighter, narrowing almost to a point. Breathing hard, I rounded a bend and arrived at a landing much larger and better lit than the lower ones. At once, I stopped.

Before me spread an enormous hall, its walls lined with flaming torches and glittering objects, its ceiling vaulting high overhead. But my attention was fixed on the center of the hall. Rhia had been captured by a warrior goblin! His tongue flitting around his gray-green lips, the goblin had pinned her arms behind her back. His burly hand covered her mouth so that she could not cry out again.

"Welcome to our castle," thundered a powerful voice.

I swung around to see a large man, his face as stern as chiseled stone, seated upon a red throne that shimmered eerily. His mouth seemed etched in a permanent frown. Grim though he was, he looked darkly handsome as well. Beneath the gold circlet he wore on his brow, his black eyes glared intensely. Over his face and body wavered some strange shadows, although I could not tell what caused them.

Gathered around Stangmar's throne stood five or six ghouliants, their faces as hollow as corpses'. Two Fincayran men stood among them, their coal black hair brushing against the shoulders of their red robes. One of the men stood tall and thin, like a great insect, while the other was built like the stump of a thick tree.

Recalling what Cairpré had told me, I scanned closely the faces of the two men, wondering if one of them might actually be my own father. Yet as much as I had once longed to find my father, I now dreaded the prospect. For I could only despise a man who would serve a king as wicked as Stangmar.

I just want to know him, I had said to Branwen at our last conversation. *It is better you do not,* she had replied. Alas, if he had fallen to the state of the group before me, I now understood why.

Rhia, seeing me, struggled ferociously to free herself. The warrior goblin merely wheezed in laughter and held her more tightly.

"We suspected you would come here eventually," declared Stangmar with his fixed frown. "Especially with your friend here to bait the trap."

I started, wondering why he should care where I was. Then I realized that Stangmar still believed that I wore the Galator, the last Treasure he had long been seeking. How I could take advantage of that mistake, I was not certain, but I resolved to try.

Rhia struggled again to break loose, to no avail. As she twisted in her leafy clothing, I caught the barest whiff of the freshness of the forest we had left behind.

I stepped closer, planting my staff on the stones to help keep my balance on the slowly spinning floor. "Let her go. She has done nothing to harm you."

The king's eyes burned, as the shadows danced over his features. "She would if she could. As would you."

At this, both of the Fincayran men nodded in agreement, while the ghouliants in unison laid their hands on the hilts of their swords. The taller man glanced at me, his face tight with worry. He leaned toward the king and started to say something, but Stangmar waved him silent.

Just then the ghouliant from the dungeon marched up the stairs behind me. Although his face had been savagely scratched, he showed no sign of bleeding. In one of his hands he held Trouble by the talons, so that the upside-down bird could only flap his wings and whistle angrily.

"Another friend, is it?" Stangmar's shadowy face turned to a pair of ghouliants. "Go see if there are any more."

Instantly, the two soldiers rushed past me and descended the stairwell. I then remembered that I had lost track of Shim. I could only hope that my small companion had found a secure place to hide.

Frantically, I turned from Rhia, smothered in the arms of the warrior goblin, to Trouble, dangling helplessly in the grip of the ghouliant. "Set them free!" I shouted to the king. "Set them free or you will regret it."

Stangmar's frown deepened. "We are not accustomed to taking orders from a mere boy! Especially when that boy also threatens our royal person."

Despite the continuous wobbling of the revolving castle, I stood as tall and steady as I could.

Then Stangmar leaned forward in his throne. For an instant the shadows departed from his face. With his square jaw and intense eyes, he looked even more handsome, while no less rigid, than before. "Nevertheless, your valor impresses us. For that reason, we shall be merciful."

Suddenly the shadows reappeared, moving frantically across his face, his chest, and the gold circlet on his brow.

"We know what we are doing!" he growled, though it was not clear to whom. Regally, he waved to the goblin holding Rhia. "Set her free, we command you. But watch her closely."

The warrior goblin grimaced, but obeyed. Roughly, he shoved Rhia onto the stone floor in front of the throne. Trouble, still hanging upside down, screeched wrathfully at the goblin. But he could do no more.

"What about the hawk?" I demanded.

Stangmar leaned back in his throne. "The hawk remains where he is. We trust him as little as we trust you! Moreover, keeping him as he is will encourage you to cooperate."

My spine stiffened. "I will never cooperate with you."

"Nor will I," declared Rhia, shaking her brown curls.

Trouble screeched again, making his own position clear.

For the first time, Stangmar's frown eased slightly. "Oh, you shall cooperate. In fact, you already have! You have brought us something we have long desired. You have brought us *the last Treasure.*"

I winced, but said nothing.

Shadows flickering over his face, Stangmar spread his arms to indicate the objects displayed on the walls. "Here in this hall we have collected many articles of legendary power. Hanging on the wall above our royal throne is Deepercut, the sword with two edges: the black one, that can slice into the soul, and the white one, that can heal any wound. Over there is the famous Flowering Harp. That silver horn is the Caller of Dreams. Beside it, you can see the plow that tills its own field. No more will these Treasures or the others pose any risk to our sovereignty."

His face hardened as he pointed to an iron cauldron set by the opposite wall. "We even have the Cauldron of Death."

At the mention of this object, the two men in red robes traded knowing glances. The taller one shook his head somberly.

"Yet the one Treasure we have most wanted is the one not hanging from our walls." Stangmar's voice boomed inside the hall, drowning out even the steady rumble of the spinning castle. "It is the one you have brought us."

I knew that he would soon discover that I did not have the Galator. Emboldened by the certainty of death, I squared my shoulders. "I would never bring anything that could help you."

The grim king observed me for a moment. "You think not?"

"I know not! I once carried the Galator, but it is no longer with me. It lies beyond your grasp."

Stangmar, his face shadowed, eyed me coldly. "It is not the Galator that we seek."

I blinked. "You said you were seeking the last Treasure."

"We are indeed. But the last Treasure is no mere item of jewelry." The king clasped the arms of his throne. "The last Treasure is my son."

A wave of horror flowed through me. "Your . . . son?"

Stangmar nodded, though his face showed no joy. "It is you I have been seeking. For you are my son."

XXXVII

DEEPERCUT

Dark shadows played across the king's features, while his large hands squeezed the throne. "And now we must complete the promise we made before you fled with your mother."

"Promise?" I asked, still reeling from Stangmar's revelation. "What promise?"

"Do you not remember?"

I looked morosely at the man who was my father. "I remember nothing."

"That is fortunate." Stangmar frowned more deeply than before. The shadows wavered on his face, even as they spread slowly down both of his arms. The king clenched his fists, then pointed to me and issued his command. "Throw him into the Cauldron."

In unison, the ghouliants turned toward me.

Trouble, still in the grasp of one of the ghouliants, beat his wings and struggled to free himself. His enraged screeches echoed in the cavernous hall, rising above the rumbling of the spinning castle.

"No!" cried Rhia, jumping to her feet. Quick as a viper, she leaped at Stangmar, closing her hands around his neck. Before his guards could come to his aid, the king wrestled himself free and threw her back to the stone floor. She landed in a leafy heap at the boots of the warrior goblin.

Rubbing the scratches on his neck, the wrathful king stood up. His entire body writhed in shadows. He barked at the goblin, "Kill her first! Then we shall deal with the boy."

"Gladly," rasped the goblin, his narrow eyes alight. He reached for the hilt of his sword.

My heart pounded. My cheeks burned. Rage surged through me, the same violent rage I had felt against Dinatius. I must stop this from happening! I must use my powers!

Then searing flames engulfed my mind. The stench of charred flesh. My own flesh. My own screams. I feared those powers, no less than I feared the Cauldron of Death.

The warrior goblin, grinning savagely, slowly lifted his sword. Its blade glinted in the torchlight. In the same instant, Rhia turned toward me, looking at me with sorrowful eyes.

A new feeling, more powerful even than my rage and fear, filled my heart. I loved Rhia. Loved her spirit, her vitality. *You are all that you are,* she had said to me once. Then the words of the Grand Elusa, spoken within her glowing crystal cave, came back to me. *The last Treasure carries great powers, greater than you know.* My powers were my own. To fear, perhaps, but also to use.

The goblin's powerful shoulders tensed for the blow. Trouble screeched again, fighting to free himself from the ghouliant's grip.

But what about my promise? Again I heard Rhia's voice: *If someone gave you special powers, they are for you to use.* My mother, her sapphire eyes piercing into my soul, joined in. *All God asks is that you use your powers well, with wisdom and love.*

Love. Not rage. That was the key. The same love that caused the Galator to glow. The same love for Rhia that filled me now.

Make your move! commanded the voice of Domnu. *In chess, as in life, your choice will make all the difference.*

Just as the warrior goblin started to bring down his sword on Rhia's head, I focused all of my concentration on the great sword Deepercut, suspended from the wall just behind the throne. The flames rose again in my mind, but I persisted, pushing them back. Beyond the gleeful snort of the goblin, I heard nothing. Beyond the sword and the iron hook that held it, I saw nothing.

Fly, Deepercut. Fly!

The iron hook burst apart. The sword ripped free of the wall and flew toward the goblin. Hearing it slice through the air, he turned. Half a second later, his severed head rolled onto the stone floor.

Rhia screamed as the heavy body fell on top of her. Stangmar roared in anger, his face a mass of shadows. The two red-robed men cried out and stepped back in fright. Only the ghouliants, their faces utterly blank, stood watching in silence.

In the commotion, I let go of my staff and raised my hands high. Deepercut spun through the air toward me. With both hands, I seized the silver hilt.

The ghouliants, seeing this, drew their own swords. Moving as a single body, they rushed at me. Suddenly the voice of the king rang out.

"Stop!" His downturned lips released a long, low snarl. "This duel is ours. No one else's." The shadows roiled across his body. For an instant, he hesitated. Then, with a violent shake, he declared to someone only he could see, "We said this duel is ours! We need no help."

Bounding down from the throne, he swiftly retrieved the sword of the fallen warrior goblin. Glowering at me, he slashed his blade through the air. Only then did I notice that the shadows had again departed from his face. Stranger yet, when I glanced at the red throne, the dark shadows were still there, hovering just above the seat. I felt gripped by the feeling that, somehow, those shadows were watching me closely.

"So," he taunted, "you have *the powers*, do you? Just like your grandfather before you." He took a pace toward me. "But even with all his powers, your grandfather could not escape a mortal death. Nor will you."

I barely had time to lift Deepercut to block Stangmar's first swipe. The swords clanged, echoing among the stone arches of the hall. The force of his blow made my sword vibrate down to the hilt. My hands strained to hold on. I realized that Stangmar had the triple advantages of greater strength, more skill, and—even with my improved vision—better eyesight.

Despite all this, I fought back as well as I could. Although the spinning floor and its constant vibration threw off my balance, I pressed the attack. Slashing wildly, I parried and dodged. Sparks flew when our blades clashed.

Perhaps my sheer ferocity made Stangmar cautious. Perhaps Deepercut itself somehow strengthened me. Or perhaps Stangmar was merely toying with his prey. Whatever the reason, it seemed as we worked our way up and down the hall studded with precious objects, that I was actually holding my own.

All of a sudden Stangmar drove down on me. With a powerful blow that rang through the hall, he smashed into Deepercut. The sword ripped from my hands and clattered to the stone floor.

The king brought his sword to my throat. "Now we shall keep our promise." He indicated the terrible Cauldron by the wall. "Go."

Still panting, I stood my ground. "Who made you promise to kill me?"

"Go."

"And why should that promise mean so much to you, when you have broken all of your promises to your own people?"

"Go!"

I folded my arms. "You promised Rhita Gawr, didn't you?"

Stangmar's frown hardened, even as the shadows danced over the throne. "Yes. And you would be wise to speak of our good friend with respect. Now go!"

I looked imploringly at the man whose eyes and hair mirrored my own. "Can't you see what Rhita Gawr has done to you? To your realm? He wants you to poison your lands. Blacken your sky. Terrify your people. And even . . . kill your own son!"

As I spoke, the mysterious shadows thrashed wildly on the throne.

Stangmar's face reddened. "You have no understanding of these things. No understanding at all!" He pushed the tip of the sword against my neck.

With difficulty, I swallowed. "Rhita Gawr is not your friend. He is your master, and you are his slave."

Eyes aflame, he prodded me toward the Cauldron.

"Would Elen—your wife, my mother—want this?"

Stangmar's rage boiled over. "We will spare the Cauldron and strike you down with this very sword!"

With that he lifted his weapon to whack off my head. Seeing my opening, I concentrated on Deepercut, lying on the floor just behind him.

To me, Deepercut. To me!

But I was too late. The sword had only just begun to move, tilting up on one edge, when the grim king planted his feet firmly to deliver the blow.

As his rear foot came down, however, it grazed the upturned

blade of Deepercut. The black edge, with the power to slice deep into the soul, pierced his leather boot and pricked the base of his heel.

Stangmar cried in agony and crumpled to the ground. The shadows flailed, seeming to shake the very throne. The ghouliants, swords drawn, started to come to the king's aid. But he raised his hand. Abruptly, the soldiers halted.

Slowly, Stangmar lifted his head. He gazed up at me, his face growing softer by the second. His jaw loosened. His eyes widened. Only the frown did not change.

"You spoke the truth," he declared, speaking with difficulty. "We—that is, I—confound this royal speech! I . . . am no more than a slave."

The throne rocked violently from side to side.

Stangmar turned to the thrashing shadows. "You know it is true!" he cried. "I am nothing more than your lowly puppet! My head is now so filled with your threats and delusions that it spins as incessantly as this cursed castle!"

At that a chilling, hissing sound arose from the shadows. They ceased their wild movements and started shrinking, congealing into something still darker.

The king struggled to stand, but the wound had made his whole lower body immobile and he fell back. Somberly, he faced me again. "You must understand. It was never our—that is, my—intention that Fincayra should come to this! When I made that first promise, I had no idea what grief it would bring."

"Why?" I demanded. "Why did you ever make a promise to Rhita Gawr?"

Stangmar's brow furrowed. "I did it . . . to save Elen."

"Elen? My mother?" All at once, I remembered her final words about my father. *If ever you should meet him, remember: He is not what he may seem.*

"Yes. Elen of the Sapphire Eyes." He took a deep breath and exhaled very slowly, his elbows propped against the stone floor. "When she gave birth to you on the shores of Fincayra, it broke one of our oldest laws, one handed down by the spirits themselves, that no one with human blood should ever be born here. Otherwise, humans would have a birthright to a world that is not their own! The punishment for this high crime has always been harsh but clear. The half-human child must be exiled forever from Fincayra. And, what is worse, the human parent must be thrown into the Cauldron of Death."

He tried again to stand, with no success. The ghouliants, who appeared increasingly agitated, started toward him again. The ghouliant holding Trouble joined with the others, his sword in one hand and the struggling hawk in the other.

"Stop!" ordered Stangmar. "I do not need your miserable help."

The ghouliants obeyed, though they continued to watch warily, fidgeting with their swords. Meanwhile, the shadows on the throne continued to shrink. As they condensed, they grew thicker and darker, like the center of a gathering storm.

Stangmar shook his head. "I did not know what to do. How could I condemn to death my own fair Elen? She lifted me higher than the trees I once climbed as a child! Yet I was the king, the one responsible for enforcing the laws! Then Rhita Gawr first came to me. He offered me his help, in exchange for my help in solving a problem of his own."

"What problem was that?"

Stangmar looked away. "Rhita Gawr told me that he had learned in a dream that his gravest danger would come from a child who was half human and half Fincayran. So, knowing of you, he believed that as long as you lived, you would pose some sort of threat to him."

My whole body trembled, even apart from the quaking of the floor. "So you agreed to kill me instead of her?"

"I had no choice, don't you see? Rhita Gawr promised to protect Elen and all of Fincayra from any punishment by the spirits for this violation of the law."

"And you promised to throw me in the Cauldron!"

"I did. Sometime before the end of your seventh year. For that entire time, I kept my promise a secret from Elen. I only told her that the spirits had agreed that she need not die, and you need not be exiled. She was so relieved, I could not bear to tell her the truth. She trusted me completely."

His voice took on a faraway tone. "As it happened, during that seven years, the alliance with Rhita Gawr grew more and more strong. And necessary. He alerted me to the giants' plot to overrun Fincayra. He helped me to cleanse our land of dangerous enemies. He gave me a castle where I could be truly safe. He . . ."

The words trailed off as the king slumped lower. "He made me his slave."

Touched by his anguish, I completed the story for him. "And when Elen—my mother—found out that she had been spared only so that I could die, she fled Fincayra, taking me with her."

Stangmar gazed at me in despair. "So in the end, I lost you both."

"And so much more," added Rhia, standing next to the corpse of the beheaded warrior goblin.

I nodded, then turned to the ghouliants. For some reason, they had drawn closer about the throne, surrounding it with their bodies. Yet despite the nearness of the other soldiers, Trouble continued to wriggle and flap his wings fiercely. The ghouliant who held him did not seem to notice that one of the hawk's talons had almost pulled free.

"Too true," admitted Stangmar. "Rhita Gawr has assured me that if I can find my half-human son and put him to death, my power will then be complete. But what he really means is that I will have done his bidding—ridding him of whatever threat you might represent. So who, I ask, is ruler now?"

At that instant, the ghouliants stepped in unison away from the red throne. Parting like two curtains, they revealed an impenetrable knot of blackness writhing on the seat. Darker than the Shroud itself, the shifting knot released a shrill, shrieking hiss. With the sound came an icy gust that chilled me to the marrow of my bones.

"Rhita Gawr!" shouted Stangmar, desperately trying to raise himself off the floor.

The knot of darkness leaped off the throne, flew past Rhia, and landed on the floor next to Deepercut. Before I could even take a breath, it wrapped itself completely around the silver hilt. Like a dark hand of evil, it raised the sword and slashed at Stangmar, slicing one side of his face from ear to chin. Blood streaming down his jaw, the king howled in pain and rolled to the side.

Suddenly Stangmar froze. His expression began to change from terror to wrath. His eyes narrowed, his frown tightened, his fists clenched so hard they went white. Then, to my shock, he grabbed the other sword and jumped to his feet. He stood beside me, proud and strong despite his bloody face.

"Help us!" I cried.

But instead of aiming his sword at the black knot holding Deepercut, he pointed it straight at me. "You are a fool, boy! We are not so easily defeated as that."

I backed away. "But you said——"

"We said nothing of importance," he declared, with a wave toward the undulating mass of darkness that was Rhita Gawr. "Our friend here has healed us! By striking us with the edge that can heal any wound, he has cured our whimpering soul. And in doing so he has brought us back to our senses. We know who our enemies are, and now we will strike you down!"

Rhia started to charge at the king, but two of the ghouliants stepped in front of her. She tried her best to dodge them, but they blocked her path.

As Stangmar drew back his sword, preparing to run me through, Rhita Gawr gave another shrieking hiss. Stangmar faltered. Slowly, he lowered his weapon.

Looking somewhat ashamed, the king shook his head. "We would not fail you again," he protested. "We were deceived! Deluded! Allow us to fulfill our promise to you now."

An angry, ear-splitting hiss was Rhita Gawr's only answer. As Stangmar looked on obediently, the pulsing knot of darkness lifted its own sword once again. Swinging the blade around, Rhita Gawr prepared to end my life.

Just then, another shrill cry filled the hall. Trouble had finally broken free from the ghouliant's grip. As the soldier tried in vain to pierce the hawk with his sword, Trouble soared toward the ceiling of the great hall.

Swooping up to the highest possible point, the merlin released a screech that echoed from every wall. He careened sharply in the air, pausing for a split second above our heads. Then this small but spirited creature, whose life ever since our first meeting had consisted of one brave deed after another, did the bravest deed of all.

At the very instant that the sword started slicing toward me,

Trouble beat his wings mightily and plunged faster than an arrow into the very center of the black mass. Taken by surprise, Rhita Gawr let go of the sword, which flew across the hall, skittering over the stones. As the cold arms of blackness wrapped around Trouble, he slashed and pecked and whipped his wings furiously. Hissing and screeching, the dark knot and the merlin rolled over each other on the floor.

Desperately, I searched for some way to help Trouble. But how? I could try wielding Deepercut, but he and Rhita Gawr had embraced each other so tightly that I couldn't possibly hit one without hitting the other. I could try using my powers to strike a different kind of blow, but that would surely fail for the same reason. My heart burst to watch—yet that was all I could do.

Trouble fought on valiantly. Still, Rhita Gawr's chilling embrace and superior strength proved too much. Slowly, inexorably, the mass of darkness was swallowing the bird. Consuming him, bit by bit. First his talon. Then his wing. Then half of his tail. And, in a few more seconds, his head.

"Oh, Trouble!" wailed Rhia, still flanked by the ghouliants.

With a final, piercing whistle, the merlin lifted his head as high as he could, then plunged his beak right into the uttermost heart of the blackness. Suddenly, a thin edge of bright light surrounded the grappling pair. A strange, sucking sound rent the air, as if the wall separating two worlds had been ruptured. Both the dark mass and the hawk it had consumed grew swiftly smaller, until only a tiny black speck remained, hovering in the air. An instant later, that too disappeared.

Trouble was gone. Though he had somehow taken Rhita Gawr with him, I was as sure that the wicked spirit would one day return as I was sure that my friend would not. My sightless eyes brimming with tears, I bent to pick up a lone feather that had come to rest on the floor by my feet.

I slowly twirled the banded brown feather between my fingers. It was from one of Trouble's wings, the same wings that had borne me aloft not so long ago. Those wings, like myself, would never fly again. Gently I slipped the feather into my satchel.

Suddenly the point of a sword pushed at my chest. I looked up to see Stangmar, half his face and neck smeared with blood, scowling at me.

"Now we will fulfill our promise," he declared. "And in the way it was meant to be done. So that when our friend returns, he will know beyond doubt where our loyalty lies."

"No," pleaded Rhia. "Don't do it! This is your chance to be a true king, don't you understand?"

Stangmar snorted. "Waste not your breath on such lies." He turned to the ghouliants. "Guards! Throw him into the Cauldron."

XXXVIII

ANCIENT WORDS

Instantly, the ghouliants not guarding Rhia tramped across the hall, converging on me. Swords drawn, faces emotionless, they began marching me toward the Cauldron of Death.

I did not even try to resist them. Whether from the loss of Trouble or from the continuous shaking of the floor, my legs felt wobbly and weak. Moreover, even if my powers could have helped me now, I had no heart to try anymore. My only thoughts were of the empty place on my shoulder.

Rhia tried to run after me, but the soldiers restrained her.

Grimly, Stangmar watched. He stood as rigid as a statue, his eyes smoldering, his hand squeezing the hilt of his sword. The dried blood on his face had turned the same color as the Blighted Lands of his realm.

Pace by pace, the procession drew nearer to the Cauldron. It seemed to glower at me as I approached, dark and silent as death itself. For a moment I considered throwing myself into it willingly, in the hope that I might be able to destroy the Cauldron as well as myself. But even that small satisfaction would not be mine, for the ghouliants were flanking me so closely that they would surely have killed me before I broke free.

Crestfallen, I turned to Rhia. Reaching through a gap between two of the soldiers, I extended a bent forefinger toward her. Although her eyes were clouded, she returned the gesture, symbolically wrapping her finger around mine for the last time.

The ghouliants stopped just short of the Cauldron. Although it reached only up to my waist, its iron mouth yawned so wide that a fully grown man or woman could easily have fit inside. And within that mouth lay only blackness—even thicker and deeper than the Shroud. The ghouliants shoved me almost to the Cauldron's rim, then turned to Stangmar, awaiting his orders.

Rhia pleaded with the king. "Don't, please!"

Stangmar paid no attention. His voice rising above the rumble of the ever-spinning castle, he gave his command.

"Into the Cauldron!"

At that instant, a tiny figure dashed out of the shadows near the stairwell. With only a fleeting glance at Rhia and myself, Shim sped across the floor, his small feet slapping on the stones. Before the ghouliants realized what was happening, he clambered up to the rim of the Cauldron. He hesitated for a fraction of a second, then threw himself into its mouth.

A thunderous explosion shook in the hall, rocking the revolving castle to its very foundation. Although the spinning never ceased, the power of the blast caused the rotations to wobble erratically. I tumbled to the floor, as did Rhia and several of the ghouliants. Torches fell from their mountings, sizzling on the stones. The Flowering Harp swayed precariously from the wall, held by a single string.

As the sound of the explosion reverberated among the walls, as well as the Dark Hills beyond, I regained my feet. What I saw was the Cauldron of Death, split into two great halves. And there, in the center of the destroyed Cauldron, lay the body of the little giant.

"Shim!" I bent over my companion, tears again filling my eyes. My voice a mere whisper, I spoke to the corpse. "You always wanted to be big. To be a true giant. Well, a giant you are, my friend. A giant you are."

"What treachery is this?" Stangmar slashed his sword through the air as he raged at the ghouliants. "We told you to find any other intruders!"

Angrily, he grabbed one of the ghouliants' swords and thrust it straight into the soldier's belly. The ghouliant shuddered, but did not utter any sound. Then he slowly pulled the sword out again, facing Stangmar as if nothing had happened.

Stangmar strode up to me, still kneeling at the edge of the shattered Cauldron. His face taut, he raised his sword high above me. As I turned toward him, my head tangled with black hair so like his own, he hesitated for an instant.

"Curse you, boy! The sight of you—and the cut of that cursed blade—has awakened feelings in us. Feelings we thought we had forgotten, and wish only to forget again! And now our task is twice as wretched. For though we must do what we must do, the pain will be all the greater."

Suddenly, Stangmar's mouth dropped open in astonishment. He faltered, stepping backward in fright.

For within the remains of the Cauldron, a strange thing was happening. As if a gentle breeze had started to blow through the hall, the hairs on Shim's head were stirring, quivering. Slowly at first, then with increasing speed, his nose started to grow larger. Then his ears. Then the rest of his head, neck, and shoulders. His arms too began swelling, followed by his chest, hips, legs, and feet. His clothes expanded with him, growing larger by the second.

Then came the greater miracle. Shim opened his eyes. More

amazed, perhaps, than anyone else, he groped at his expanding body with his swelling hands.

"I is getting bigger! I is getting bigger!"

By the time Shim's head was pushing against the ceiling, Stangmar recovered his senses. "It's a giant!" he cried to the ghouliants. "Attack him before he ruins us all!"

The nearest ghouliant dashed forward and ran his sword into the part of Shim's body that was closest. That happened to be his left knee.

"Oww!" howled Shim, clutching his knee. "Stingded by a bee!"

Instinctively, the once-little giant curled himself up into a ball. This only made him an easier target, however. The ghouliants gathered around, poking and stabbing him with the fury of an angry swarm. Meanwhile, Shim's body continued to expand, with no sign of slowing. Before long, the pressure of his shoulders and back against the ceiling made it start to buckle. Chunks of stone rained down on us. A hole opened in the ceiling.

One of the towers on the battlements fell, crashing into Shim's still-growing nose. But instead of making him curl up tighter to escape harm, the blow made something else happen. It provoked his wrath.

"I is angry!" he thundered, swinging his fist, now nearly as large as the king's throne, through a section of wall.

Stangmar, visibly frightened, started backing away. Following his lead, the ghouliants also retreated. The two Fincayran men, who had been cowering by the throne, dashed madly for the stairs, tripping over each other in their haste.

I ran to join Rhia, pausing only to retrieve Deepercut, which lay near the stairwell. Together we huddled in a far corner that seemed safe—for the moment, at least—from falling stones.

Then, for the first time in his life, Shim had a very giantlike experience. He saw his attackers running *away* from him. And the gleam in his enormous pink eyes made it clear that the experience was one he just might enjoy.

"I is bigger than you," he bellowed. "Muchly bigger!"

Shim, whose hairy feet alone had swelled bigger than boulders, stood up. He stretched his body to its fullest height, bringing down another piece of the ceiling. With a vengeful grin spreading over his gargantuan face, he began stomping on the ghouliants. Each of his stomps shook the entire castle, and sections of the floor itself began to give way.

But the deathless soldiers survived even these crushing blows. After each attack, they merely stood, shook themselves, and resumed slashing at Shim's feet with their swords. Shim's eyes flamed with rage. He stomped harder than ever. The more the ghouliants scurried beneath him, the more weight he threw into every step.

As I sat with Rhia in the corner, fervently hoping that Shim would not move to our end of the hall, I watched crumbling pieces of the ceiling crash around him. He was clearly angry—and clearly enjoying himself.

Then, beyond the sound of splintering stones and stomping feet, I began to hear a strange, rhythmic sound coming from somewhere beyond the castle. Distant at first, then closer, the sound swelled steadily. I suddenly realized that it was the sound of voices, the deepest voices I had ever heard. They were singing a simple chant, consisting of three profoundly low notes. And there was something else about the chant, something familiar, that stirred in me a feeling I could not quite identify.

Then an enormous face, craggy as a cliff and wearing a shaggy red beard, appeared in the gap in the ceiling. It was followed by another, with curly gray hair and full lips. And another, with skin as dark as a shadow, a long braid, and earrings made from chariot wheels. Each of them nodded in greeting to Shim, but remained outside the castle walls.

"Giants," said Rhia in wonderment. "They have come."

Indeed, rising from their secret hiding places all across Fincayra, the giants had come. Responding to some long-awaited call, perhaps the explosion from the Cauldron of Death, they had lumbered out of the darkened canyons, remote forests, and unknown ridges of this land. Bearing huge, flaming torches, they arrived from many directions. Some wore heavy nets of stones, which would have allowed them to rest unnoticed in fields of boulders. Others still carried branches, even whole trees, on their flowing manes. And others, perhaps because they were too foolish or too proud to disguise themselves at all, wore vests and hats and capes as colorful as the fruited trees of Druma Wood.

Swiftly, the giants arranged themselves in a circle around the castle. Following Shim's example, they began stomping the ground together, with the combined force of an earthquake. All the while, they lifted their voices in the rhythmic chant, singing in their most ancient language, the language of Fincayra's first people:

> *Hy gododin catann hue*
> *Hud a lledrith mal wyddan*
> *Gaunce ae bellawn wen cabri*
> *Varigal don Fincayra*
> *Dravia, dravia Fincayra.*

In a flash, I recalled hearing my mother sing the very same chant. But was that memory from our time in Gwynedd, or from sometime before? Had I, perhaps, even heard it as a baby? I could not quite tell.

Somehow I caught the feeling, perhaps from that vague, uncertain memory, that the meaning of this chant had something to do with the timeless bond between the giants and Fincayra. With the notion that as long as one lasted, so would the other. *Dravia, dravia Fincayra. Live long, live long Fincayra.*

The more the giants danced by the light of their great torches, the more the castle crumbled. While the stones behind Rhia and me continued to hold, other sections of the wall were buckling. And as the castle's walls weakened, so did its enchantment. The spinning started to slow, the rumbling to fade. Then, with a grinding scrape of stone against stone, the castle came to a wrenching halt. Pillars and arches collapsed, filling the air with dust and debris.

At that moment, the ghouliants, whose power had sprung from the turning castle itself, released a unified shout—more of surprise than of anguish—and dropped wherever they stood. I could not help but think, as I viewed their bodies sprawled among the stones, that their faces at last showed a touch of emotion. And that the emotion was something akin to gratitude.

With the death of the ghouliants, Shim climbed through a missing section of wall and joined the rest of the giants outside. As I listened to the pounding of their heavy feet all around the castle, I remembered more ancient words. Words that had foretold this Dance of the Giants:

> *Where in the darkness a castle doth spin,*
> *Small will be large, ends will begin.*
> *Only when giants make dance in the hall*
> *Shall every barrier crumble and fall.*

Shim, I realized, had been saved by an older form of magic. Older than the Shrouded Castle, older than the Cauldron of Death, older perhaps than the giants themselves. For even as his act of courage had destroyed the Cauldron, his very footsteps in running across the stone floor of the hall had begun the dance that would destroy the castle in its entirety. *Small will be large, ends will begin.* The Grand Elusa had told Shim that bigness meant more than the size of his bones. And now, through the bigness of his own actions, he towered above the battlements of this crumbling castle.

HOME

The wall behind us started to groan. I turned to Rhia, whose tattered suit of vines still smelled of the forest. "We must go! Before the whole castle collapses."

She shook some chips of stone from her hair. "The stairs are blocked. Should we try to climb down somehow?"

"That would take too long," I replied, leaping to my feet. "I know a better way." Cupping my hands around my mouth, I shouted above the din. "Shim!"

Even as a crack split the wall, a face appeared through a hole in the ceiling. The face would have been familiar if only it had been many, many times smaller.

"I is big now," boomed Shim with pride.

"You got your wish! *To be as big as the highlyest tree.*" I waved to him to bend closer. "Now put your hand through that hole, will you? We need a ride out of here."

Shim grunted, then thrust his immense hand through the hole in the ceiling. The hand came to rest on the floor beside us, though so near to a chasm that only one of us at a time could squeeze past to climb into Shim's palm. Rhia chose to go first.

While she carefully worked her way around the chasm, I hefted Deepercut in my hand. Although its silver hilt still felt cold from the clutch of Rhita Gawr, the twin edges gleamed with a luster that reminded me of moonlight on the rolling surface of the sea.

Suddenly I remembered the Treasures of Fincayra. They too must be saved! Whatever time remained before the final collapse of the castle, I must use it to find the Treasures that had not already been destroyed by falling debris.

"Come on!" called Rhia, holding onto Shim's thumb.

"You go first," I answered. "Send Shim back for me." As she watched me worriedly, I cupped my hands and shouted toward the ceiling. "All right, Shim. Lift!"

As Rhia rose through the ceiling, I placed Deepercut on the safest looking slab of stone I could find. Immediately, I began prowling around the remains of the once-cavernous hall. Crawling over tumbled columns and the corpses of ghouliants, dodging falling chunks of stone, stepping over fissures snaking across the floor, I moved as swiftly and carefully as possible. All the while, beyond the groans and crashes of the castle, I could hear the ongoing pounding of the Dance of the Giants.

In short order, I found the Flowering Harp, with all but a few strings intact, and a glittering orange sphere that I guessed must be the Orb of Fire. Quickly, I carried them over to Deepercut and returned for more. Near the toppled red throne, I discovered my own staff, a treasure at least to myself. At the far end of the hall, I uncovered the half-buried Caller of Dreams, as well as the hoe that Honn had said could nurture its own seeds.

All in all, I found only six of the Seven Wise Tools. After the hoe, I located the plow that tills its own field, although it proved almost too heavy for me to lift. Then I discovered a hammer, a shovel, and a bucket, whose powers I could only guess. Last of all I turned up the saw that I knew from Honn's description would cut only as much wood as needed. Although part of the handle had been crushed by a huge chunk of stone, the tool remained usable.

I had just deposited the saw with the other Treasures when Shim's face reappeared through the hole in the ceiling.

"You must comes!" he thundered. "This castle is readily to fall in."

I nodded, though I still wished that I had been able to locate the missing one of the Seven Wise Tools. Not knowing what it might look like had only made my task of finding it more difficult. Even so, as Shim lowered his great hand and I began loading it with the Treasures, I occasionally paused to scan the hall for any sign of the seventh Wise Tool.

"Is you done yet?" Shim bellowed impatiently.

"Almost." I hurled the last of the objects, my staff, onto his palm. "Just one more minute while I climb on."

"Quickerly!" called Shim. "You might not haves another minute."

Indeed, as he spoke, I felt the stones of the floor under my feet shift drastically. I started to climb onto his hand, giving a final glance to the hall.

Just then I spotted, in the shadows behind a smashed pillar, something that made my whole body tense. It was not the missing Wise Tool. It was a hand, groping helplessly. The hand of Stangmar.

"Comes on!" Shim implored. "I can sees the ceiling about to fall."

For an instant I hesitated. Then, even as a section of the ceiling came crashing down beside me, I turned and raced across the floor of the foundering castle. The crumbling of the walls, floor, and ceiling seemed to accelerate, as did the chanting and stomping of the giants outside.

When I reached Stangmar, I bent over him. He lay chest down on the floor, the gold circlet still on his brow. A large slab of stone had fallen across his lower back and one of his arms. His hand, now clenched into a fist, had ceased groping. Only his half-open eyes revealed that he was still alive.

"You?" he moaned hoarsely. "Have you come to watch us die? Or do you plan to kill us yourself?"

I gave my answer by reaching over and gripping the slab. With all my strength, I tried to lift it. Legs trembling, lungs bursting, I felt not even the slightest movement in the stone.

As the king realized what I was doing, he eyed me with scorn. "So you would save us now to kill us later?"

"I would save you now so you might live," I declared, though the floor beneath us started to sway.

"Bah! Do you expect us to believe that?"

Concentrating hard, I heaved, calling on all the powers within me. Perspiration slid down my brow, stinging my sightless eyes. At last, the slab budged just a little, though not enough to free Stangmar.

Before I could try again, the floor burst open. The two of us tumbled into the darkness below, amidst the rising roar of the castle's final collapse.

All at once something broke our fall. Stangmar and I rolled together in a heap. At first I had no idea what had caught us, except that it was far softer than stone. Then, as the light from the giants' torches returned, I viewed the ruins of the castle below us, as well as a familiar face above us. And I understood.

"I catches you!" crowed Shim. "It's a goodly thing I has two hands!"

"Yes," I replied, sitting in the center of his palm. "A goodly thing."

The giant's enormous mouth frowned. "The wickedly king is with you." He roared with rage, "I will eats him!"

A look of terror filled Stangmar's face.

"Wait," I cried. "Let us imprison him, not kill him."

Stangmar gazed at me with astonishment.

Shim growled again, scrunching his mountainous nose with displeasure. "But he is bad! Completely, totally, horribly bad."

"That may be true," I replied. "But he is also my father." I turned and looked into the dark eyes of the man beside me. "And there was a time, long ago, when he liked to climb trees. Sometimes just to ride out a storm."

Stangmar's eyes seemed to soften ever so slightly, as if my words had cut almost as deep as the blade of Deepercut. Then he turned away.

Shim set us down on a knoll of dry grass at the edge of the hill where the Shrouded Castle once stood so formidably. Then he stepped away, the ground shaking under his weight. I watched him sit down, propping his back against the hillside. He stretched his immense arms and gave a loud yawn, though not so loud as the snore that I knew would soon come.

Seeing Rhia nearby, I left the crumpled form of Stangmar to join her. She stood looking westward, beyond the castle ruins, toward a faint line of green on the distant horizon.

Hearing the crunch of my footsteps, she spun around. Her eyes, wide as ever, seemed to dance. "You are safe."

I nodded. "As are most of the Treasures."

She smiled, something I had not seen her do for some time.

"Rhia! Am I mistaken, or is it growing lighter?"

"You are not mistaken! The Shroud is going the same way as the castle and the ghouliants."

I pointed toward the giants, who had ceased their chanting and stomping. Singly and in clusters of two or three, they were beginning to drift away from the ruins. "Where are they going?"

"To their homes."

"To their homes," I repeated.

Peering across the hillside, we observed what was left of the Shrouded Castle. While much of it had been crushed in the Dance of the Giants, a ring of mammoth stones remained standing in a stately circle. Some of the stones stood upright, others leaned to the side, and still others supported hefty crosspieces. Whether the giants had placed the stones in this fashion, or had simply left them standing, I knew not.

In silence, as the first rays of sunlight started piercing the sky above the Dark Hills, I contemplated this imposing circle. It rose like a great stone hedge upon the land. It struck me that this ring of stones would make a lasting monument to the fact that no walls, however sturdy, can forever withstand the power of what is true. Vision that is true. Friendship that is true. Faith that is true.

All of a sudden, I realized that I could remember my own childhood in this very place! On this very hill! *Only when giants make dance in the hall, Shall every barrier crumble and fall.* The prophecy, I now understood, had not applied only to walls of stone. My own inner walls, that had cut me off from my past since the day I washed ashore on Gwynedd, had begun to crumble along with those of the castle.

First in gentle wisps, then in surging waves, memory after memory came floating back to me. My mother, wrapped in her shawl before a crackling fire, telling me the story of Hercules. My father, so confident and strong, leaping astride a black stallion named Ionn. The first time I ever tasted larkon, the spiral fruit. The first swim in the River Unceasing. The final, sorrowful minutes before we fled for our lives, my mother and I, praying that the sea might somehow deliver us to safety.

And then, from my distant childhood, came the words of a chant called the Lledra. It was a chant that had been sung by my mother long ago, just as it had been sung by the giants themselves today:

> *Talking trees and walking stones,*
> *Giants are the island's bones.*
> *While this land our dance still knows,*
> *Varigal crowns Fincayra.*
> *Live long, live long Fincayra.*

"Rhia," I said quietly. "I've not yet found my true home. Nor am I sure that I ever will. But, for the very first time, I think I know where to look."

She raised an eyebrow. "And where is that?"

I waved toward the circle of stones, luminous in the swelling rays. "All this time I've sought my home as though it could be found somewhere on a map. And now I remember a home that I once knew. Here, on this very spot! Yet, at the same time, I have the feeling that if my true home exists anywhere, it isn't on a map at all. More likely, it's somewhere inside of myself."

Her voice wistful, she added, "In the same place that our memories of Trouble are found."

I reached my hand into my satchel and pulled out the feather. Softly, I stroked its edge with my finger. "I have an idea of what happened to him when he vanished. I can't quite believe it—but I can't quite dismiss it, either."

Rhia studied the feather. "I have the same idea. And I think Arbassa would agree."

"If it's true, and his bravery opened the door to the Otherworld—then he and Rhita Gawr must have fallen through that door together."

She smiled. "It wasn't a journey Rhita Gawr had planned! But it gave us the chance we needed. So if it's true, Trouble is somewhere out there right now, still soaring."

"And Rhita Gawr is out there too, still fuming."

She nodded, then her face turned serious. "Still, I'm going to miss that hawk."

I dropped the feather, watching it spin slowly downward into my other hand. "So will I."

Rhia kicked at the brittle grass under our feet. "And see what else we have lost! This soil is so parched, I wonder whether it will ever come back to life."

With a slight grin, I announced, "I already have a plan for that."

"You do?"

"I think the Flowering Harp, with its power to coax the spring into being, might be able to help."

"Of course! I should have remembered."

"I plan to carry it to every hillside and meadow and stream that has withered. As well as to one particular garden, down on the plains, where two friends of mine live."

Rhia's gray-blue eyes brightened.

"I was even hoping . . ."

"What?"

"That you might want to come along. You could help revive the trees."

Her bell-like laughter rang out. "Whether I come or not, this much is clear. You may not have found your true home. But I think you have found a few friends."

"I'd say you're right."

She watched me for a moment. "And one thing more. You have found your true name."

"I have?"

"Yes. You remind me of that hawk who once sat on your shoulder. You can be fierce as well as gentle. You grab hold with all your strength and never let go. You see clearly, though not with your eyes. You know when to use your powers. And . . . you can fly."

She glanced toward the circle of stones, gleaming like a great necklace in the light, then turned back to me. "Your true name ought to be Merlin."

"You can't be serious."

"I am."

Merlin. I rather liked the name. Not enough to keep it, of course, though I knew that names sometimes had a strange way of sticking. *Merlin.* An unusual name, to say the least. And all the more meaningful because of the sorrow and joy it brought to my mind.

"All right. I shall try it. But only for a while."